PLANETFALL

Also by Emma Newman from Gollancz:

Planetfall
After Atlas
Before Mars

PLANETFALL

EMMA NEWMAN

This edition first published in Great Britain in 2018 by Gollancz

First published in Great Britain in 2018 by Gollancz
an imprint of the Orion Publishing Group Ltd
Carmelite House, 50 Victoria Embankment
London EC4Y 0DZ

An Hachette UK Company

1 3 5 7 9 10 8 6 4 2

A CIP catalogue record for this book is
available from the British Library.

ISBN 978 1 473 22385 1

Printed in Great Britain by Clays Ltd, St Ives plc

www.enewman.co.uk
www.gollancz.co.uk

For Kate, and everyone who loved her

ACKNOWLEDGMENTS

This book was written amidst the thrilling terror of book launches and the chaos of moving house, out on submission during a period of terrible health, bought on the same day as the most awful news was broken to me, edited while grieving and published while finding a way back to the world.

I doubt I could have survived all of that—let alone find myself here, writing this—without the constant and loving support of my husband and countless cuddles from my son, who understands the value of such things. You are both pillars of strength for me. Thank you.

Thanks also to my friends Gareth L. Powell, for reassuring me that the book would find a home when I needed to hear that most, and Adam Christopher, for keeping me sane in this writerly life. Well, saner than I would have been without him.

Thanks to my agent, Jennifer Udden of DMLA, who has seen me through the worst year of my life and sent me the best GIFs at the best times.

Thanks to Rebecca Brewer, my editor at Ace/Roc, who has

perfectly understood what I was aiming for in this book and given me some much-needed confidence again.

I would also like to thank Dr. Rachel Armstrong for speaking at the Clarke Awards in 2013 and inspiring several ideas that found their way onto these pages. Your speech gave me hope that there are still amazing people out there doing amazing things for the benefit of humanity.

To anyone who, like me, suffers from an anxiety disorder, I want to say this: It is hard. You are brilliant. Be kind to yourself. As my late best friend, Kate, said to me once, "Treat yourself like you would treat me." She was wise, so please, treat yourself with the same love and kindness you devote to your best friend.

And that brings me, last but not least, to Kate. Oh, I miss you, darling. Thank you for giving me all you did, loving me so deeply and believing in me so much. This book, and all the books I will ever write, is for you.

1

EVERY TIME I come down here I think about my mother. I don't want to; it just happens. My brain has decided it's a critical subroutine that must be executed when the correct variables are in place: (when time = predawn) + (when physical location = beneath the colony) + (when physical act = opening the door to the Masher) run "unpleasant memory of mother #345."

My hand is pushing the door open and I'm back at my old lab and she's following me in, her heels clicking on the tiled floor. I've prepped the equipment to run one hour before her arrival so there's something to show straightaway. She never was a patient woman.

"Is that a printer?" she asked, and I nodded. It started then—I know it now that I'm looking back—that tightening of my gut as I dared to hope I might impress her.

"Yeah." I smiled.

She didn't. "Like the one I have at home?"

"Better."

"What's it printing?"

"My latest work."

She went up to the plasglass and peered through, seeing nothing but a few millimeters of tissue. She turned to me with her nose slightly wrinkled. "What is it printing?"

"A new pancreas," I said. "For Dad."

"Oh." She'd hoped I was making something she could hang up in the hallway of her inert home. "I didn't realize you were involved in this sort of thing. I've seen it on the news."

And that was the moment I knew I'd been stupid to hope for anything. "The gene therapy isn't working out for him. There's an unusual base pair sequence in the—"

"Renata—" She holds up her hand. "You know I don't understand this kind of thing." The hand lowers to rest over her heart. "I'm an artist."

I wanted to say that my colleague had called me that when he saw the final model I'd compiled for the print. I wanted to ask her why she wasn't even the tiniest bit worried about Dad's cancer. They were married once; surely an echo of something remained. But all I said was, "I'm making him a new pancreas with cells cultured from a cheek swab and it's actually fucking cool. I'm going to save his life. And thousands of other people who can't—"

"I don't think it's right."

"How can it be wrong to save a life?"

"Where does it stop? Making a person? Making copies?"

"Actually, they've already locked down the ethics on that, after the guy over at Princeton—"

"It's going too far, all this science. Where's the beauty? Where is God in all of this?"

"Everywhere," I whispered. "Especially here."

She didn't hear me.

This is where I take a deep breath and look at the Masher instead of the lab in my past. I run a hand over the alloy and rub my fingers together. I know from patching into the environmental sensors and the color of the walls that the humidity levels are within satisfactory parameters, but I still do it. The alloy is the same gray-blue as my mother's eyes. That must be the memory trigger. I used to wish I'd inherited them, but thank the Lord I didn't. I wouldn't want to see my mother's eyes looking back at me in the mirror. I have my father's dark brown eyes and his tight curly hair and his flat nose. It was genetically inevitable, but it was still a disappointment to her. It's obvious in the postbirth footage I lifted from the family server. It's the only time you see her. Days later she was the one doing all the filming. Drawn back. Getting the composition right, one step removed from her own retinal cam.

I walk from one end of the Masher to the other, peering through the plasglass at the sorted discards from the homes above instead of human tissue. I feel just as excited now as I did back then.

"What have you got inside you today, Mash?" I ask. I don't know why; there's no voice recognition or synthware or any kind of UI. There's no point; the sorter is the only part with any AI and it's not that clever. It doesn't need to be to sort materials.

In the ceramics section an interesting curve in the collected pile catches my eye. I press the nubbin at the bottom corner of the door and it slides open. It's a vase, I think, the design riffing off a Möbius strip aesthetic. The bacteria are destroyed by the household chute on the way down, so I know it's sterile and safe to take out.

I turn it over a few times and rub my thumb over the shiny white surface. It tells me two things right away: the creator is a learner—they always want to play with Möbius strips when they get to a certain phase of the CAD training program—and their printer is going to break down soon. The imperfections in the surface are obvious to me; if it were my printer it'd be stripped down and cleaned right away, but these people don't notice the signs. They know I'll turn up and fix it when it breaks and that's enough for everyone. Except the Ringmaster.

Even though the design is crude and the vase flawed, I rescue it from its fate. Someone with the potential to be a good visengineer tried so hard to make it an interesting shape. I need something to remind me there are still people creating for the love of it. I put it on top of the unit and rummage through the rest of the abandoned ceramics, but nothing takes my fancy, so I slide the door shut and move on to the plastics compartment. I've had time only to open its door when a message marked "urgent" arrives for me.

I don't even question who it is from; only the Ringmaster has manners bad enough to tag any message that way. I decline voice contact—the acoustics would give away my location—and indicate that I'll accept only text. He'll think I'm on the toilet or having a shower. The only other times most people accept text-only is if they're making love with someone boring, and he knows there's no chance of that.

Ren—come to the west gate. Now.

I close the Masher compartment, actually interested. What's Mack doing there? He never goes to the western edge of the colony.

With a simple thought command, a virtual keyboard appears in front of me, overlaid across my visual field. What's going on? I type back.

Someone's coming.

What's that supposed to mean? You want to have a meeting at the west gate?

No. Someone's coming *toward* the colony. From outside.

The v-keyboard disappears, my implant thinking it's not needed anymore when the words fly from my brain and I stand there, motionless, too stumped by what he's sent to respond.

Ren? What are you doing? Come now!

I think of the Masher and call up the menu, starting the machine off as I struggle to process what he's said. I watch as the contents on the other side of the plasglass are rendered into the base powders they were printed from. By the time the last specks of it all have been sucked back into the communal feeds, the Ringmaster has sent three more messages and is starting to swear. He never swears.

Abusing my privileges, I access the cloud and look up what patterns he's downloaded in the past twenty-six hours. When I see the one for the automatic pistol delivered to his home printer less than twenty minutes ago, my mouth goes dry.

I call up the v-keyboard again. Sorry. Getting dressed. On my way.

I can't help but speculate about what it means. The only

other people on the planet were never supposed to come here. And as soon as I think that, my heart races and I feel sick and I want to go home and curl up and not go outside for a week.

But I can't give in to that impulse right now. I focus on walking up the slope toward the exit, forcing my mind to imagine going to the western gate. The thought of crossing the streets, of walking past homes and people looking out at me hurrying past, sweating and shaking, makes me feel worse. Why call me there? What does he want me to do? He's already printed the solution.

The hatch down to the Masher's hub is only a couple of meters from my home. At least if he's looking out for me, I'll come from the right direction. A few early risers might be mooching around inside their pods, but it's too early to be outside and social. The hatch drops back into place and locks automatically, the seam between it and the path already fading as the gap is filled by the repair cells already growing.

It's cool, with a gentle breeze, and if I try hard enough I can imagine it's the edge of Paris in late April. I keep my head down and look at the crystal beneath my feet. I think about when Pasha grew this path, when we debated the most efficient mechanisms to make it durable but not slippery when wet. I remember printing the lattice underneath that he used as a base to train the crystal and keep it exactly where we wanted it. I remember the arguments over the color it should be and that twat whose name I can never recall asking if we could engineer it to look like it was made of yellow bricks. I had to look that up on the cloud. He was a pop culture historian and that was his contribution to the colony aesthetic? Why did the Ringmaster approve his place on the ship?

And then I see it: the western gate. Nothing more than a

couple of symbolic pillars designed by Pasha's wife, Neela. I like her style; it's simple and elegant. I helped her to print them, but she thought them up. She liked the freedom given by the fact that no one cared about them on that side of our settlement; it was the side farthest away from God's city.

Mack is standing there, the only other person out and about at this time, looking away from the colony. I can see the mountains in the distance and the vast plains between. The figure he's watching is probably half a kilometer away, hunched over and moving slowly. The landscape is still relatively wild beyond the gate, with long grasslike plants.

"Do you know who it is?" I ask as I approach, more to signal that I'm there than anything else.

"A man, in his early twenties or so," he replies. "The proximity alarm woke me up. I thought it was an animal."

The man is staggering toward the colony. "Is he sick?"

"No obvious symptoms. Look for yourself."

I shake my head. "I disabled the zoom in my lens. It gives me migraines and—"

"He must be from the others," he says, not interested in me and my nervous babbling. "One of their kids. He must have walked for weeks."

My palms are slick with sweat and I want to go home. "What do you want me to do?"

He turns and looks at me for the first time, a slight twitch around his left eye indicating he's switching to normal focal range. He's looking haggard with the stress of it all. Mack hates the unexpected almost as much as I do, but his clothes are smart, his black hair tidy and his beard neat. He has to present himself at his best, even when he thinks there's just an animal to scare off the boundary.

"Do you think we should shoot him?" he asks, looking down at the gun resting on his palm, like a child he was holding has just crapped in his hand.

"Why are you asking me that? Why not Zara? Or Nabiha or Ben? They—"

"Because you were there."

I close my eyes and I think about the vase I left on top of the Masher. I think about whose printer is likely to break down next and remind myself not to mention that I knew it was going to happen; otherwise—

"Ren. What if he's here to ruin everything we've done here?"

"*We've* done?" It comes out like a croak.

"Yes, *we*." His voice hardens. "Should I shoot him and make sure he—"

"Oh for fuck's sake, Mack, I'm an engineer! Not your conscience!"

His mouth drops open at my outburst and I regret the words. He just doesn't want to be the only load-bearing object in this messy structure.

"I haven't got any binoculars," I say in the calmest voice I can muster. "Look at him again and tell me what he's carrying."

"A pack, not a big one," he replies after a few moments of scrutiny.

"Any sign of a gun?"

"No."

"Any bulges around his midriff?"

"What, like growths or—"

"Like explosives," I reply and he grimaces before looking back at him. "They wouldn't have the tech for anything more subtle than something they could make from—"

"Nothing like that," Mack cuts me off again.

"Does he look . . . I don't know . . . angry?"

Mack shakes his head. "He looks desperate. Oh, look at him."

The young man is waving both arms, like one lost at sea when sighting a chance of rescue. Mack looks at me, and when our eyes meet, we both know we can't kill him.

"Shit," I say and he nods. "Come on, then—let's go bring him in. If we're quick, we'll get him to your house before anyone notices."

2

I HAVEN'T GONE out of this gate for a long time. There's nothing on this side of the colony that interests me and the sensor net maintains itself. There are animals that range nearby sometimes, but they tend not to come any closer than the edge of the zone monitored by the long-range sensors. I agree with Kay's theory that God's city emits something that keeps them away, but she's still looking into it all these years later. Like all of us, she gets distracted by other experiments. It's low priority.

"What do we say to him?" Mack asks, dragging my focus back to the young man.

"I was going to start with hello and then see how it goes," I reply. I'm trying to sound light and relaxed because I don't want to push the magma chamber of unspoken shit into an eruption. I'm barely handling it as it is.

"He must have been born after Planetfall," he says, his pace fast but steady. "He doesn't look old enough to have been born on the ship and there weren't any babies in their pods."

"Small mercies," I whisper and thankfully he doesn't hear. When I glance at him to check whether he's looking pissed off at me, I see the sweat on his forehead and how white his lips are against the black of his beard. "Are you sure he's alone?"

He looks at me like I'm an idiot. "I checked that."

"But you didn't see him coming."

"I haven't checked on them for a long time. I thought . . ."

He doesn't finish the sentence, but the unspoken half lingers between us. We thought they were dead. We thought we had killed them.

The urge to turn around and go home and tell everyone to fuck off until it's all over bears down on me. I can feel guilt and fear and ten thousand questions I've asked myself since Planetfall rising up with the contents of my stomach and I want all of it to stay deep down where it should be.

"We stick to the story," he says with the firm edge in his voice that means he's made up his mind and it's not up for discussion.

"But he'll know what really happened."

"Stick to the story," Mack says again and I don't have anything else to say. There are too many unknown variables to make any useful predictions and I try not to speculate these days. "Let me do the talking," he adds.

As if I wouldn't do that anyway. He's the Ringmaster. He knows what to say to the crowd and to the latecomer without a ticket. I just maintain the rigging and make sure the tent doesn't collapse on us all.

The sky is now the same deep blue as that of a Mediterranean summer and when I look straight up and see a couple of clouds I can almost believe I'm on Earth again, like my brain cannot help but return to its default setting. Ahead of us the highest mountain nearby, dubbed Diamond Peak by the more romantic members of the colony, will soon be tipped by the sun rising over that exact point. They have a silhouette reminiscent of the Alps. It's only when I look at the details here—the way the seeds are shaped on the grasses we're walking through, the slight sparkle of the silicates in the soil beneath our feet that give it a magical quality and the hard shells of unfamiliar creatures tucked between the stalks—that I remember we're so far from home.

The stranger has sunk to his knees, the exhaustion setting in now that he knows we're coming to him. As we pick up the pace, he falls forward onto his hands, his black hair hanging straight. I can see his pack now. It's a basic design from the survival pattern folder on the local server of each of the Planet-fall pods. It has a built-in water filtration mechanism and a more primitive version of the porous fabric we use on houses in the colony, designed to absorb water and push it, via an osmotic mechanism, to the internal filter. He's probably been living off dew and rainwater for the whole journey—and his own urine, if he had any sense in the dry spells. I have no idea what he would have done for food; there are gels designed to produce fast-growing fungi but not enough packs to sustain such a trip.

He's thin and his clothes are worn and patched in several places. We knew their printers would fail, and without access to the cloud they had no way to run complex diagnostics. None of the people in that group were printer specialists and so unlikely to have any specs or spare-part patterns on their personal servers. The clothes he's wearing are basic survival patterns designed to be durable and breathable with a sensor net built into them designed to help the body's homeostatic system in adverse conditions. The built-in transmitter must have failed; otherwise it would have pinged our network when he was five kilometers away.

Mack and I break into a run when he collapses, disappearing in the tall reed-thin plants. While we run, I check the network to see who's awake and whether there's any talk of Mack and me leaving the gate, but no one seems to have noticed. The sun is rising and in a couple of hours the air will be teeming with insects. I don't have any protective clothing nor repellents on me and I wonder how this man survived without them.

I half expect him to be dead by the time we get to him, but the pack is rising up and down and his head is turned to the side. I think of the parasites and organisms in the dirt only millimeters from his mouth and nose and the millions of microscopic assailants he can't possibly be protected against.

"We're here," Mack says as we stop and kneel down on either side of him. "You're going to be all right."

"Hi," the young man says with a slight American accent as he struggles onto his hands and knees to tip back and rest with his backside on his heels. He sweeps his hair off his face and both Mack and I gawk at him.

He looks like Suh. He looks like the Pathfinder.

I can see her in his eyes, his lips, the shape of his chin and cheekbones. The genetic signature of her Korean heritage is written across him and I want to laugh and cry and kiss him a million times and hide my face with shame. He is an echo of her beauty. He smiles at me uncertainly and I see her again that day at the observatory, holding the piece of paper in her hands.

"Holy crap," she said and held it out to me. "It's real. It's a real thing. It's . . . it's a real place."

I took it and scanned the numbers, but astronomy wasn't in my repertoire. Then I noticed a string of numbers that were more than familiar—just the sight of them made me feel nauseous. They were the first things she wrote when she woke from her coma, before she even spoke or asked where she was or why she was in the hospital.

"It's a place, Ren. There's a planet in the exact location the numbers describe." She laughed, the first time she'd laughed since the day she wrote them down. "Isn't it wonderful? We know what it means now!"

I shook my head. "No, I don't think we do."

All these years later, this stranger has tears in his eyes too. "I knew it wasn't true," he says. "I knew it was real and I knew you wouldn't kill me."

Mack is speechless for the first time in the forty-odd years I've known him.

"Of course we're not going to kill you," I say.

"My name is Lee Sung-Soo." He grasps my hand tightly and I can't help but squeeze back. "My grandmother was the Pathfinder."

I want to take a moment to let it sink in, but Mack is obviously struggling and I need to make this boy think everything's all right. "I'm Ren—Renata Ghali—and this is Cillian Mackenzie, but we all call him Mack."

He smiles at me—I want him to never stop and I want to never see it again, all at once—and then he looks at Mack, who musters one of his warmest smiles as he shakes Sung-Soo by the hand.

"How did you find us?" Mack asks.

"The planet's topography was on one of the pod servers," he replies. "I pieced together some of the things my parents said and worked it out."

"What did they say?" Mack is trying not to look terrified. I've known him too long to be fooled though. That clench in his jaw says it all.

"About the mountain and the plain below it, the things the Pathfinder saw before we got here." His gaze shifts to focus behind us. "That's it, isn't it? That's God's city."

I nod. "Not the bit at the bottom—that's the colony—but the rest is."

"It's . . . amazing," he says and then laughs. "That sounds so stupid. They said it was all a lie, but here I am looking at it!"

"Where are the rest of the people who . . ." Mack doesn't know how to describe them.

Sung-Soo's eyes lose their joy. "They died. I'm the only one left."

Mack takes the pack from his shoulders and puts it on his own back; then we both take an arm, wrap it over our shoulders and hoist him up between us. There's barely any weight to him at all.

We head back toward the colony, and I can't help but look up at God's city, just like Sung-Soo does but with less wonder. I'm used to it now, but it still draws my eyes up.

It stretches above the colony like a huge forest of ancient baobab trees tangled around one another, forming an organic citadel. The outer membranes of the structure are black, to absorb the most sunlight, and at this time in the morning the nodules at the top of the structure are spherical.

"It changes with the weather," I tell him as he walks between us. "When it gets hot, the nodules in the upper levels grow tendrils and look a bit like dendritic cells. It increases the surface area to—"

"To manage the heat," he says, nodding. "My father taught me some of my grandma's knowledge."

Mack's silence feels like a fourth person stalking us through the grasses.

"We'll take you to Mack's place," I say. "To check you over and let you rest."

"Thank you. Can I stay? There's nothing to go back to. There was a storm . . ."

I glance at Mack. He's staring up at the top of the city and doesn't notice. I know where his mind is. I don't want to go there. "Of course you can. Right, Mack?"

He snaps his head to look at me. "What?"

"Sung-Soo can stay, can't he?"

"I don't have any objections," he says diplomatically. "But you must understand, we have to speak to the rest of the colony and give them the chance to ask questions and voice any concerns."

Sung-Soo nods. "Very fair. I can hunt and I can carve well and I'm strong, when I'm rested."

Hunting and carving? Such primitive words. I slip my hand down to hold his and feel for calluses. When I find them, I'm relieved, but why? Did I think he was lying? What else could they have done to survive?

"It's going to be fine," I say, and Sung-Soo smiles as if I meant the words for him.

3

MACK IS GRADUALLY steering us in a different direction for the return journey so we'll go around the outside of the colony and enter at the north gate, right next to his place.

We're silent as we trudge through the grasses, Sung-Soo exhausted and malnourished, Mack and I trapped in our own little spirals of guilt and dread. He's taking us on a route that makes it far less likely we'll be spotted, but there's still a chance. He's probably trying to work out what to tell everyone else and buying time to figure that out at his own pace.

I'm trying to make something more like a mental flowchart out of the tangled mess of what-ifs and thens in my mind. I give up. We've learned so many times that, no matter how carefully we plan, something unpredictable will destabilize the system.

The northern gate is again just a couple of pillars, but more ornately designed than the western one. There are stylized plants and flowers intertwined with overly fussy representations of the skeletal structures that form the frames of our houses. I think it's a bit childish and overdone as a representation of our aspirations to live as sustainably and naturally as we can, but the majority liked it. I think "majority" is one of my least favorite words. It's so often used to justify bad decisions.

Mack's place is based upon one of the round designs, looking like an igloo with spokes coming out of it to end in half-submerged bubbles. We're experimenting with a new membrane on the outside of the central hemisphere and it's looking good; several of the native species we've planted on it are thriving.

Half of the structure is aboveground, the rest submerged below. As Mack touches the patch to the right of the door I can't help but check on the transition between above- and belowground. Some of the earlier experiments with the new coating resulted in unexpected interactions with the soil, but this variant seems okay.

"Are those . . . fish?" Sung-Soo points at one of the windows.

"Yes," I say, refreshed by his wonder at the things I barely notice now. "We harvest energy from sunlight using the aquarium algae. Some of the other houses do that through the outer skin—" I wave a hand at some of them. "But Mack likes fish."

The door opens and its motion makes Sung-Soo dig his heels in a little. "Is it . . . alive?" he asks, staring at its edges compressed against the door frame.

"Sort of," I answer. "It's based on a heart valve, loosely speaking."

He lifts his arm from my shoulder; I let go of his hand so he can brush the structure with his fingertips. "What is it made of?"

"A composite organic material, a bit like cartilage."

"Come inside," Mack says, eager to get him out of sight.

The door sighs shut behind us and the lights come on, bathing the main living area in the daylight spectrum. There are familiar comfy chairs and the central sunken fireplace for when Mack wants some primal reassurance given by control over fire. I'm drawn to the antique orrery displayed above the nook housing his home printer, the only trinket he brought from Earth.

Sung-Soo watches the walls change color as they react to the carbon dioxide we're exhaling, shifting from pale blue to a warm peach.

"House: privacy," Mack says and the inner glass of the aquariums turns opaque.

"Have you got a health kit handy or shall I print one?" I ask as Mack guides Sung-Soo to one of the chairs.

"I've got one in the other room."

"I'll make your chair dirty," Sung-Soo says and Mack shakes his head at him.

"It cleans itself; it's fine. Don't worry about a thing." He goes off to his bedroom and I note he takes Sung-Soo's pack with him.

"What's that for?" Sung-Soo asks, pointing at the large bowl-shaped impression at the center of the room.

"It's a fire pit," I say and he nods.

"That I understand."

"We don't need them for warmth; the house maintains whatever temperature we want. Lots of us feel comforted by a fire, that's all. Would you like me to light one?"

He shakes his head. "I'm warm enough, thanks." He reaches down to brush the carpet. "Is this a plant?"

I nod. "A kind of moss. It's part of the house's ecosystem."

Mack returns with the small case and I reach for it. He passes it over after a moment's pause, realizing that I want to do the assessment. It's not that I don't trust Mack. I just want to be sure it's done properly.

I run the roller over Sung-Soo's forehead and down the right side of his cheek. Normal temperature so no infection. A good start.

"I'm going to take a blood sample. It won't hurt. It's the fastest way to see how well you are."

He just nods and rolls up his sleeve. "I've had them before."

I take the penlike syringe from the case and press the blunt tip against his arm. The display at the end of the "pen" helps me locate the vein and numbs the skin there. I click the button at the side and the needle goes in, filling the internal vial with his blood. When it's full, the needle withdraws and the device deposits a tiny bit of skin sealant. When the display goes green, I lift it off his skin and place the pen into the analyzer part of the case.

"I'd like to extract your DNA," I say, adhering to ethics even though Mack is standing behind him with his finger over his mouth. "I'm sorry . . . You do know what that is, don't you?"

Sung-Soo raises an eyebrow. "Of course I do."

"Sorry." It's hard to know what they taught him.

"What do you want with my DNA?"

"Well, everyone in the colony has their genome on file, so it's easy for the colony medical program to recommend treatment or referral to a specialist." I glance up at Mack, who's frowning at me now. He's too tense and he'll give something away if he's not careful. He's lucky I know how to put on a show. "I'm curious too. I don't understand how you survived, to be honest. Did your . . . group develop anything to help you adapt to the environment here?"

He shakes his head. "No. A lot of us died. My father thought it was because of allergens, but none of them knew enough to be able to do anything about it."

His father was a linguist. That was why he was with us that

day. I can't look at Sung-Soo, so I busy myself with the analyzer even though it's already doing what it should.

"And I don't mind about the DNA," he adds with a smile. "Thank you for asking me first."

I add the command to do a full genome extraction from the sample. "It'll take a little while for the information to compile and for me to have a proper look at it."

"Are you a geneticist?"

I nod. "And an engineer. That's what I trained in first. They work well together." A gentle beep from the unit tells me the first set of results is through. As I examine the data, Mack comes and sits down across from Sung-Soo.

"Can you tell us more about what happened to your group after Planetfall?" he asks. "We would have looked for them if we thought they'd survived."

Careful, Mack, I think, hiding my concern by keeping my eyes on the display.

"They all had different stories," Sung-Soo replies. "My father lived longer than my mother and he told me that half of them went mad before I was even born. Some killed themselves; some died from reactions to stuff like plants or things in the air. There were a lot of deaths. Especially of the babies."

I hear Mack swallow.

"He said the Pathfinder was wrong. There was no God, no city, nothing here. He said she was mad and they didn't want to be part of her colony and live her lies. So they ran away."

There's a tremble in his voice and his eyes are filled with anger.

"He lied to me though. I never believed him. I couldn't believe my grandmother would do such amazing things and it all turn out to be crap."

"What else did he say about the Pathfinder?" Mack presses.

I want to leave and the strain of fighting that urge is giving me a headache.

Sung-Soo is silent for a few moments. "He . . . he said she was dead." Now he looks tearful. "I've been too afraid to ask. Is that true? Is she dead?"

"No!" Mack says cheerily and pats his knee. "She's in God's city, communing with the creator."

Sung-Soo's face is happiness and relief incarnate. "Can I see her?"

Mack shakes his head. "None of us can, I'm afraid, but once a year she sends us a message. The next one is due in a few days. You're just in time!"

I don't think Sung-Soo knows how to process the news. His expression fluctuates between hope and sadness. "Why only messages?"

"Because God hasn't finished with her yet. When the time is right, when we are ready as well as her, she'll be returned to us."

How many times have I heard him say that? This time it makes me want to scream. But I push it down, as I always do. Better this way. Better for everyone.

"You've got a slight electrolyte imbalance and you're mal-nourished but not dangerously so," I report, eager to change the focus of the conversation. "That's no surprise really. Mack, I've sent a request from the health kit to your kitchen to make him a shake to help replace some of the nutrients." I look back at Sung-Soo. "It won't take long. You need rest and a few good meals and you'll feel a lot better. It's incredible, really."

"How did you survive?" Mack asks.

Sung-Soo smiles. "I know what I can and can't eat here. Don't you?"

"Well . . . yes," I reply. "But only because we could test things first."

"So did we. Sometimes it didn't end well."

I'm desperate to analyze his genome. There has to be something in him that's adapted, but to do so in one generation? It seems . . . incredible.

"We had a lot of problems with allergies in the early days here," I say. "We knew we would, and took precautions, but we couldn't live in environmental suits forever. We managed to engineer retroviruses that modified our DNA to handle the new microbes and allergens here. We're modifying it all the time, of course, and sometimes we're caught out, but we haven't lost anyone yet." Sung-Soo says nothing and I worry I've sounded smug. "So, what I'm trying to say is that once I understand your genome, I can make sure you're properly optimized for survival here."

"More than I am already?"

"Yes."

"I was sick a lot when I was a kid," he says. "But at least I survived."

"How old are you?" I ask.

"I think I'm twenty-two."

"Your mother was pregnant in the Planetfall year?" Mack sounds appalled. He doesn't want to think there was a pregnant woman aboard. Stupid man, there wasn't one; we'd have known. Sung-Soo would have been conceived after Planetfall.

The three of us fall silent then. "How old are you?" Sung-Soo asks me.

"Nearly seventy," I say and watch his eyes widen. "I know I don't look it. We've been working on some interesting things here."

"You said something about a storm," Mack says before he has to reveal how bloody old he is. He's so vain.

Sung-Soo looks past us into the fire pit. "It hit when we were moving the camp to avoid the floods that came every year. We didn't realize how bad it was going to be." He stops and covers his face.

"Your shake is ready, Mack," a synthvoice calls from the kitchen and Mack goes to collect it.

I don't know whether to rest a hand on the poor boy's shoulder or just leave him to it. I've never been very good at this sort of thing.

"I lost everyone there. Do I have to talk about it?" he asks.

"No, no, of course not," I say, not wanting to make him suffer any more than he must have already.

Mack returns with a tall glass filled with the shake. I drink a lot of them. They're surprisingly satisfying. Sung-Soo takes a hesitant sip and then comes to the same conclusion.

He downs the contents and hands the glass back to Mack with a smile. In moments his head tips back and he slumps out cold.

I lurch forward to take his pulse, but Mack grabs my wrist.

"I gave him a sedative," he says. "He'll be fine."

"What did you do that for?"

"We need to talk about what we do next. You don't believe him, do you?"

I stand and move away to the window. Mack joins me. Faint shadows of fish cross his features as I try to fathom what he's suspicious of.

"Which part don't you believe?" I ask.

"You know how angry his father was! He said he was going to tell everyone when we completed Planetfall. Do you really think he didn't tell his own son?"

"He must have changed his mind," I reply, watching Sung-Soo's chest rise up and down slowly, fearful he'll wake and hear us. "What did you give him?"

"The same stuff that knocks me out for eight hours," Mack replies. He can't remember the drug's name.

Paranoid, I hurry over to Sung-Soo and check he really is unconscious. Mack can be an idiot sometimes; there was no guarantee that the drug would have the same effect on a boy who survived everything this planet's biomass had to throw at him. When I'm satisfied he is asleep, I return to Mack. "Maybe he didn't want his son growing up knowing the truth. It's about as shitty as the truth comes, after all."

Mack stares at the boy. "You trust him?"

I shrug, remembering how I felt after discovering the calluses on his hands. "I don't know. All I do know is that if we throw him out of the colony, or some other despicable thing, I'll never forgive myself. Or you, for that matter. Let's give him the benefit of the doubt. He's Suh's grandson, for fuck's sake!"

"Tell me what comes of the genetic analysis," he says, capitulating. "I'll let him sleep it off, then help him clean up and I'll think of a way to break the news."

"He'll need somewhere to live."

"He can stay with me while a place is built. I have room," he offers.

I'm relieved. "I'll be back when I have some answers," I say, and after one last look at Sung-Soo I take the health kit and leave Mack to it.

4

I HATE FEELING this way. As I walk away from Mack's place I can feel that horrible fluttering in my chest like a swarm of flies is trapped behind my ribs. I used to dream about them inside my chest, laying eggs in my heart and the maggots chewing their way through it until my chest burst open. The only thing that drowned out their buzz was my screams as I woke. I haven't had that nightmare for a long time. I fear that will change now.

I try to focus on the health kit's tiny orange light indicating the analyzer is still at work, to think about an improvement to the membrane I'm testing on the outside of my house, to focus on the feeling of my toes inside my shoes and the sound of the soles against the crystal path, but nothing calms the swarm. Something terrible is going to happen. I need to go home. I need to—

"Ren, is Mack okay?"

Nick's voice makes me cry out and I nearly drop the kit. I

clutch it to my stomach as he approaches. He looks concerned, but also excited. Something unusual is happening and he thrives on being the first on the scene.

"Mack?"

He's looking at the health kit. "I saw someone help you carry him into his house. Is he hurt?"

Either he caught the briefest glimpse of the back of us or he's trying to trick me into lying. I can't handle this. I don't know what to say.

Now he's frowning. I'm not usually caught out so easily. I haven't had a chance to get my head straight.

"He . . ." I look at the kit to avoid his eyes. He means well, I remind myself. He doesn't realize I find his interest irritating. He probably believes he's being personable and caring about the community. I think he's overcompensating.

Then I feel guilty. I've defended Nick so many times when people have grumbled about him. In the early days of the project so many people treated him so badly I felt shocked to the core. It made me realize I lived in a bubble, a world where all the people I interacted with every day were highly intelligent and accepting and had evolved past so much of the bullshit that still plagued swathes of society. When Nick arrived, having bought his place with an obscene amount of money, these highly intelligent people treated him with sneering disdain and open hostility. It reminded me that we're still apes. Still evolving.

"Is it bad?" he asks with a hushed voice and takes a step closer.

Don't touch me, I think as he reaches a hand toward my shoulder.

"It's—"

A sound behind me makes him look past my face and his hand drops to his side. I see confusion in his expression and twist to see Mack hurrying out of his house. Shit.

Mack's head is down and he's marching swiftly toward the central Dome with his hands in his pockets, whispering to himself. I check the network and see his status as "busy—private." He's either having a private conversation with someone else or dictating a message. He prefers to use voice rather than the v-keyboard. He laughs at me when I use mine, saying I look like a poor mime trying to look like I'm playing the piano. I never rise to the bait though. It may look stupid but at least people can't lip-read or listen in. There are at least a hundred or so people in the colony with augmented hearing good enough to eavesdrop on him now if they chose to. Luckily Nick isn't one of them.

"Oh, he seems fine," Nick says and looks at me pointedly. He wants to know who the third person was.

"Yeah, Mack's okay," I say.

Why is he going to the Dome? He goes there only for group meetings and there are none scheduled for today. As soon as I think that, I get an icon in the top right of my field of vision asking if I want to check.

"Ren, what's going on?"

With a glance to the upper right I select the option and the schedule appears to float over Nick's jacket. There's a new entry. But before I have a chance to check it, an urgent message arrives, the icon for that larger and flashing in the way I find so annoying. Nick looks away and I suspect he's got one too.

I open it. Obviously from Mack. I didn't anticipate the content though, nor the fact that he's sent it to every member of the colony.

Fellow citizens, I apologize for the hour and the urgent tag
but there's a need for a colony-wide discussion of an event
that occurred this morning. It seems there were survivors

of the tragic accident that happened during Planetfall. The child of one of those survivors has made it to us and has asked to live with us at the foot of God's city.

The envelope icon has started to flash in the corner of my vision. It does that only when there are more than ten unopened messages.

That child is Lee Suh-Mi's grandson. His name is Lee Sung-Soo.

"God in his mercy!" Nick exclaims moments later. He must be at the same part as me.

If you have any concerns about Sung-Soo, or objections to his joining us, I want you to follow the protocol for any colony-wide issue, namely contacting your group leader, who will bring them to the council meeting I've scheduled in ten minutes. Apologies for not giving more notice, but this is just as unexpected for me as it is for you and I think it's imperative we deal with any concerns as soon as possible, for Sung-Soo's sake. The meeting will be open on the public stream and the public tag for this topic is "Newcomer." Sung-Soo is not connected to our network.

A flash appears bottom right, indicating a new trending tag. I don't have to look it up to know what it is. Interesting choice of word. Would I have picked the same one? It's less loaded than "survivor" or "stranger" but has a subliminal effect of assuming he's going to stay. After all, Mack didn't pick "visitor." Nor "guilty reminder," but that would just be stupid.

I'm sure lots of people will be keen to meet him. He's had a
very difficult journey and I ask that people respect his need
for the time and space to recover. We need time as a
community to take in the news and resolve any issues we
may have before he's introduced to everyone. Thank you for
your understanding. I'm in the Dome now but ask you to
discuss this in your groups and direct any questions to your
councilor rather than my private stream. Thanks, Mack.

When I pull my attention from the message, I notice Nick
staring at me. "So that's who it is," he says and looks at Mack's
place.

"Aren't you group leader this month?"

He nods and realizes he can't just go and bang on the door.
He has to go home and be available to anyone who wants to
speak to him in person as well as online. He leaves and I set
the health kit down at my feet before calling up the v-keyboard.

Thanks for the heads-up, Mack.

I don't expect him to reply; he's probably being inundated
despite his request. But he does.

We couldn't keep it a secret. I saw Nick poking his nose in
and had to make a call on it. We knew we would have to tell
everyone eventually. Come to the Dome. I want you here,
you were with me when we found him.

He knows I hate meetings. No.

Ren, don't be a pain in the arse.

People are going to realize he's in your house. I'm going to stay with him in case he wakes up. I don't want to get involved in the politics. That's your bag.

I could do with some support.

You'll be fine. Give me access to your house. I want to keep an eye on him. Look, Carmen is already coming over. You want her banging on the door to wake him up when we're not there?

There's a pause. I can see her talking to Nick, having intercepted him on the way home. It's going to be everywhere in less than—

A door opens behind me. "Ren, is the grandson at Mack's place?"

Mack?

I've given you access. Keep up with the meeting, in case I need some info, OK?

I pick up the health kit as the v-keyboard disappears and hurry over to Mack's place, pretending I can't hear ten different people calling my name. I shut down my stream and my in-box. I just can't handle being connected right now.

I press my palm to the side of the door and the house "tastes" me. I can hear footsteps as the door opens but I don't turn around. "It's being discussed at the meeting," I call over my shoulder and let the door close behind me.

Ignoring the knocking, I put the health kit down on a nearby table and look at Sung-Soo. Mack has taken his shoes off, eased his legs up onto a footstool grown out of the moss and covered him with a blanket.

The moss looks inviting, so I take off my shoes too and let my feet sink into its cool green softness. The knocking eventually stops and I make sure the windows are still set to privacy before making my way to sit near him.

The only sound is our breathing. I watch him sleep, feeling . . . everything. No, not everything. I don't feel relaxed and I don't feel hopeful. Watching someone sleep can be the hardest thing in the world.

I'm back at the hospital in Paris, watching Suh sleep. There are monitors and wires and beeps that serve to remind me that her rest is anything but normal. I cried a lot. I talked a lot too, hoping she could hear me, clinging to some romantic notion that the sound of my voice would somehow call her back into my world.

We were just flatmates then. I already loved her, of course, but no one else knew back then. Not even her.

Watching someone in a coma is a special kind of prison made of love and hope and despair. Sometimes other people come and sit in the prison with you, but you can't have a real conversation. You can talk about coffee or what the sleeper did or didn't do and what that might mean and what the doctors have said, but nothing else. People who don't know the rules learn fast. For those who have no words left for one another there are magazines more than thirty years old, relics of a paper age kept for this kind of prison where no one is allowed to get online and talk about their vigil.

And you're always alone there, even if other people are sitting around the bed and watching the comatose with you. There's nothing to say after the daily update and so you're left there in your private little hells, unable to leave in case they wake up when you weren't there.

So you talk to the sleeper when there aren't any other visitors and you pray and you cry and you sit there, numbed, for hours until one day they either slip away completely or open their eyes and give you the only key out of the prison.

I sat with her for two months. I lost my placement and I nearly lost our flat, before Dad intervened when he realized what was going on. That was back when he wasn't angry with me. That was before the cancer too.

I blink and look around Mack's living room to remind myself I'm not back in that prison again.

5

I'VE BEEN INSIDE every house in the colony—I helped to build most of them—but Mack's is my favorite. It has just the right balance of space and coziness. Not too big, not too small. Room to breathe but still with the feeling of being held.

I walk away from Sung-Soo toward the bedroom, thinking that his pack must still be in there. I want to look inside. I want to see what he's been using to survive and if there's any food or clues to explain how he could have traveled so far alone. It doesn't occur to me that it's a breach of privacy until the pack is in my hands.

I sit on Mack's bed. It's an expanse of crisp white cotton with a patch of dust on it left by the pack. I bounce up and down a couple of times, half to recall what it's like to sit on a bed like this, half to see if the springiness of the sponge we grew two years ago has endured. It feels good and I wonder if he's shared it with anyone lately.

The pack is heavy on my lap. It's certainly weathered

enough. Enough for what? For his story to ring true? Where else would he have come from?

Fumbling with the Velcro, I wince at the sound of it ripping apart. This is wrong but I don't stop myself pulling the inner layer open. There's a waterproof jacket scrunched up, filthy, smelling of mud and sweat. I could close it and put it back where it was but I'm pulling it out, committed to the crime now.

One of the petri dishes that would have contained the gel is the first thing I see underneath, its lid intact. As expected, none of the gel is left. There's something inside, so I pull it out to inspect the contents in the light. I recognize the six nuts still in their shells. They grow on bushes in dry soil and we can't eat them without being horribly sick. They contain a protein we can't digest.

Perhaps he was using them as bait for hunting. I put them on top of the crumpled jacket and pull out a canister with some water left in it, its lid with a valve fitting to connect to the reservoir collected in the pack's filter. There's a thermal sheet folded neatly and a small bundle of something like leather tied tight.

The bow is easy to pull loose and the skin unravels. There are all sorts of small mammals it could have come from. Two knives fall onto the moss. One is large with an impressive blade, probably used for hunting. The second is very small with a worn handle that looks too imperfect to have been printed. Did someone craft it? I wrap both of them up again and retie it, resting it on top of the pile.

There are a couple of jumpers and another pair of trousers, all stinking and crusted with dirt. I pull them out expecting to find more underneath only to find nothing more than powdery soil. I look for pockets I must have missed. There are none.

I put everything back as close to how I found it as I can manage. A notification flashes that the meeting is about to begin, and thanks to Mack's "critical" tag I'm forced to actively notify the network that I won't be present. It's like he's forgotten everything about netiquette in the last hour. I don't shut it out completely though, mindful that he wanted me to keep an eye on things. We both know he's on his own really. But I find myself keeping the stream open and minimalized, my own settings watching for mentions of my name by default. I know most of the questions will be about what happened this morning and then the rest are relatively predictable: Can we be sure he's the only survivor? Why didn't we know they were there? I want to hear Mack's response to that one when it comes up, so I add that to the session alert parameters.

The pack has left a dark smudge on my trousers. I stand, putting it back on the bed, smooth out the divot I left and then brush the dirt off my clothes. Beneath the ambient guilt of going through Sung-Soo's things is an uneasiness, like the pack's contents have given me emotional indigestion.

Something is missing. He spoke of carving and I saw a small knife that looked like it could be used for whittling (is that what they used to call it?), but no carvings, not even small ones. I shake my head. Why would he carry anything like that? It would weigh him down and he was busy surviving. But that bit of mental grit doesn't disappear.

He wouldn't have had time to sit and carve trinkets while traveling, but before he would have. Did he really have nothing he wanted to keep after hours of crafting before he set out to find us? Before—yes, that's it—there is nothing in that pack from his life before. Nothing of his parents, of the others who survived at least some of the years he's been alive.

But he wouldn't want to carry it over a thousand kilometers. I tell myself that other people aren't as sentimental as I am. He didn't have the luxury of keepsakes. Every gram carried had to help him survive. He's lost his people and then been forced to leave everything behind.

I couldn't have done that. I would have to take a lock of hair at least. But perhaps he didn't even have that. A pebble, then, a pebble from the place he was born, something to root him.

When I had to pack before we left Earth it was a thousand tiny agonies strung together. I can still see the empty metal box in front of me, only half a cubic meter in volume.

"That's all we get?" I put a hand on Mack's shoulder, stopping him from leaving.

"It's all we get. Even Suh."

I suspected he would sneak on an extra one for himself and he saw that in my frown. "It's all been worked out, Ren. No exceptions. Not even Nick can take more than that."

"He tried, then?"

Mack laughed. "Of course he did. Offered two million per locker if he could take more. He couldn't understand it wasn't like excess baggage or his country's government. You got an upgrade, didn't you?" He tapped the side of his head and I nodded.

I'd got a faster chip, a better lens and as big a personal server and cloud storage space as I could afford. All my photos, films and music were there already.

"Well, then." He shrugged. "You can print everything else you need once we're on the ship."

I looked around my room at the pictures my mother had painted, the antique microscope my grandfather had left me and the hand-stitched embroidery lovingly crafted by my grandmother. The shells collected at the beach on the day I first felt my baby move inside me. The casts of her feet and hands when she was only a week old, her first pictures, the three candles from her last birthday cake and her ashes. My father's notebook, given to me at my graduation, in which he had handwritten letters to me throughout my life. Every single one made me cry, whether it was about the day I took my first steps or the first time I built my own printer. He always had the foresight to plan ahead for the most beautiful things. That was why it was so hard for him. He didn't see it coming. He couldn't plan ahead for losing me that way.

How could I choose which of these to take and which to leave behind? How could I know which of these threads, weaving me into my past and my family, could be cut without unraveling the deepest parts of me?

Mack seemed to notice the things filling the room for the first time. His gaze rested on the castings, on the tiny bronze toes and fingers. "I'll have some room left in mine, I think. I'll be happy to take something if you want." It was the first time I saw something other than the Ringmaster in him. It was the first time I understood why Suh looked at him the way she did.

I should have gone to the meeting and supported him properly. I check on his stream and it's identical to the meeting one. He's fielding questions, being the perfect mix of reassuring and informative.

I'm here if you need me. My private message is met with a smiley.

I find myself staring at the pack again. Sung-Soo may not need anything to make him feel rooted. Perhaps he's more enlightened than I am. Perhaps he's always looking ahead, eyes on the horizon.

There's no map.

That's the other thing missing. How could he have made that trip without one? Quite aside from the sheer distance covered, there would have been obstacles that could have thrown him off course if he was using simple navigation techniques.

Perhaps he's chipped. Perhaps they found a way to do it. I go back into the living room and kneel in front of him. He hasn't moved. There's a speck of dried shake on his chin and his eyes are still beneath the lids in his dreamless sleep.

It takes me a minute or so of reaching toward his scalp and then pulling back before I can bring myself to run my fingertips through his hair and feel the skin behind his ears. The violation makes me shiver but I am compelled to feel for myself. I should wait until we do a full scan.

There's no sign of anything and my attention turns to his wrists. Nothing is strapped to them and then before I realize what I'm doing I'm patting down the pockets in the rest of his clothing.

I snatch my hands away. What am I doing? Then I see a thong of leather tied around his neck, tucked beneath his top. I pull on it, whispering an apology, and a carved pendant the size of my thumb is revealed. It's a tree, artful, beautiful, one of the native species that remind us of oaks. There's even a little creature realized in its branches with just enough nicks and chips out of the shape to give it large-eyed character. The leather is threaded between two branches.

I don't know what it's carved from. It looks and feels a little like soapstone, with an iridescence that reminds me of the inside of a paua shell I had to leave behind on Earth, given to me by the father of my child. Purples, blues and indigo swirl through it. I wish it were mine.

Reverentially I ease the pendant back behind the fabric and drop it softly onto his chest. He did take something with him.

A gentle beep from the health kit pulls me away. The light is now green and I download the genome to my server rather than the colony one. I want to know first.

I run the quickest, dirtiest analysis, thinking that I'll get myself a drink while the program chugs away and then drill down into the data once the meeting's over. I don't reach the kitchen. The first results flash up a notification that stops me midstride. The genome is contaminated and the program recommends immediate quarantine. When I query why, the response makes me shake: Verify sample taken from Homo sapiens subject.

I'm still standing there, one foot in the air, wondering what the hell that could mean when the software monitoring my stream pings that the question I was interested in has been asked by Nick. He's there in person, being on the council, so I open the full feed and see the Dome's interior with practically every colonist in the central amphitheater. It's big enough to seat everyone, with rings of soft mossed seating running up the slopes. I have the choice of several cam locations, rigged as it is to be recorded and broadcast for all sorts of entertainment as well as the meetings.

I pick the cam closest to Mack, wanting to see what he does. So many faces looking at him expectantly. I was right not to go. I would have been freaking out by now.

"Because I thought you used Atlas to scan for them," Nick continues.

"I did," Mack replies. "The same bank of sensors and camera equipment we used to locate God's city. As many of you know, we looked for them for weeks, taking shifts to watch for any movements or hints they might have survived, but there was nothing."

"Were you looking in the right place?" a man calls from the back, out of shot.

"Of course we bloody were," Nabiha retorts. "I was the one who found the crashed pods. We all saw the pictures that Atlas took of them. And before anyone asks, we know there's nothing wrong with Atlas's array because I tested it only last week."

"Sung-Soo himself has told us there are no other survivors and he implied a nomadic lifestyle, which could account for why we lost them. But the most important thing to focus on now is the man recovering in my house. Does anyone have any objections to his being welcomed into our community?"

I shut down the live feed, seeing Mack's living room properly again and the health kit's green light. I can't tell him anything now, not while he's there in front of them all.

I sit down so I can focus on my v-display without risk of tripping over something. I have a tendency to do that when I get engrossed. I open the analysis program and confirm the source of sample is *Homo sapiens*, male, approximately twenty-two years old. I then call up the data that prompted it to suggest Sung-Soo is anything other than that.

When I drill down, I recognize some of the key markers in the DNA as indigenous. Stupidly, I look back at Sung-Soo, at his fingers and toes almost black with dirt. He's human. He's Suh's grandson. I run a cross-match against her stored genome data and that of his parents, just to be certain, and there's ample evidence that's the case. I'm shocked by the identity of his mother. Lois and Hak-Kun? They never got along. Perhaps the trauma brought them closer together.

But there's something else's DNA in him too, and enough of it to trigger the program's warning. I cross-match the alien DNA with our growing database and the closest thing it matches to is an organism similar to a tapeworm. It makes my stomach flip with worry.

The full medical scan is the only thing—short of my stripping him off, which even I won't do without his permission—that will show if anything is physically amiss. I want to do a full analysis of his secondary genome too. I have to wait for Mack to come back, or wake Sung-Soo early and take him there himself. He should probably eat something soon anyway.

I check the network for the locations of the colonists and it's obviously the best time to take him to the medical pod. Everyone's either in the Dome or in their homes, watching the feed. I'm surprised there's no one camped outside waiting for the first glimpse of him, but I think Mack's open approach is helping demystify it all.

I print a stimulant that will counteract the sedative. As gently as I can, I pull down his lower lip and dab the paste on to the moist skin near his gums. Within a minute his eyes are opening and he stretches. The first thing he notices are his missing shoes and the new footstool.

"You fell asleep."

"I needed it, I think," he replies. "Where's Mack?"

"Telling everyone else about you. How do you feel?"

"Hungry." He looks around the room. "Where are my things?"

"I'll get them for you."

I retrieve the pack and check the stream. There are no objections and they've already moved on to making plans for building him a house, even preparing a chip for him, should he want one.

When I give him his pack, he rummages inside and pulls out the petri dish containing the nuts. He chucks a couple into his mouth and holds out the rest toward me.

I watch him chew, swallow and then frown as he realizes I'm confused. "They're good," he says, popping another into his mouth.

"We can't eat them."

"Who can't? Why not?"

"Humans," I say and then realize how terrible that sounds. "I mean . . . people here, in the colony, can't eat those. It makes us ill."

He stares down at the nuts. "You sure it's the same ones?"

When I nod, he shrugs, unconcerned. "More for me, then."

6

BY THE TIME I've got Sung-Soo to the medical center, Kay is ready and waiting with everything fired up and ready to go. She's been following the stream from her lab, thankfully; otherwise her leaving the meeting at the Dome after my call would have sent the gossip dogs loose among us.

Kay has one of the best smiles on the colony, a mixture of dimples and the promise of a fantastic sense of humor. Even after all the years since we had our fling, I can still remember the feel of her body against mine and the way she blew raspberries on my stomach whenever I tried to leave her bed. Her skin is slightly lighter than my father's was, her hair a wild afro explosion pulled back into a tight ponytail now that she's on duty. She doesn't hide her delight when meeting Sung-Soo and shakes his hand warmly with both of hers. That smile has a predictable effect upon him and I see him relax in moments. That's why I took him to her instead of Dr. Lincoln.

"You look like your grandmother," she says to him as she leads him over to a chair. "Did Ren tell you that?"

Sung-Soo shakes his head. Once seated he looks around the room at the minimalist equipment and the three empty beds. His gaze lingers over some of the covered trays next to one of them, no doubt the swabs and other things Kay will use in the tests.

"No need to be nervous," Kay says, sitting opposite him. "All I'm going to do is take a few samples from you so we can map your secondary genome and take a look inside you to make sure everything looks tickety-boo."

Sung-Soo's hands slap over his stomach protectively. "Inside me?"

Kay's glance at me reveals her brief discomfort. She's realizing just how divorced his life has been from ours. "I don't need to do anything invasive. There's a scanner, over there. You'll just lie down and relax; you'll feel a slight tingling in your skin, that's all."

He nods and after a beat says, "Secondary genome? I thought Ren already did all that genetic stuff."

"I'll take swabs from your skin, inside your mouth, and a stool and urine sample." Kay's voice is light and pitched exactly right to put him at ease. "From those, I'll be able to identify your microbiome—the bacteria that lives in and on you. We all have it—in fact that bacteria keeps us healthy—we just think yours will be different from ours because you grew up somewhere else."

I've already sent the first findings to her and told her about the nuts, so she must be desperate to get started. She's hiding it well though. Lincoln would have had him swabbed by now, not giving a shit about putting the boy at ease. After a brief stab of paranoia I check on his location and he's at the Dome. I can't imagine the meeting lasting much longer and wonder if he'll already know that I've brought Sung-Soo to the other doctor. I'm not looking forward to the next time I see him.

"Will you stay, Ren?" Sung-Soo asks and I nod.

"Of course."

Another look from Kay. She can see he trusts me. She doesn't know how little I deserve that. I pull over another chair so I don't have to hide that from my face.

She takes the swabs first and the only time Sung-Soo will let me out of his sight is when he has to go to the bathroom with a sample cup and reddening cheeks. Once the samples are loaded for processing and the extraction started, Kay has Sung-Soo lie down to start the scan.

"Does everything look okay?" he asks. "Where can I see my insides?"

"Try to keep still," Kay replies and returns her attention to the scan.

When Sung-Soo looks to me, I smile. "Only Dr. Reed can see the scan. It's supposed to be that way. Anything to do with your health remains confidential between the doctor and you."

If he were chipped, Kay could share what she sees overlaid across his body, if she considered it a risk worth taking. There have been times when patients have demanded to have the scan's results shared to their vision through the cloud, only to freak out at the sight of something perfectly normal. There aren't any physical screens in here to show Sung-Soo what's going on and I feel the gulf between our experiences widen. It must seem bizarre to him.

"My father could see things that weren't there," he says. "And a couple of the other older ones, but none of us that were born after they landed."

"Do you want to be chipped?" I ask and he frowns. "Do you want to be able to see things like we do?" I clarify.

"I don't know," he says and looks at Kay. "What's wrong?"

He's perceptive; at first glance I would think there was only concentration on Kay's face, but she's concerned about something.

"Nothing's wrong," she replies, a beat too slow. "You're just very interesting, that's all."

The words make me feel sick. Sung-Soo's attention goes back to me and all I can do is try to smile as reassuringly as I can.

"Show Ren," he says. "Make her see what you can. Please."

Why does he trust me so?

"I can explain everything once the scan is done," Kay says.

"I want Ren to see it now."

Does he want to see my reaction? Perhaps that's it. Perhaps he can see that Kay is harder to read than I am. She pauses the scan with a flick of her right index finger and turns to me.

"Are you comfortable with that?"

I shrug. "I don't understand this stuff as well as Dr. Reed does," I say to Sung-Soo. "I don't think I'll be much use."

"Please," he repeats and Kay nods.

She sends me a ping from her place on the cloud, and after I've followed it, passed a security check and agreed to various confidentiality clauses, her view of the scan's live feed is overlaid across Sung-Soo's body. As I'm trying to make sense of it I see her fingers moving in my peripheral vision. She's using a v-keyboard and in moments a private message arrives from her.

There's an organism living in his gut. Don't freak out when you look at it. It's indigenous and I'm not sure if it's parasitic or symbiotic yet—that's what I'm trying to work out.

Like a tapeworm?

I'll be able to tell you more soon. Keep him calm.

"We're trying to work out how you can eat those nuts," I tell him, aware of his scrutiny. "It's a hard puzzle, but nothing to worry about."

"I feel fine," he says to Kay. "I walked here. I'm fit, just tired."

"How long did it take you?"

"About two months."

Kay looks at me. She opens her v-keyboard. Did he have a map we could follow back?

No sign of anything like that. He says he pieced together some clues from what he'd heard his father say about the Pathfinder's visions and used the pod's computer to work out the direction from the first scans we did of the surface.

While the analysis is crunching I'll take a look at his brain. I had no idea there was anything between Lois and Hak-Kun.

I don't reply to that. The scan is complete. We take longer to examine the results than it takes to create them. I watch as she zooms in on his brain and enlarges it, identifying major structures and exploding them out like a construction blueprint. I know most of them, but not everything about what they do and how they interact with one another.

Huge hippocampus! she types to me. His spatial memory must be phenomenal.

"Do you mind if I ask you some questions?" she asks him. When he shakes his head, she begins to quiz him on how they lived, from what they ate to where they built and what they used.

I can feel the need to leave increasing. I haven't had a chance to take this in properly. It's all happened too fast. I need to be by myself and fit a better lid on the huge, bubbling pot of emotions boiling inside me.

He answers all the questions without giving any sense of feeling invaded by her curiosity. Why is she fussing about this and not the thing living in his gut? I can't help but think about the awful stories Dad used to tell me about what his grandparents dealt with as frontline medical care providers. What was it called . . . the worm that came out of the blister? A guinea worm! I had nightmares for weeks after he told me about that and refused to drink water from anything other than our house supply, which I knew was off-grid and filtered multiple times, even though we were living in France by then. I can hear his laughter when he realized I refused to drink the water from the table jug at one of the most expensive restaurants in Paris because I feared it contained larvae.

"Renata—" My dad's laugh made the people at the tables around us smile; it was the warmest, happiest sound of my childhood. "They eradicated the disease years ago. There haven't been any reported cases for over two decades and even when it was widespread, they didn't get it in Paris."

I must have been nine or ten. My feet only just touched the floor when seated in those restaurant chairs. He and my mother had split up by then.

"But what if someone kept a worm in a jar and forgot about it and tipped it down the toilet and then spread the eggs over the city and—"

"We don't drink the same water we flush down the toilet. You know that. This is just a worry-thought, Ren. Remember what we said about worry-thoughts the other night?"

I'm filled with a wrenching need to speak to him again, to hear his gentle voice. He knew just what to say to make me feel safe, not only from the external but also my internal world. That scared me more than anything, sometimes; the noise of my thoughts, the sense that even the space inside myself wasn't safe.

"Ren?" Kay asks. "Are you okay?"

I blink and realize there's unread text in our chat window.

Nomadic, as I thought, her message reads. You see this kind of hippocampal enlargement in people who have to remember details across large geographical areas.

"Sorry, I was miles away there." I feel stupid. Kay is frowning at me, confused by my lack of interest. Usually I devour anything she sends my way.

I realize that Sung-Soo's hand is resting on mine. He's looking up at me with the strangest expression and I have no idea what he's thinking. "You're missing someone," he says.

I pull away and shut down the shared scan results. "I need the . . . I won't be a minute."

Once I'm locked in the bathroom, I put the lid of the toilet down and sit, hunched over, wrapping my arms about my body. Of course he knows how to recognize that. His father must have looked like I did, every fucking day.

I pull up my sleeve and pinch my forearm, focusing on the pain from that until the urge to cry subsides. I will not lose control again today. I will not think of anything except making sure Sung-Soo is okay and that whatever is inside him isn't a long-term threat to his health or anything that could cause a problem for us.

I take a deep breath and flush the toilet for effect. I wash my hands for the same reason, but it also calms me. Then I go back to them.

"Could you take a look at the first results through from the analyzer?" Kay asks and I nod. "Ren is faster than I am," she explains to Sung-Soo.

"Are you okay, Ren?" he asks and I nod, tired of the question.

"I'm fine. Let me take a look at this stuff. I'll just be sitting here, right next to you, okay?"

I work on the data from his stool and urine samples first, concerned about whatever it is inside him. Between the data from the bacteria within it, the actual content of the stool itself, and the traces of indigenous DNA woven in with his blood sample, I manage to ascertain that, whatever it is, it's not putting anything like eggs or anything reproductive into what he excretes. That could change, of course, but I'm still relieved nonetheless. It's putting something into his blood though. I look at the scan and see the thing nestled in his digestive tract, in the same kind of place a tapeworm would be happy—another parasite that haunted my childhood nightmares once I learned of it. It looks a bit like a grub and isn't big enough for him to be able to feel it.

I don't want to risk taking a biopsy and have it release something toxic, and I don't want to put Sung-Soo through a procedure, no matter how painless it would be. I can't see anything that indicates something that would be poisonous to us through contact or ingestion, even without the same microbiome as he has. I have enough genetic data to begin modeling the interaction between his body and the organism and decide that's the best course of action for now.

I only realize how long I've been working when I hear a gentle snore. Sung-Soo is asleep where he was lying, a blanket now drawn over him. There's an IV bag hung up next to him, probably to get his electrolytes sorted out. Kay is sitting on the other side of the room working away. I check on the meeting stream and see that it finished over an hour ago. There were no objections to Sung-Soo being accepted into the colony.

A message from Mack—mercifully without an "urgent" tag—asks if everything is okay and I shoot off a quick message giving him an update before going over to Kay. I don't give any details, mindful of confidentiality.

"I don't think that thing inside him is a risk to anyone else," I say in a whisper.

"Agreed. I think it's a symbiotic relationship," she whispers back. "My theory is that it provides him with the immune system benefits that kept him alive when lots of the others born in their camp died. He probably ingested an egg or larva and it stayed, taking a portion of nutrients from his food, including the proteins from those nuts. I saw something like this in an animal I dissected last year. That's where the genome data on the server came from."

"What shall we tell Sung-Soo?"

She rubs her forehead. "Nothing until we have a comprehensive picture of what it does. I want to be certain it doesn't have any other effects on him that haven't been picked up in the initial scan. I'm going to keep him here for a few more tests, okay? I've seen the model you started. I'll put any more data I get into it, okay?"

I hesitate, feeling like she's taking over. But this is within her remit more than mine. She has to make sure he's not a threat to the colony's health and she'll have a better idea about how his microbiome will interact with ours.

"I'll keep you posted, Ren," she says, brushing my arm with her hand. "The moment anything comes up, I'll ping you."

"Okay," I say, thinking of the vase I abandoned some hours ago. For a moment I consider going to get it, but it's too risky at this time of day. "Let me know when he wakes up," I add as I head for the door.

"Ren—" She hurries over as I reach for the touch pad. "Don't feel guilty."

I tense, thinking she's overheard something, or somehow—

"Because we all looked for them as best we could. It's not your fault."

I look away, unable to manage the relief that she's just as clueless as everyone else. "Thanks."

"Come over for a drink when you can," she adds, knowing better than to wait for an invitation to my place. "Anytime you want. It's been a while."

There's a change in the way she's looking at me, the way her hand rests on my shoulder. But there's no room inside me for anything like that now. "I'll try," I say. "But I reckon things will be busy for a while."

She nods and kisses my cheek. "See you soon, Ren."

When I step outside, I feel the breeze cool the skin where she kissed me. Lots of people are outside, chattering to one another excitedly, in person and in the streams. I check for any trouble brewing but there is none; they just want to see Sung-Soo and they've realized he's inside.

Now they're all looking at me.

"Is he in there?" Zara calls from the rapidly gathering crowd.

I don't know what to do. Will they all try to go in to see him? I hear a little beep from the other side of the door. Kay has noticed the crowd and locked the door. A second later, a message arrives from her.

Tell them he's here for tests and recovery and that he's
doing fine. No visitors yet though.

"He's being cared for by Dr. Reed," I begin and watch the worry spread. "He's absolutely fine. Really. No visitors yet."

"We're going to hold a welcome party," Nick says, coming closer. "Can I just pass on the invite?"

"No," I say too quickly. "Send it to Dr. Reed and she'll pass it on. He's asleep at the moment and he might not be up for it."

Poor man. If I'd walked all that way, the last thing I'd want was a party thrown in my honor.

"It's an open invite," Nick adds. "We'd love to see you there, Renata."

"Are you free for a drink now?" Zara asks and Nick scowls at her.

Oh shit, they want to milk me for information. "Not right now," I say. "And thanks for the invite," I say to Nick. "I'll . . . do my best to be there."

Before I even finish the sentence, the envelope icon is flashing again as private messages pour in. I shut it down and try to think of a decent enough excuse for getting away from them as soon as possible.

There's a ping with a "maintenance" tag attached. As Nick strides over, pushing his way past others to reach me, I open it. Carmen's printer has broken down. There's a personal note attached. You can hide in here if you want.

Her house is mere meters away and I can see her at the window. She raises a hand when she sees me look over and then mimes having a drink. Hers is not the port of choice, but there's a storm brewing here and she's offering the closest sanctuary.

"Carmen's printer has broken," I say. "I need to fix it. See you all at the party, maybe."

7

CARMEN'S PLACE HAS marble flooring that gleams beneath the dozens of bright, starlike lights floating beneath her ceiling in baubles filled with helium. There's enough light coming from the windows, which are bigger and clear plasglass instead of the murky aquariums that Mack favors, but she likes the sparkling. All of her home's energy is absorbed through the outer skin of the house, which looks like a shiny black marble half embedded in the earth, its surface broken only by the curved windows.

The inner space is totally open plan, aside from a bathroom partitioned off with a slab of polished granite. She shares her home with a different person every year. There's about a hundred or so who do that, believing that it's the best way to keep different groups knitted together in an expanding colony. She has two daughters, one of whom is asleep in her cot on the far side of the room. The other must be at the crèche or with her father perhaps. The other father is living with another man in the group now. I couldn't imagine having to share my space with anyone, let alone having to get used to a new person every year.

"You looked like you needed a hideout," she says, coming over to kiss me on each cheek, as is her way. I try not to think of the germs she's left on my skin, nor of the possibility that some left by Kay's kiss are now about to invade Carmen's body when she next licks her lips.

"I did," I say. "Is your printer really broken?"

"I cracked the casing, just in case anyone checks up." She grins. "Can't have them thinking we're colluding."

"What would we collude over?"

"Nothing. Would you like a drink?"

"Water, please."

I watch her walk over to the kitchen area, which is nothing more than a countertop and a couple of hot plates for when the mood to cook takes her. There's a food printer and a few other gadgets hidden behind gleaming panels of crystal. I don't know how she copes with all the sparkling. The outside world must seem very dull and matte to her children.

She slides one of the panels across, finds a glass shaped like a lily and fills it with water from the dispenser next to the printer. I know the water is pure; I built the filtration system. The glass isn't one of her design; she only uses downloadable templates.

"Thanks," I say and drink most of it straightaway, not appreciating my thirst until now. She refills it for me before getting one for herself and then beckons me over to join her as she sits on the wide white sofa.

I perch at the other end of it, feeling like I'm taking sanctuary from wolves in a bear's cave. "How are the girls?" I ask, having forgotten their names.

"Fine, fine," she says. "So tell me all about him."

I knew it was coming. "Is that the price for my rescue?"

She sniffs. "Mack answered everyone's questions, but didn't say what he was like. Is he savage? He must be, living without any access to the cloud."

"People don't become feral just because they're not chipped!"

"I didn't think he would be." Her smile makes me curse myself. I resolve to not give any more away. "Will he be at the party?"

"I've no idea."

"Mack said he can talk, like us."

"Carmen, he wasn't raised by gorillas!"

Leaning back, she sips from her glass. I have the feeling she's building up to something. "So he understands how we live. Enough to join the colony, at least."

"Is there something that's worrying you?"

Carmen puts the glass down by her feet and sits on the edge of the sofa, suddenly focused and businesslike. "You must have thought about the timing of this."

I keep quiet. Does she mean how long it took for us to discover they'd survived, or something else?

"It's less than two weeks before the next message from the Pathfinder." When I keep silent, she sighs and says, "Renata, don't you think it auspicious that her grandson—one that we didn't even know exists—comes here in time to receive her message?"

"'Auspicious' is a loaded word."

"What would you use?"

"Coincidental."

It's not what she wants to hear. There's the tiniest shake of her head. "You don't think it's significant in any way?"

"I think him coming here is significant, not the timing."

"God guided him here to us—"

"He memorized a map."

"In time to receive the Pathfinder's message," she continues, ignoring me. "And I think it should be he who takes the seed."

I rub my eyes with my thumb and forefinger. I'm too tired for this shit. "Carmen, there are rules about this; you know that." I don't say anything about how I feel about them, how much I dread the event nor how the ritualization of it all makes me sick to my stomach.

"Rules that *we* made, not God."

"They were made for good reasons."

"But this sign from God should take precedence over anything Mack decided was the way to do things over twenty years ago!"

I don't like the sound of this. "It wasn't just Mack; it was the council, and you bloody well know why they decided this was the way." She doesn't know the true reasons; none of them do, aside from Mack and me. "And anyway, saying it's a sign from God is an interpretation, not a fact."

"It's too close to be anything but!" Carmen's cheeks are flushed and the baby is stirring in her cot, disturbed by the tone of her voice. "He could have arrived just after the ceremony, or six months afterward, but no, he comes in time to receive the seed himself. We have to acknowledge that God must have planned it that way."

The resurgence of this kind of religious talk makes the skin on the back of my neck prickle. The times it's blossomed in the colony have brought us closer to self-destruction than anything Mack has kept hidden.

"I don't want there to be any religious talk," I remember Suh saying at the first meeting with Mack.

He stared at her for a moment, half laughed and then fell silent when he realized she was serious. "You have half the planet saying you're the next prophet, you've said yourself that you want to build a spaceship to find God, and you don't want anyone to talk about religion?"

"You said the whole world is talking about me when we spoke on the phone," she replied. "What's the other half calling me?"

"Mad," I said as he squirmed. "Messiah complex, mostly. Some of the kinder ones are theorizing that you can't handle being a late-blooming genius, so you're claiming a divine element as a defense mechanism."

Suh shook her head, closed her eyes for a moment and then looked at Mack. "What do you think I am?"

"Ambitious," he replied without hesitation. "Brilliant. Fascinating."

"Do you believe in God?"

"No."

"Ren does."

He looked at me for the first time. "And you are?"

"My best friend," Suh answered for me. "And before the coma, about twenty times more intelligent than me."

He didn't stop looking at me. "And what do you think?"

"I think that something has sent a message through Suh."

"God?"

"I want to go with Suh," I replied, dodging the question. I hadn't made up my mind yet. Some days I thought she was mad; some days I found myself weeping at the local church, thanking God for choosing my best friend. "What I think is going on isn't important."

He nodded at that. "True. It's what investors think that counts. Unless you happen to be a billionaire?"

"No," I said. "But I'm an engineer, so I can help."

Mack smirked. "That's like looking at the national debt of the United States and saying that you've already had a friend promise to pay back a dime."

"Ren is very gifted and I trust her. That's the thing that worries me about all this." Suh waved a hand at the tentative drawings she'd made of the craft that went on to become Atlas. "If this is going to happen, we need to bring in people I've never met, but who will have heard of me. I've had death threats. How can I trust them?"

Mack steepled his fingers in front of his chin. "You want to travel millions of miles into outer space, and it's that that worries you the most?" He smiled with that gleam in his eye. "I'll worry about the people; you worry about whether you know where we're going."

"Where *we're* going? You want to come too?"

"If you'll have me. I can put in twenty million dollars by the end of today, another ten when I've liquidated some assets. I wouldn't have offered to fund-raise for you if I didn't believe in the project."

"I thought you offered to fund-raise so you could earn your fee," I said, not liking the way he was obviously trying to charm Suh.

"I'll waive my fee, on one condition." He was focused fully on Suh again. I wasn't important. "You let me help you choose who comes on board. I'll make sure that none of the crazies get anywhere near this."

Suh didn't even hesitate. "Agreed. And remember: no religious talk. We focus on the science and downplay anything else I might have said when I wasn't being careful."

"So you don't think you're building a ship to find God anymore?"

"I didn't say that," she replied, glancing at me. "I just don't want that to be the only thing people are thinking about when they're considering joining the project."

We argued that night. I couldn't understand why she trusted

Mack and she couldn't understand why I was so upset. I couldn't articulate the reasons back then because I couldn't admit my feelings about her. She got her way, of course. And her instincts were correct about him, though it took me several years longer to admit that.

He did an excellent job of screening candidates, but there was always a risk of zealotry in some of the people accepted onto the ship. Carmen's profile certainly showed leanings toward it, but we engineered our way of life to try to keep it in check. I wonder if this is the beginning of destabilization, the start of the allergic response to the new social pathogen.

No, I shouldn't think of Sung-Soo like that.

"I think that interpreting events as signs from God is a slippery slope," I begin but she cuts me off before I can finish.

"But that's what the Pathfinder did! You followed her—we all did. How can you do that and live at the foot of God's city and reject this sign?"

"Don't you remember what happened the last time people said stuff like that?" It's a low blow, but I want her to think about what she's doing.

"Of course I do. But this is completely different."

I stand up. I can see there's no reasoning with her and that she's built up enough steam in her own head to start something off. Mack needs to know and I can't warn him while I'm here. "I should fix that casing."

"Renata." She stands too, taking care to calm her voice after a glance at the child starting to fidget herself awake. "Please at least think about this. I'm not the only one who sees it this way."

"What about Marco? He's been preparing himself for the last six months. Do you think it's okay to tell him it's all for nothing?"

Marco was living apart from us, a mile away on the other

side of God's city, cut off from the cloud and our network, with only a medical app monitoring his health, programmed to alert the doctors if there is anything outside of normal parameters. He is living as pure a life as he can, as agreed upon in the year after the first message seed was "found."

"He would understand."

"I don't think he would, nor his group, nor the people who thought he was the best candidate. Look, Carmen, none of this is up to me. I'm sure the council will consider this." I put some space between us by going over to the printer.

"Oh, they will. I've already notified my group leader and there's a stream debating it right now."

Shit. This isn't going to go away. "Can you give me temporary privileges?" I point at the printer and in seconds I receive a ping to that effect. It's only a hairline crack in the plasglass and takes less than five minutes to fix. She watches me the whole time, occasionally taking a breath to say something but then deciding not to. The baby settles again and I head toward the door.

"Will you at least consider her grandson as a candidate?" she asks and I stop.

"Next year," I reply. "But not before the next ceremony."

"If God wanted him to have the seed next year, he wouldn't have guided him to us in time for this one."

"You were the best astrophysicist in Europe," I say, pressing my hand against the pad on the door frame. "I would stick to interpreting data that can be verified objectively. For all our sakes."

8

SEVERAL HOURS LATER I'm curled up on my bed, my back pressed up against a pile of clothes I need to sort through, looking at the vase I've reclaimed from the top of the Masher. It took a while to find the perfect place for it, and even though it's precariously balanced, it looks right there. I wonder about who made it again. That makes me think about the failing printer, which brings thoughts of Carmen's words back to me. Why doesn't she see what she's doing?

I told Sung-Soo we hadn't lost anyone yet. That was only a half-truth. We haven't lost anyone to anaphylactic shock or accidental poisoning, but we have lost someone to something worse.

It started in the same way; that's why Carmen infuriates me so. How can she not remember the streams filled with speculation about what God would want us to do? Can't she remember what Liam yelled at everyone the last night we saw him?

"How does Mack know what God expects? He doesn't even believe in him! What if this is the last test? What if the

Pathfinder is waiting for us to join her? I've had dreams too! I've spoken to her too!"

Liam was losing it and we could all see him unraveling in front of us. He wasn't eating properly nor attending to his share of the work that needed to be done. His partner had been in one of the pods that failed to land with us. Oh God, I can still hear the sound of his screaming when he was told.

I did that to him.

I access my server and review the colony's energy consumption data, but the numbers aren't enough to crowd out the guilt and memories of Liam's feet swinging back and forth, back and forth.

I close the file and crawl over to the plate of food I've been trying to eat all evening. I haven't had a proper meal all day and the last thing I need is for Kay to get a notification that something is wrong with me. I pick at the meal, but it's not what I need. The only thing that will satisfy me isn't food and it isn't in the colony. It's in God's city, and I know I have to go back there tonight.

The party for Sung-Soo has already started and Mack has pinged me twice. I just can't face it. Not after today. This time a message arrives. Sung-Soo keeps asking where you are. Are you coming, Ren?

Tell him I'm not feeling—

I delete that. If I tell anyone I'm feeling ill, they'll come over.

I'm shattered, Mack. Tell him I'm sorry but I just can't—

I'm being crap. I should be there. I delete the half-written message and check the network. Everyone seems to be there;

at least there's a hell of a lot of chat about it on the public stream and everyone with their location markers set to "public" is in the Dome. That's a skewed sample though; the kind of people who don't mind everyone else knowing where they are twenty-six hours a day are the kind of people who like parties.

Either way, my absence is being remarked upon and there are several mentions in my personal stream asking when I'll be there. People are talking about how lovely Sung-Soo is and how much he reminds them of the Pathfinder.

"Fuck!" I say to the ceiling and notice a crack in the coating. It isn't changing color in response to my carbon dioxide. "Fuck," I say more quietly at the sight of it.

I can't find any clean clothes, so I print a new set of trousers and a loose top. I manage to locate a belt and pull it free from the pile of stuff on top of it. A quick brush down and it looks like it's just been printed. I run a hand over my head. My hair is too short to need any styling, but it will need a wash soon. I pull a couple of tangled curls apart, look at the corkscrew-like hair that comes away and blow it off my finger.

Half an hour later I'm walking down the path to the Dome. The colony is silent except for the sound of insects and other distant creatures calling to one another outside the boundary. God's city looms over me as I walk, brightly lit with pockets of phosphorescence. They give the illusion of people living inside the pods with lights on in their homes. For the first few days that's what we thought it meant, but there's no one living in those lit spaces. No one like us, anyway.

I bring my attention back to the path ahead. It's better than looking up at the topmost point of the citadel and the space most brightly lit. Now that I'm closer to the Dome I can see people moving on the other side of the plasglass, dancing by the look of it, along the uppermost row of the tiers.

I stop, wondering if I should print myself some MDMA or something else that will take me out of myself. Half of the people dancing are probably off their face on something or other. But then I think of Sung-Soo and how it might freak him out if I'm acting differently. Besides, I don't want to lose the whole night. I'll stay for an hour or so, enough to be seen and to support Sung-Soo; then I'll go home and prep for a run into God's city. I need to have a clear head for that. One should never break a sacred law when under the influence of psychoactive substances.

The silence endures, even when I'm only meters away from the door. I allow myself a moment of quiet pride in my ability to build structures with that level of soundproofing before letting the door sensor taste me.

I enter the entrance hall, referred to as "the airlock" by most people. Once the door behind me has closed fully, the one in front opens onto the auditorium. The sudden burst of music and laughter and shouting makes me shrink back for a moment. When the people closest to the door see me hesitate, the urge to leave increases, but in moments they've come and pulled me in and a drink is put in my hand before the second door has closed behind me.

I sip it, uncertain of what it is. Some kind of cocktail. It's nice and I'm tempted to knock it all back, but I've made up my mind about how I want the rest of the night to go, and I don't want to be distracted.

I don't need to look for Sung-Soo and Mack; they're at the heart of a tight cluster of people in the center of the amphitheater, orbited by others desperate to get closer but unable to. I can see only the tops of their heads, the people are pressing in so tight. Mack looks up at me, presumably after seeing a mention of my arrival in the stream, and beckons me down.

By the time I've reached the lowest tier, Sung-Soo has

wriggled his way through the cluster and comes toward me, arms outstretched. He's clean, wearing new clothes, and looks so much better. His hair is sleek and shining in the Dome's light and he actually looks delighted to see me.

"Sorry I'm late," I say, but the words are swamped by the tsunami of music. He just embraces me and I find myself returning it. His hair against my cheek reminds me of Suh.

9

I STAY AT the party longer than I thought I would. Sung-Soo has an infectious laugh and it is refreshing to see someone other than Mack hold court. Everyone loves him and not just because of the connection to Suh.

There was a sense of awe surrounding him because of that, something he worked hard to dispel. He was delighted by everyone and everything and so drunk by the time I left that Mack had to steer him home, singing all the way.

I stopped after one drink and danced a lot, mostly with Sung-Soo, sometimes with Kay, who was trying to tell me about the model results at the same time. She gave up soon enough and we almost kissed at one point, but I pulled away, not wanting Sung-Soo to see. Kay wasn't bothered, thankfully, probably thinking it was my tendency toward privacy. It wasn't, and the reason has been bothering me since.

I didn't want Sung-Soo to think I was attached to someone. As I pull on my black gloves, pressing the seal between them and the edges of my sleeves, I'm annoyed with myself. I'm not some teenager, swept off my feet easily. I'm more than three times his age, for heaven's sake! It's just because he reminds me of her. And that in and of itself is appalling. I heft my pack into place, sickened by my attraction to him. Another reason why a trip to God's city is all the more imperative now.

The colony is just as quiet as it was when I left my house earlier that evening, but now it's because everyone is at home, either carrying on the party with a few friends in private or collapsed on their beds. At least the days of hangovers are over. I set my status to "asleep," just in case, and then move as quickly and silently as I can to the eastern gate.

Even in the starlight I can see its polished metal gleaming. There's titanium, gold, silver and all manner of other metals that make up its different parts. I've never liked it. It's too busy and ostentatious. I won't pass through it to avoid the sensors; I'll cut through between Nick's and Pasha's houses. There's no physical boundary to cross, no wire to cut, just the barrier of sacred trust to push myself through.

It's nights like these that I miss the moon. All those years I barely paid attention to it, giving it nothing more than a glance or perhaps a quiet moment when it was particularly full and golden, hanging low over the Champs-Élysées. Sometimes I find myself looking for it before I remember there isn't one to be found.

The stars are amazing though. People still lie outside their houses on some of the warmest nights, just to look up at them. Before arriving here, we'd never known the pleasure of looking up into such a full sky. On Earth there was too much light pollution and on Atlas there was only one observation window. On the journey there were very strict rules about how long someone could stay on the viewing deck over the trip. It wasn't just the matter of sharing with a ship full of people; it was the radiation too. We were so deprived of sky by the time we arrived, so starved of gazing into the distance. We had the simulation rooms, of course, designed to stop us from going mad and giving our eyes and brains scenery to process as we always had, but it wasn't the same. Full immersion playbacks of time outdoors were only any good for solo cravings.

I think the sky helped all of us in those early days. There were a few who found it too much, staying in the landing pods for days until the rest of us realized and coaxed them out. When we all got used to it, the nighttime sky and its crushed diamond brilliance was something we never wanted to lose. We voted unanimously against any kind of bright lighting outside the homes—even the Dome can be made opaque on nights when only a small number of people are using it.

Tonight, the stars are gradually being covered by cloud and the darkness is welcome. I don't need anything to guide me; the path glows with its own soft phosphorescence and I know the point to leave it without getting too close to Nick's house. Once away from the walkway I stoop a little and hurry along like someone obviously up to no good. It's a habit probably acquired from all the games I've played over the years. Some part of my brain believes this is what my body should do in these circumstances, and I don't fight it.

Both Nick's and Pasha's houses are dark. In moments I'm past them, and the short, springy heather-like plant that covers most of the colony outside of the paths is replaced by the longer grass I associate with the wild space beyond the boundary.

God's city is still lit in places, and will be so until the last hour before the dawn. The tendrils that grew from the nodules during the day are now fully retracted, some visible only by the way they obscure the stars.

Its base is like the foot of a black mountain made of thousands of rubberlike roots twisted and tangled around one another. In the daylight, it looks like it's growing out of the ground, but in the starlight it looks like rock, like it has always been there and always will be. I know this place better than anyone in the colony, and if any of them knew what I'm doing, I have no doubt I would be expelled, regardless of how much they need my skills.

We know so little about God's city, and that's a travesty, considering how the vast majority of the colony is made up of scientists. I find it hard to believe that I'm the only one who sneaks in there—surely my curiosity burns just as much as the next person's. Somehow Mack's manipulation, right from Planetfall, has managed to keep the colony's curiosity in check. He's managed to find a way to keep people reverent enough to stay out of that place without tipping them over into religious dogma—at least he had until Sung-Soo arrived. Still, it's not like his arrival is pushing people to demand access to the city. They've bought into the circus so entirely, so deeply, they're not even questioning it anymore. But I know the truth. I'm immune.

Even so, I still don't understand God's city, and I agree with his desire to keep people out. It's dangerous, in more ways than one. It looms over the colony and remains just as mysterious as the first day I saw it. I may know what is at the top of it, and I may know what the interior is like in places, but I can't say I understand it. Everyone else seems happy to wait for Suh to return and deliver an explanation to them on a platter. Perhaps it's easier to do that than to face the fear of what they could find in there. Perhaps Mack is too good at what he does.

The base of the city is only twenty meters or so from the colony boundary and I cross the distance quickly. My heart is pumping faster now, my body filled with the thrill of the illicit.

Soon any thoughts of possible punishment are crowded out by the anticipation of what I'll find within. I'm already feeling better, more focused and less anxious. Now it's all about finding the particular bunch of three tendrils twisted and looped slightly farther out than most.

I find it by touch as much as by sight. My hands know the bumps and gnarls as well as I know the colony and soon I'm standing in front of the giant loop that pushes out from the mass like an arched flying buttress. I don't know if it was designed to do that or if it's a flaw. Either way it helps me to find a way into the tangle.

Contorting myself to slip between the gap made by the arch and the rest of the base isn't a problem. There's a hollow large enough for me to stand, albeit a little stooped. I'm not looking forward to the next part and have to ready myself for the inevitable claustrophobia as I feel for the circular shape and its central depression.

I happened across it by chance only a week or so after Planetfall. We were all scouting and working out the best location for a permanent colony rather than the temporary camp formed by the pods we'd landed in. Mercifully I'd been by myself; otherwise I wouldn't have been able to keep it a secret. When I was asked if I'd found anything of note, I said no. I was already withdrawing then, so worried about letting anything slip out that I just kept everything to myself.

That was the second major lie I told that week. It gets easier, in some ways; now I lie without expending any effort. But I think each one has its own weight. One alone may barely register, like a grain of sand in the palm of one's hand. But soon enough there's more than can be held and they start to slip through our grasp if we're not careful.

I'm always careful.

Once I've found the large dimple I'm looking for, it's simply a matter of taking off my glove and pressing my hand against its center. It opens, the dimple revealing itself as the point of closure for a ring of muscle-like mechanisms that open on contact.

The tube beyond isn't lit until I touch its edge. The same ethereal glow that radiates from some of the nodules above appears at intervals, revealing the interior. It pulsates slightly and is covered in a thin coating of a clear, mucus-like substance. It reminds me of an esophagus, only curving upward instead of down.

As I put my glove back on I take a deep breath and then roll the edge of my hat down until the thin fabric covers my face and all my hair. I cover the gap in the fabric for my eyes with a pair of goggles and make sure the seal is tight against my skin. I pull the respirator from the clip on my belt and put that on over the fabric covering my mouth and nose. It sends a ping confirming the air filtration mechanism is functioning correctly. But even though I know I'm protected and that the climbing ropes will still be there once I get inside, I pause. I shouldn't be doing this.

"This is wrong, Renata."

My father's voice had dropped to a lower register, one within the vocal domain of disappointment. Even though I was in my late twenties I still felt the same twinge in my chest that his disapproval elicited when I was much younger. It irritated me. When would I stop being a child?

"Wrong? That's a bit judgmental, isn't it? You make it sound immoral."

He sat down on the one good chair in the apartment, the only one that wasn't patched or being held together with gaffer tape. Furniture manufacturing was still embedded in the mass production factory model then and we couldn't afford any replacements after pouring every last penny into the project.

The seat was too low for his long legs, bringing his knees up high. He rested his elbows on them, looking like he could spring up any moment, far from relaxed. "I think it is." As I took a breath to argue, he added: "Not the project. Whatever fools want to do with their money is up to them, and I know a lot of new advances are being made as a result of Atlas. I've seen the propaganda that Cillian Mackenzie is piping out. I'm talking about you going with them."

I wasn't expecting that. We hadn't really talked about it in the early days. He was so busy, traveling from country to country, always embroiled in tense political negotiations between governments fighting over dwindling water supplies and failing to plan for the end of fossil fuels. I never understood how he could deal with the uncertainty of it all.

He'd come to the apartment when I told him I was planning to leave once Atlas was ready. I'd been dreading telling him and yet the words just came out right in the middle of a conversation about algae, of all things. He dropped everything and came over right away. He didn't even do that when I graduated.

"Why would it be wrong?"

"Because you're needed."

"Mum doesn't need me. She only cried because one of her vacuous friends was there and she wanted the attention. You don't need me. I know you'll miss me; I'll miss you." I had to stop then, choked by the thought of it.

"I'm not talking about us. I'm talking about the world. Bad enough that you left WHO for this, but to leave completely?"

I think I groaned then. "Dad, I'm not the only visengineer in the world, you know."

"No, but you're one of the best. You've single-handedly

removed the need to depend on gene therapy and organ donation—"

"Don't exaggerate." I sat down, automatically keeping my weight off the back left leg of the chair that had already broken once. "I stood on the shoulders of a lot of people. Nobody does anything single-handedly anymore."

"You're underestimating yourself. You were the one who brought disciplines together in that particular combination. I would be dead and hundreds of other people would be dead now if it wasn't for you. If you leave before you reach your prime, this generation loses one of its best. What you do could have such an impact on so many people, Renata. I would rather it benefit millions, rather than a cult of a thousand."

I couldn't sit still. "It's not a cult!" I said as I jumped to my feet and wrapped my arms about myself. "You've met Suh—she's not like that!"

"Cults come in all shapes and sizes."

"It is not a cult."

He didn't pursue it. "Answer this, then: why do you want to go?"

"To see what's there."

"That's selfish. And irresponsible. I'd like to go snorkeling in the Great Barrier Reef, but I probably won't get a chance because there's too much to do."

I started to pace. "I'm not going to let your martyr complex dictate my choices! There's evidence to suggest that this trip is what we were made for—what our evolution has been leading us toward all this time and—"

"Evidence?" He shook his head. "I can't believe you'd let yourself be sucked in like that. There have been cults saying we come from an alien planet for over a hundred years! Are you sure Atlas is actually being built up there? There was a cult in Spain that sucked millions from its members to build a spaceship and all that bastard was building was a luxury mansion on a private island!"

"Of course I'm sure! I'm part of the team. We get reports every week. And they're not faked."

He pulled back and stood by the window, staring out at the stone wall opposite as if it were a view of the Eiffel Tower. "Have you asked yourself if there are other reasons you want to go?"

It was the first time we'd ever really argued, and I felt sick. "There are lots of reasons."

"Have you considered that you might be running away?" He turned and pointed at the bronze cast. "There's nothing better to distract ourselves from grief than a new project big enough to consume every moment. Have you stopped since she died? Have you let yourself—"

"That's got nothing to do with this. Have you thought that your being so upset about this might have everything to do with your choice instead of mine? Now that we've only got a year or so, are you regretting all the years you put everything else before me?"

I expected him to be angry and defensive or to cut the conversation dead and leave. Instead, he just stood there, looking so much older than I'd appreciated before. "I do regret that. But I don't regret what I've done with my life, Renata. If Atlas is real, if you go with those people, will you be able to say the same?"

10

THE COMPRESSION OF the esophageal entrance is enough to ground me in my body again. I keep my eyes closed like a child who's been told to, on pain of having a surprise present spoiled—desperate to look but obeying the rule. I'm not only prolonging the moment of purest anticipation; I'm also preparing myself for transition between the outside and the citadel interior. I've found that if I take this part slowly, I tend not to vomit. At least, not immediately.

I fumble for the climbing rope and grip it tightly. Its surface is roughened and I'm certain now that the interior is attacking the fibers. Now I want to open my eyes even more; I want to see if my experiment has yielded any results.

Only after counting to sixty (and then ten more to be certain) do I slowly open my eyes. The tunnel is a dark reddish brown, larger than the one I've just been sucked through, and the mucus covers everything here too. The valve is trying to close on one of my ankles and I hurriedly pull it free, even though I know it would just open again as soon as it detected an obstruction.

The glowing light that was pulsating up the tube I've just been spat out of is rippling up and down the tunnel. One moment the movement makes it look like the space is contracting, and then it changes, tricking my brain into thinking it's twisting counterclockwise. I kneel down with closed eyes and squeeze the rope between my knees. After a swift voice command, the goggles filter out the particular part of the spectrum that the phosphorescence inhabits and trick my eyes into thinking the tunnel is uniformly lit. It takes a few seconds for the software to smooth out the image, but it works well enough. If only we'd known to do that the first time we came here.

Once it's done, I look around for my experiment. I last came here about two months ago and it was the first time I left something behind. I didn't leave the experiment in plain sight, in case someone else in the colony is doing the same as me, so it takes a minute or so to locate the fold of membrane I chose as a marker. Once I see it, I pull myself along on the rope, still on my knees, feeling like I'm moving up a slope of about fifteen degrees or so. I know that can change in an instant though, so even though I don't really need the rope to progress, I keep my grip strong.

I hear the first of the noises as I reach the pellets and it takes me a moment to steady myself. It begins as a low moan and in seconds develops into a high pitch like an eagle's cry. So many times I've panicked, thinking that an inhabitant has found me and is alerting others to my intrusion, but no one ever comes. No one lives here. At least, I don't think they do.

There are only two of the four pellets left, the ones made of stainless steel and glass. They seem unchanged. The two others I left with them were made of bone carved from a creature I'd found dead and the other a ball of dried mud. I spend a little while hunting for them, thinking they might have rolled somewhere else, but I can't find them. Have they dissolved? Has this place digested them?

Another screech makes me shudder. Is it trying to tell me I shouldn't be here or am I simply trying to assign some kind of meaning to a random sound? When I listen intently, I can hear distant rumbles like my empty stomach. Nothing that sounds synthetic—or rather . . . manufactured. They seem just as organic as this slightly sticky intestine-like interior.

I leave the pellets where they are, curious to see what happens over time. Even though there's a part of me that wants to leave and go home to curl up and try to forget the day, I can't leave until I've found something to take with me. So I pull myself onward, getting occasional flashes from the tunnel as the frequency of the light shifts and the goggles have to adjust the incoming data processing to keep the image smooth and protect the visual centers in my brain. Without them I'd be in the throes of a migraine by now.

After the second time I came here, I didn't return for a few years. I had to focus on the colony. No, that's what I told myself, but it was as much about not focusing on what happened at the top of this city. For a long time I couldn't even look at the place without feeling distressed. Walking around the colony without looking up when facing certain directions became normal. At least I can look at it now—and enter it— without being afraid I'll give something away.

I can't remember why I came back. Perhaps it was simply a matter of having formed enough emotional scar tissue to cope. Perhaps my curiosity steadily built up its own pressure until it became more powerful than the avoidance.

The first few times I tried to map it out, first with memory alone, then with the help of my chip when I lost faith in my ability to understand the place. All the chip did was confirm that, once I move away from the initial tunnel attached to the valve I came in through, everything changes. I don't know if there's a pattern; I can't make it here regularly enough within controlled parameters to measure that, but either way, I never know where I'm going to end up. The only thing I can be certain of is that I won't be able to reach the top room again.

Only this rope and this part of the tunnel seem to be a constant. I've followed it as far as I can to a place where the rope disappears into a slimy wall, as if a new one has grown around it, trapping the rope in place but not severing it. Eventually it will rot, and would have already, had it not been made of the most resilient artificial fibers and coated to resist extreme conditions.

Being inside God's city feels like walking through the intestines of a gigantic creature, the way the tunnel twists and turns like a section of digestive tract and the mucus too, all creating a sense of being inside something alive. Even though our homes are grown from organic materials, this place feels closer to the interior of a living thing, a creature perhaps, something that straddles both plant and animal and impossible to classify in any Earth-based system of knowledge.

Not for the first time, I imagine God's city as an animal, squatted deep in the Earth, unconcerned by lowly creatures like me crawling through it occasionally. I've seen nothing to suggest it's anything but organic and suspect it's simply a wonder of synthetic biological construction, like our homes but on a bigger scale and designed by an alien mind.

The tunnel suddenly tilts in the opposite direction, as if an invisible hand has grasped the section of intestine I'm clambering about in and lifted it into the air. My knees go out from under me and I'm on my stomach, pressed against the rope that I'm now gripping with both hands. All I can do is hang on and try to get some purchase with my boots, but the floor that is now wall is too slippery and spongy. The pellets roll past me and I doubt I'll ever see them again. There's nothing to stand on, nothing to dig into, and I know I'll fall soon.

It's never changed orientation so sharply before and I try to keep my breathing steady. The closed valve that forms the way back out again is now a meter away, set into the wall above my head. I'm not strong enough to pull myself up by the strength of my arms alone. I try anyway. I manage to pull my chin a few centimeters up the rope, knowing that if I let go with one hand to move it to a higher hold, I'll lose my grip. I try to wrap my legs around the rope, but can't feel where it is through my protective clothing. If I can just hang on until it changes back, I won't be trapped inside.

The muscles in my hands start to burn and I have time to swear before they give out completely and I half slide, half fall downward. My fingers gouge tracks into the tunnel, the gloopy residue collecting beneath my fingertips, and the goggles are soon coated with the stuff too. A warning flashes up from the air filter mask's software; it's getting clogged and I'm not carrying an air supply. It can't filter through such a thick layer of mucus and I panic, abandon the useless attempt to stop my slide with my hands, and instead try to wipe off the gunk covering the mouthpiece with frantic inefficiency. I twist as I do so, managing to get the tunnel against my back so nothing more accumulates over my headgear.

My feet hit something and the impact jars through my body, making my knees buckle. As I pitch forward, somehow one of my hands finds the rope again and I cling on to it, my panicked breaths making the filter mask pull in tighter with each intake. Whatever broke my fall is solid beneath my boots and seems stable enough to support me as I shiver and struggle to put the mess of primal reactions back in their place.

Once the worst is over, I try to wipe a glove on a patch below my left armpit that is relatively free of the slime and then clean off the goggles, leaving a thin smear the coated plasglass can cope with. Soon they are clear and I get the filter mask functioning well enough for me to take stock and work out what to do next.

I'm on some sort of ledge that forms a circle in the tunnel and I realize it's the rim of an open valve. I've been through several of these here before, but when the tunnel is horizontal and they form doorways instead of things to land upon precariously. They remind me of heart valves, clashing with my simplistic sense of being inside a creature's gut. Usually these valves retract fully into the wall, but this one is different, thankfully.

The tunnel starts to tip again, back into the orientation it was before, so all I need to do is press my back against the wall and then relax as it gradually returns to being the floor again. I sit up when it's still and there's nothing to suggest it will move again anytime soon. The ledge has returned to being a door frame again and I spot the glass marble as it rolls down the side toward where I am, tracking slowly through the gloop to stop near my right leg. The steel one is still missing, but now I don't care about either of them. I'm just glad to be able to walk back to the exit valve—once I'm confident my noodle-like legs will cooperate.

My gaze wanders as I recover, and I spot something thin and metallic about thirty degrees up the edge of the interior valve, sticking out from where the former ledge meets the tunnel. I've never seen anything else metallic in here before, but I don't know its every detail. I usually strike out to find the nearest room, moving quickly before the way back to the rope changes so I don't get trapped. At the thought of that, I glance behind myself, just to check that the way back out of God's city is still where I think it should be. Once I'm reassured, I shuffle over to the object and give it a cautious tug.

It comes free with a quiet squelch. In moments the valve closes and I realize this bit of detritus has kept it open and prevented the valve from fully retracting into the wall. If this strange little thing hadn't been there, messing with the mechanism, I could be anywhere by now.

It's made from two bits of metal, only a few millimeters in diameter, each one about ten centimeters long and hinged together in the center. It's hard to make out the detail with such high filters on the goggles, but the edges of two prongs seem to have been snapped off, or at least aren't finished in a way I'd associate with something made.

I jolt. This has been made—it's hinged—it isn't something that could have grown and isn't something that fits with any of the other artifacts I've previously recovered from the city. I've found things like pots and a variety of other objects that I haven't been able to fathom an original function for, but none of them metal. They're made of either wood or ceramics and look handmade.

From what I've seen of this place and the things contained within it, I have to conclude that whatever this thing used to be part of, it must have been brought into God's city by someone else. I try to think of our first group and the equipment we carried, but nothing comes to mind that would explain this.

I move the two lengths of metal, testing the hinge. It's only slightly corroded. I have a good memory for most things, but I don't have a huge amount of confidence in my recollection of what we brought in with us that day. The only way to be sure is to look at the footage we took before leaving Atlas for the first time. I can't bear the thought of it. I don't want to see Suh's face, not now. It will only make things harder again.

It's time to leave. I've got something to take home and I don't want to be here the next time the tunnel decides it wants to move again, but the mystery of it won't let me go. How did it get here? What was it part of? By the time I reach the exit valve, the hinged metal pieces held tightly in my hand, I resolve to call up the footage as soon as I'm outside.

I take a few deep breaths before stepping onto the valve's center. It opens and I drop a meter or so before hitting the side of the tube. I hold the last breath I took as it closes above me. I'm expelled in a horribly biological fashion and dumped on the ground like a lump of shit.

I sit beneath the twisted tendril buttress and pull off the goggles and filter with relief. The smell of the mucus is sharp in my nostrils, reminding me of fried mushrooms, but soon enough it passes. I'm covered in the stuff, so I peel the protective suit and gloves off, rolling it into a tight bundle mucus side in, ready to be stuffed into the chute for the Masher as soon as I get home. I'll brush off the boots once the mucus has dried and give them a good clean. I've worn them in now; if I print a new pair they won't be nearly as comfortable. I'm glad I wore light trousers underneath this time, and a T-shirt. The cool night air is pleasant on my skin, but I need to shower before I can feel free of the evening's adventure.

Not yet ready to go back to the colony, I retrieve the mystery object from the place I left it to undress and wipe it clean as best as I can. I feel its edges in the darkness, making a mental note to wash my hands as soon as I'm able and not to touch my face or lips before then. I access my archive on my personal server, but when it comes to actually opening the file, I can't do it. I haven't looked at that footage from first Planetfall for over twenty years. Perhaps I never will.

Instead, I pull up my visengineering design window and approach the problem from another direction. I create a virtual replica of the artifact and ask the program to run comparisons with any print patterns stored on the cloud.

I wait as it runs the check, leaning against one of the thick tendrils. Starlight reaches in as a cloud breaks and I tilt my face to it with eyes closed. It was stupid to go into God's city alone. It always is. But I know I'll go back there again when the urge becomes too intense to ignore.

A ping notifies me that there are no exact matches but it provides several partials. I scroll through them and none seems right. The material would be wrong for most of them and the scale doesn't work for most of the others. I widen the parameters to match for custom patterns printed on Atlas before Planetfall, using my engineering security code to gain access. Another abuse of privileges; I'm not doing it to fix anything or at the request of the Ringmaster. I don't care. I already know that people print bizarre dildos and busts of the people they have crushes on and all sorts of other embarrassing personal designs. None of them, it seems, can explain the artifact.

It's possible it was part of something one of the initial landing team brought with them from Earth, something that hasn't ever been printed. I try to let my thoughts wander, hoping they'll stumble across some memory that will satisfy the question, but I end up dozing off.

The alarm that wakes me is silent, a signal sent directly into my brain from my chip, and it wakes me in an instant. It's a horrible mechanism, flooding the body with adrenaline and the sure knowledge that an immediate response is necessary. It's the highest level neural alert—within safe parameters anyway—and I only have it in place for one eventuality: someone getting too close to my house.

I sit up, feeling the twinge in my back caused by slumping inside the twisted hollow. I'm cold and there's a pale gray light coming through the gap instead of starlight. Dawn. I rub my face and then access the sensor array implanted at twenty-centimeter intervals around my house, one ring of them set ten meters out, the second set five meters closer. They detect a sudden increase in pressure from above caused by anything over twenty kilograms. It's set to ignore me, thanks to an automatic ping from my chip whenever I get close.

The data suggests an adult has crossed both boundaries. The system has already matched it against the last known weights of the colonists and a list of about twenty names comes up, all at the slender end of the inhabitants. Then I get a ping from my house software saying someone has requested access who isn't entered into the colony record. I don't need to call up the camera feed from the door. It must be Sung-Soo.

"Fuck," I whisper and then feel terrible for swearing so close to a holy place. The emotion fades quickly when I question feeling bad about saying a word while willing to go clambering about in there. Guilt sometimes comes from stupid places.

After digging a shallow pit in the soft soil accumulated in the hollow, I dump the filthy protective gear, including the goggles and mask and the piece of hinged metal, covering them up as best I can. I'll come back for them later.

The house pings me another entry request. I scramble out from under the buttress and run as fast as I can out into the wild grasses. I don't want to approach the colony from this direction. I don't want Sung-Soo to know I've been here. Almost as much as I want him to get the fuck away from my house.

11

I'M PANTING BY the time I get to the edge of the colony and enter from the direction I want him to see me coming from. I can feel the sweat on my forehead and top lip. I wipe it from my face, feeling a blast of coolness in my armpits as the early-morning breeze brushes the damp patches of my T-shirt. My sweat is particularly sharp smelling and I wonder if it's because of the panic, both inside God's city and right now.

I slow to a brisk pace, caught between wanting to catch my breath and needing to get there as fast as I can. What could he want at this time of the morning, for God's sake?

I cut in to the boundary between the southern gate and Kay's house, half jogging past the obscured windows and the people still sleeping inside. There's no sound except the wildlife staking out territories and calling for a mate. The sounds are different here than on Earth, but the purpose seems the same. "This is my patch!" they scream. "I want sex! Come and shag me! I'll give you strong babies!" It's the same stuff humans say most of the time. We just dress those needs up in fancier linguistic clothes.

When my house comes into view, Sung-Soo is leaning against one of the windows, hands cupped either side of his face to shield out the light as he peers in. Even though there's no way he can see inside, I'm still irritated. Why do people do that when there's no answer at a door? Do they expect to see the resident in there, feet up, oblivious? Are they checking they're not being snubbed, rather than whether the resident is at home?

Sung-Soo straightens his back as he steps away from the curve of the dome. My place was one of the first dome-shaped structures here; now about sixty percent of them have the same shape and basic design. None of the other houses—as far as I know, anyway—have the additional rooms and cubbies I've created beneath mine.

I hurry as he leans back in and smells one of the tiny plants growing from the soil covering most of its surface. As I watch, his head tilts and I know he's seen the patch that's dying.

"Sung-Soo!" I call and he turns, stepping away from my house quickly.

"I thought you would be in," he says as he comes toward me.

"Just went for a jog." The lie fits well with the sweat.

God's city looms behind him and I can't help but think of the things I've stashed away in their shallow grave. I force myself to focus on his eyes—on his grandmother's eyes. I look away again.

"I was worried I'd got up too early. Can we start right away?"

"Start what?"

"My house. Mack said we'd build it today and that you're the one who makes them."

He looks like a child. His excitement and eagerness crash

against me like waves, and like the beach I steal the energy from them. "Right now?"

"Do you have something else planned? Mack said you'd be free."

"Did he say that last night?" When he nods, I click my tongue. "Hang on a sec."

I call up the v-keyboard and dash off a note to Mack. With a petty thrill, I tag it as "urgent, top priority," and send it. If I'm expected to build a house at dawn, you should bloody well be awake too.

"How about you give me a few minutes to get myself sorted out?" I suggest.

"Good, yes, I'd like to see what your place is like inside."

"Why?" I asked that too quickly.

"Mack said you can make houses different inside. They can be whatever you want. I thought that, seeing as you make them, your house would be the best."

A sharp, twisting cramp shoots through my gut. "It's not." I force a smile. "It's like my grandma always used to say: the cobbler is the worst shod."

His eyebrow rises and I realize he has no idea what a cobbler would be. Half of the people in the colony are probably just as clueless.

"The cobbler was the person who used to make shoes in the . . . a long time ago. The saying explains that the person who makes something for everyone else rarely has the time to make the good ones for themselves."

"Oh! But that doesn't matter. I've only seen Mack's place and the Dome. Yours doesn't have to be the best to be useful."

For what seems to be the longest moment I just stand there, unable to think of a way to dissuade him. Everyone is so used to me, it's been a long time since I've been put on the spot like this and I'm out of practice. I engineer things to avoid this kind of situation coming up in the first place.

A ping from Mack gives me the chance I need. I read the message and feel my shoulders drop with relief. "Mack's waiting for you at his place. He's making breakfast for us both. I'll clean up and be right over. Then we'll start, okay?"

He glances back at my house and shrugs. "Okay."

I don't move until he's gone past me, and after I take a couple of steps I pause to make a show of stretching my calf and thigh muscles out. Sneaking a peek from the corner of my eye, I see him look behind himself, no doubt hopeful for a glimpse into the house as I enter it. When he sees I'm nowhere near it yet, he picks up the pace and is soon out of sight.

I close my eyes and tip my head back, feeling the backwash of the adrenaline leaving my body ragged. The last thing I want to do today is create. Keeping everything where it is, tucked away and hidden from sight, demands all the creativity in me.

I go toward the house and think of Kay, of her kissing my neck at the end of a party in the Dome, years ago. "Let's go back to yours," she whispered.

"No, your place is better."

She pulled away from me. The position of her hand on my thigh shifted, just a tiny amount, enough to tell me she was changing her mind about where she wanted it to go next.

"I've never been inside your house, Ren, not once in over a year. I don't want us to go back to mine."

"It's not tidy."

"I don't care."

"And it's not as comfortable as yours. Your bed is better."

I kissed her, trying to make her think of the original agenda again, trying to make her primal desires work to my advantage. "And it's closer."

"A whole two minutes closer." She shifted along the moss seat, putting a distance between us so she could look at me properly. "Why won't you let me in?"

"Another time. It's a tip—I'm . . . I'm such a slob, really."

"I'm not just talking about your house."

Then I leaned back, the space between us stretching from the close intimacy of lovers to that of friends, and not happy ones at that. I could feel my walls coming up, almost a physical sensation of pulling back farther than my body had. A drawing inward.

"You never talk about before. You hardly talk about yourself at all."

"I'm not that interesting." I try to smile, but it's like adding a sprig of parsley to a mud pie.

"I've told you everything about me," she pressed. "I can tell from your body that you've had a baby. Why won't you tell me about your child?"

I stood up before I realized I had. She'd caught the edge of an emotional scab and ripped the wound open again.

"I thought sharing time and love and my body would be enough," I said, or something equally peevish. I can feel my lip curling in disgust at my younger self's taste for melodrama.

I'm glad she forgave me. She left me alone for a while and I avoided her as much as I could, embarrassed by my inability to maintain the only relationship I'd had in so many years that had satisfied my body as much as my heart. I wasn't in love with Kay, even though we both tried it on for size for a while. It was like dressing up, playing at being lovers because it was what we both wanted, and neither complained, until that night at the Dome. Perhaps if I had trusted her more, let her in, we'd have become something more. But I can't do that. I can't take the risk. Once you let someone into the building, it's harder to keep them out of all the rooms. So I keep a moat around myself, like I'm some bizarre castle keep. I have to be careful to keep Sung-Soo out too.

As I reach the door, I get another message from Mack.

> We need to talk, just the two of us. We need to sort something out to keep Sung-Soo busy today.

> Okay.

> It's serious, Ren.

I sigh. Isn't everything serious now? I don't reply, not wanting to let any more of his tension leach into me. I have enough of my own.

12

IT ALWAYS TAKES longer for me to clean up than I would like. I get distracted and can never find the things I'm looking for when I need them. My buried find from God's city is stealing attention from these mundane matters too. I can't deal with Sung-Soo's enthusiasm and Mack's paranoia at the same time as constantly trying to identify those hinged pieces of metal. I need to watch that video and free up some of my own processing.

I squeeze myself between a stack of objects rescued from the Masher and the clothes I've moved to find the top I'm wearing now. I need the tightness around me, like being held, before I open the file.

The footage sits behind three layers of encryption algorithms on my personal server. I shut down any connections to the network and the cloud. It takes a few minutes to summon the courage to open the file, and it's only my irritation with myself that makes me do it in the end. The worrying about how it will make me feel has finally been ousted by the desire to stop feeling the twisting tightness in my chest. I need to be able to think of something else.

With a look and quick blink at the relevant icon, the compulsory preplay questions begin.

At the time, it seemed a good idea to record us with full immersion. To think that I believed I'd want to relive that again and again! This is why there are warnings and several levels of opting in and confirmations of intent before you can record immersively; the people who made this technology know how well human beings can fuck themselves up. All the questions amount to the same thing: are you sure you want to preserve enough detail to trick your brain into reliving it again?

Now those same protocols are asking me if I really want to fully immerse myself in something that happened twenty-two years, fifty-five days ago. Are you in a safe environment? Are you operating machinery? Are you in control of a vehicle? Most of the questions are redundant: the chip knows I'm doing none of those things but the software forces them anyway. It wants me to really understand the risk. I do.

Would you like to prepare a message for your health care provider in the event of an adverse reaction?

That one is a hangover from several cases where people recorded their own heart attacks and other near-death experiences and then played them back to themselves in some sort of weird therapy craze and had heart attacks. Idiots. I give a negative response. I don't want Kay or anyone else to know I'm doing this. I've wedged myself in tight enough to not throw myself around by accident.

Are you aware that deep-immersion playback can cause
depression, anxiety, dissociative disorders and increase
the likelihood of addictive behaviors?

"Yes," I reply.

Are you aware that deep-immersion playback can trigger
PTSD?

"Yes, for fuck's sake." That's what I'm afraid of.

You have tagged the selected footage as critical. You may
pause but not delete during playback. Please check your
environment for any potential risks. We recommend the use
of a tongue block. Here is a list of patterns to download to
your printer.

I skip that. I may end up a sobbing mess, but I'm unlikely
to bite my own tongue.

Finally, the little arrow floats across my vision. I clasp my
hands tight together, fill my lungs with as much air as I can
and blink twice at the arrow.

I am no longer in my hallway.

I'm in the loading bay on Atlas, just outside the doors to the
airlock and decontamination chamber. The bare metal struts
curve either side of me like the ribs of a great whale, and crates
of equipment and supplies are stacked in their hundreds only
meters away from where I stand. My body is held tight in my
flight suit, the gloves feeling thick and cumbersome after years
with nothing on my hands. The metal rim upon which my helmet
will be locked rests uncomfortably on my collarbone and I want
to pee. It's just nerves.

"Who's recording?" Mack asks.

"I am," I say, raising a hand.

"Me too," says Hak-Kun. (A flitter of panic behind the re-experience, like a tiny bird taking off in a field behind me— I forgot that he was recording too.)

"Don't film my backside." Suh twists to face me and I laugh at her, a little too loud. (Oh God above us, she is so beautiful. I want to touch her—did I touch her then? Can I feel that again?)

"Mum." Hak-Kun sounds unimpressed by her lightness.

I can't help looking down, now that she's put the idea in my head, and I trace the outline of her buttocks through the flight suit, the way her hips flare out at the tops of her thighs, far wider than her waist and shoulders. She used to hate her short legs and pear-drop shape but since the coma she's been above such things. I look away when Mack clears his throat and looks up at the list he's just called up in his own vision.

"Okay, quick roll call to satisfy the ship's log and then we'll do our last equipment check before running through the landing protocols one last time. When I say your name, acknowledge verbally, state your official role in the party and confirm consent to make Planetfall."

After we all nod, he begins. "Cillian Mackenzie, Captain, and I consent to travel. Lee Suh-Mi?"

Suh is tying her hair back, fiddling with wisps that keep slipping free like black silk. "Pathfinder, and fully consensual," she says and grins at me. (A wrench in my chest behind the excitement and fear and love.)

"Lee Hak-Kun?"

"Linguistics and xeno-communication, and I consent to this trip."

"Xeno-communication?" Lois, a tall woman whose arms

are thicker than my thighs, is snorting with laughter. "When did you make that up?"

Hak-Kun folds his arms. "I'm the one best qualified to make contact or interpret alien language, should the occasion arise."

Lois shrugs. When he looks away, she makes eye contact with me and mouths "wanker" silently. I only hope Suh hasn't seen what we make of her son. It's hard being the child of one of the most important people in history.

"Lois Stephenson?"

"Yep." There's a pause and Mack stares at her. "Oh, sorry; security and threat evaluation and I am so ready to get my ass off this ship."

Mack smirks at that and then looks at me. "Renata Ghali?"

"Pilot. I give my consent to make Planetfall." (I sound so formal, my voice so tight with nerves.)

"Winston Akembi?"

"Present, doctor, and with God's grace ready to meet him."

"It won't be a he," Suh says quietly. "Not like we conceive of it anyway." All the nerves and joviality are shoved aside by a new sense of gravitas. We are in the presence of one chosen to lead us to our creator.

"Should we say a prayer?" I ask.

"Do we have to?" Mack sighs and everyone looks to Suh for adjudication.

"Let's take a moment," she says. "You can all do whatever you need before we carry on."

Ever the diplomat. I close my eyes and whisper the Lord's Prayer as I try to manage the fear. So many years and sacrifices and doubts all leading to this moment. I feel both huge and insignificant in the weave of history's cloth. Now we discover if we've followed a madwoman or a visionary. Perhaps even a messiah.

(Now, in the moment of black silence, I remember why I'm reliving this. After the prayer, I focus my attention on those in the group, forcing myself to look at the footage as if through a lens rather than my own eyes. Keeping a sense of self separate from that of the recording for anything longer than a few seconds at a time is hard, but I'm motivated enough to keep this mental distance while the last checks are made to the suits and helmets. I have to wait until I look—looked—at each person, all the while resisting the pull of immersion to examine what they're wearing and carrying. I see nothing that looks like the source of the hinged artifact.)

We step inside the airlock and when the door closes behind us, sealing us from the ship, I jump and almost drop my helmet.

Suh reaches across to touch my forearm. "It's all going to be fine, Ren," she whispers. "Stay with me and you'll be fine."

(There's a noise and a part of me realizes I've cried out at the feel of her hand on my arm. Even through the flight suit and the thin layer beneath it, even separated by all the years and the knowledge and the lies *I can feel her again* and yet I know I never will again.)

"You won't leave me behind, will you?" I whisper back and she smiles.

"Of course not. I need you to fly us back."

(My cheeks are wet and my breath judders in and out with each sob and God I need her! I need her back!)

We put our helmets on and check our comms and air supply before and after the air is sucked out. We check one another for signs of stress, reassuring one another as best we can with nervous smiles and the occasional wink. Suh is the most calm of all of us even though she has the most to lose. If there is nothing down there, she'll be the focus of the rage and disappointment. She acts as if she has no doubts though and I take solace in that.

We're sprayed and blasted with a full decontamination routine in the effort to remove any viruses or germs that may want to hitch a ride on us down to the planet. The shuttle has already been treated and anything that might be on its exterior will be destroyed upon entry into the planet's atmosphere. The plan is to keep the helmets on from now until we get back.

"I still think it needs a name," I say as the doors open onto the short umbilical tunnel that connects the ship to the shuttle. "I've never been anywhere without a name before."

"It isn't for us to name it," Suh says, and I feel stupid, like a brash tourist complaining about a hotel breakfast on the way into a sacred temple.

(My chest is hurting. There's too much to contain. I will tear in two and my blackened, shriveled heart will tumble onto the brown moss between my feet.)

We enter the shuttle and I move to the front of the group, heading for the pilot's seat. I pause at the sight of the planet, its curve describing an arc of blue and white and green at the lower left of the window. Only I can see it. The others are strapping themselves into seats behind me, facing one another. I feel privileged and terrified and doubtful of my ability. There are ten other people on Atlas qualified to fly this thing, but Suh insisted I learn so I could go with her legitimately. I've flown more simulations in the last two months than had hot meals.

"Everyone secure?" Mack asks and I hurry to take my place. I tighten the straps over my shoulders, scanning the display in front of me and checking that everything matches the simulator.

"Starting preflight check," I say and the routine takes over. It calms me in the same way that washing my hands does.

(My throat is burning and I fear I can't keep doing this, but I have to. I have to last until Planetfall and at least until we reach God's city. Otherwise I'll have ripped myself open again for nothing.)

"Ready to detach . . . Captain." It feels unnatural, saying that, as if I'm playing an immersive military game with Mack.

"Understood, Pilot." His reply only reinforces the sense of pretension. "Detach in five, four, three, two, one, mark."

There's a clunk as the clamps release and a dreadful lurch in my stomach as we lose the gravity we stole from Atlas's rotation. My body pulls against the straps as my own weight no longer holds me in the chair. There's just enough time for everyone to comment on it before I angle the craft to begin descent. They fall silent when the light stretching back to them from the cockpit shifts as the planet fills my view.

I have to pull my attention from the clouds—clouds!—and colors of life to make sure the computer is calculating the trajectory and the numbers make sense. The data from the satellite we sent out from Atlas days before has already been examined and processed by both human and computer. I know what I'm aiming for and the shuttle's navigation software is directing me to the right place to enter the atmosphere.

I'm nothing more than a fail-safe really; the shuttle could fly itself, but by law a human pilot has to be fully trained, able to interpret the flight data and capable of manually controlling the craft if needed. That's when it hits me that we're so far from home; the law is nothing but an echo of civilization.

"We'll be entering the atmosphere in ninety-five seconds," I broadcast to the communal channel. "The temperature in here will rise, but that's totally normal and we won't cook. Does everyone remember the simulation?"

I listen to the affirmative replies. "Okay, then. Here we go."

The colors so reminiscent of Earth are soon replaced by a searing red that I only glimpse as the exterior shielding completes its slide into place. The external temperature of the shuttle soars along with the tension within. I keep my attention on the display rather than the hellish black on the other side of the window. I sweat and I pray and then we're through the worst of it and my body becomes heavy again. Eventually the shielding withdraws and I can see outside once more.

The sky is blue and below is a pillowy landscape of clouds. We could be flying above anywhere on Earth and I'm overwhelmed by a sense of coming home, even though nothing could be less accurate.

"What does it look like, Ren?" Suh sounds breathless for the first time.

"Cloudy," I reply, wishing I could find something poetic or romantic to say. "Blue sky," I add. "Just like home."

"This is home now," she says, and then we hit the clouds and the shuttle shakes with turbulence.

"This is normal," I say. "It'll probably smooth out when—"

We break through the cloud base and I see the mountains and grasslands below. I'm the first human being to see this in person, rather than a satellite image, the first to weep at the sight of its majesty.

"Ren?" Mack sounds frightened—the first time for that too.

"It's . . . it's okay. Let me show you."

I link my camera feed to the communal stream and ping each of them an invite to share. A hush descends as they all watch what I can see.

"That mountain on the right," Suh says. "The highest peak. Head toward that."

I check the data and it's the direction we need to go anyway. The shuttle changes course slightly and the peak swings into the center of the view.

"Switch to manual, Ren," Suh says.

"Why?"

"Because it should be one of us who brings us in, not a machine."

13

SUH GUIDES US over the top of the mountain range, above the place now called Diamond Peak. The rock drops away from its topmost point, sweeping down to the grassland plain below like the folds of a gray gown dragging against a green carpet.

I minimize the overlaid flight controls from my vision, knowing we're on a stable flight path for a few minutes at least. I want to see it like my crewmates do.

Then I look up from staring at where the rock meets the plain and see God's city ahead, rising from the grasslands a few kilometers away like a bizarre black flower from a giant lawn.

No one says a word. There is nothing to be said at the sight of so many answers and so many questions encapsulated in one structure. The fact that humanity debated whether life on other planets existed for so long has finally been proven ludicrous.

"That's it." Suh finally breaks the silence, as only she could. "That's God's city. That's where we need to go."

"Set down half a click away from it," Mack says.

I reopen the shuttle interface and tap the appropriate places in my v-field, identifying the best place to set down. The flurry of activity caused by a manual landing distracts me enough to calm down again and roots me back in the practical.

(There's a lull in the barrage of recorded emotions and I'm able to ready myself for the next part. I remind myself to see *through* rather than simply see again and to look closely once we land. I become aware of an ache in my hands, still clasped so tightly together, and try to separate out the movements of my hands in the recording and the desire to separate my palms from each other now. I'm not even sure I've done it when my attention is snapped back to the recording.)

It's a good landing with no reported damage from either the craft or the crew. There are no congratulations, however; we're all too fixated on the structure in front of us for it even to register.

I fumble with the straps, unable to see them very well through the curve of my helmet, and then call up the data gathered by the environmental equipment on the way down.

"It's 21.5 degrees Celsius with 34 percent humidity and the atmosphere is near as dammit to Earth's," I report. "We could breathe out there."

"But we're not going to, remember," says Winston. "I don't care what the temperature is or how friendly the air is; no one takes off their helmet, gloves or exposes any of their skin to the native environment."

We all agree. There's no way I'd be tempted anyway, but it's the kind of shit Lois would do for a dare. She's been quiet though. Mack was worried she'd be bantering and being a jackass all the way through the mission, but she's just as awed as the rest of us.

"Open the door, Ren," Mack says and I do so.

I'm the last one to emerge and take my place with the rest of them, staring up at the alien structure.

"I can't see anything that looks like guns or weapons or defenses," Lois says. "But to be honest, I wouldn't know what the fuck anything that thing uses to defend itself would look like."

"Any signs of people?" Mack asks.

"Not yet," she replies. "But they must know we're here, right? I mean, they're waiting for us, right? Right?"

Suh rests a hand on her arm. "Everything's going to be fine. We're expected."

"Okay, let's get ourselves sorted out and then we'll go and take a closer look," Mack says. "Ren, stay with the shuttle."

"What!?"

He laughs. "I'm joking, I'm joking."

I manage a smile before helping to open the compartment holding all the equipment.

(This is it, the part I've been waiting for. Did any of them bring something else along not listed on the flight manifest? Some lucky object or—)

The crate is heavy but not more so than on the ship. "It's one G here, isn't it?" Hak-Kun asks and I nod.

"It's so similar to Earth," Lois says. "That can't be a coincidence."

"It might not be as meaningful as you might think," I reply as Hak-Kun opens the crate and begins to pass out containers to the relevant people. "It might simply be that life of the kind we're used to can only flourish within certain parameters, so the results are familiar without there being some sort of intelligent design behind it."

"I thought you were a believer, Ren," Mack says.

"I'm also a scientist," I fire back, irritated with his mocking tone. "They're not incompatible."

(It's easy to tune out an argument with Mack; I've had so many over the years, freeing my attention to look at what everyone is taking out of the containers. It's mostly small boxes with sensor prongs sticking out of them, and in Lois's case a small gun that leads to a brief argument between her and Mack, which she wins. But there's nothing I can see that explains the metal artifact.)

"Is everyone ready?" Suh asks. "Okay, then. This is it."

She walks off, striking out toward God's city, and I stand there longer than the rest, watching her back as she walks away from me, tiny beneath the twisting black tendrils and pods, forging the last path of the journey.

(I know this is the best place to pause the footage, but it's hard to shut it down and no longer see her. It's like sticking a fingernail into an old cut that's bleeding once more. But I know what happens soon afterward and I simply cannot relive that again.)

"Stop footage," I say out loud and I'm back in my house, wedged in and aching. My throat is raw and the fabric over my chest is wet with tears that dripped unchecked. I wipe my cheeks with the back of my hand and tackle the gunk in and below my nose with another T-shirt lying within reach. I realize it's one of Kay's tops. I never had any intention of returning it anyway, even though her scent left its fibers long ago.

Exhausted, I rest my head against the stack of fabric beside me and realize, with a sense of utter wretchedness, that suffering that day again has brought me no closer to a solution. I have to conclude that unless one of the crew smuggled something down to the surface (highly unlikely as it wouldn't have been fully decontaminated), that bit of metal didn't come from one of us.

There is a limited set of logical explanations, and none of them satisfy me.

One is that someone else from the colony has been visiting God's city secretly, as I have. The only person I know who's been back there since that first day is Mack, and I know for a fact that he hasn't been back into that particular section again. I can't imagine anyone else breaking the rules, but I do, on a regular basis, so I have to entertain the notion that someone else has too and that they left something behind.

There's another possibility: someone else came to God's city before us. For that to be true, it wouldn't be someone else from Earth, as we were most definitely the first to achieve interstellar travel on that scale. The risk that someone could improve upon the technology Suh developed and beat us to our destination was a concern of mine right from the start of the project. When Mack came on board he fought with Suh over patents and her desire to help humanity as well as reach this planet. In the end they agreed to lock away secrets within a capsule, protected by several gov-corps, to be opened forty years after we left. Suh got to feel she had left something useful behind and Mack and I were satisfied no one could beat us here. Unless something went wrong with that capsule—unlikely considering the amount of international red tape Mack wrapped it up in—we are the only people to reach this place from Earth. If someone else was inside God's city before us, it would have to be someone from another civilization.

I shiver. Were there others who, like us, came seeking God?

14

THE QUESTION STALKS me all the way to Mack's house. I can't mention it to anyone, not even Mack, which makes it feel even bigger. At least it's enough to distract me from the emotional aftershocks still rippling out from the footage. I just hope that my face isn't too puffy from the crying.

I press my palm to the sensor at the side of his door and it opens. The smell of omelets turns my stomach as I enter and Sung-Soo looks up from an almost empty plate, grinning at me. His clear delight at my arrival is jarring. Some part of me is still stuck over twenty years in the past. I should have given myself more time to recover.

"Want one?" Mack calls from the kitchen.

"I'll have a shake," I call back.

"Can we start now?" Sung-Soo asks through a mouthful of egg.

Mack peers around the door into the living room. "Ren, please start—he's driving me mad."

"Okay. Give me access to your projector." I sit on the sofa as Sung-Soo gobbles down the remainder of his breakfast. I try not to think too much about the thing in his gut. "So, there's a much easier way for you to get an idea of people's houses," I begin and call up the interface to Mack's projector. "All the plans for each house in the colony are stored on the public server. I'll bring up some 3-D reps here for you to take a look at. Then you won't have to ask anyone if you can look inside their house."

Mack enters with my breakfast and sets it down next to me as I call up the files. "Though I'm sure people won't mind if you did want to do that."

Sung-Soo looks at me pointedly and Mack laughs. "Ren isn't people." He pats my arm affectionately. "She's very private."

I keep quiet and the moment passes soon enough. "Okay, here we go."

The plan of Mack's house appears in the air above the fire pit, rotating slowly in a translucent gray. Sung-Soo yelps and his plate and cutlery fly into the air as he leaps back, knocking his chair to the floor.

"Shit, I'm sorry." I shut it down. "Sorry, I should have warned you." I should have known it would frighten him; the pods weren't fitted with projectors. They were designed to reach the planet's surface and give people temporary shelter. There was no room for anything as frivolous as entertainment systems.

Sung-Soo picks up the remains of his breakfast, apologizing too, as Mack reassures him that no harm is done.

"That was a 'projection'?" Sung-Soo asks, using the word carefully.

I nod.

"My father talked about them. I didn't know what they looked like."

The image of Hak-Kun lifting the crate and asking about the gravity here returns with far too much clarity. Now I see him in Sung-Soo's face, instead of just Suh. I still don't see Lois though. I'd never have guessed she was his mother. He never mentions her and with a shiver I wonder if it's because she died when he was very young.

"Put it back on," he says.

The image returns and he approaches it, this time with fascination and quiet delight. I sit back as Mack shows him how to use his hands to interact with the images. Sung-Soo laughs as he expands and contracts them, gasps as he selects sections and brings them out from the whole object to inspect more closely. He reacts with the purest joy when shown how to move from the plans of one house to the next, effectively gaining insight into the whole colony with just a sideways swipe of his hand. He's enchanted by the technology in a way I never could be again.

Mack steps back and gives him a few moments to see if he's got to grips with the interface. When he sees he has, Mack looks at me and inclines his head toward the kitchen. I pick up the shake and follow him in, making myself drink some of it on the way.

"It's Carmen," Mack says, sotto voce.

"Is she stirring up trouble?"

He leans against the countertop, nudging the frying pan with his backside. He's a purist; he likes to cook with base ingredients rather than printing a complete meal. He's one of those people who says he can taste a difference and is happy to waste hours every week to achieve it.

"More than that. She's tracking my movements. Secretly. I only know because I ran a check on her activity."

Mack is one of the handful of people on the colony with

the clearance to check that sort of information. Carmen should know that it's impossible to keep tabs on him without the chance of being found out.

"She can't be thinking straight," I say. "Surely she knows you'd find out."

"Maybe she doesn't care," Mack replies, his arms folded and hands tucked into his armpits, drawn tight into himself. "Maybe she wants me to know that she's doing it."

"But why?"

"Because she thinks I'm going to break the rule and go to see Marco. To warn him maybe, or coach him in what to say to her when the ceremony is about to start. I don't know."

I shrug. "So what? You weren't planning on doing that, were you?"

He tuts. "Ren, think about it. There is somewhere I need to go in the next week and Carmen mustn't know about it."

He stares at me, raising both eyebrows. I'm lost and shake my head to indicate that. He sighs. "I need to put the seed in place. If she sees me going into God's city . . ."

He doesn't need to finish the sentence. "Oh fuck," I whisper.

"That's why you need to do it for me."

I step away, holding my hands up. "Oh no—no way, Mack!"

"You have to!" he hisses, closing the distance between us until he's only inches from my face. "You're the only other person who knows and—"

"I won't do it."

He grabs my shoulders. There's no aggression, just desperation, but it still upsets me. "So you're happy to let this happen, every year, as long as you don't have to touch it? You think you're less involved? That's bullshit! You can't just choose to stand and watch the whole of your life and let others do what you're not brave enough to do yourself!"

"I never wanted this!" It's hard to keep my anger confined in a whisper. "Just because you couldn't do it without confiding in me doesn't make me complicit!"

"You never stopped me."

"How could I? You put it all into place before I had the chance to—"

"That's bullshit, Ren. You had the chance, several times, but you know how much the colony needs this. If that seed isn't there, they'll think they've been abandoned. Do you want them to feel that?"

I shove him away from me, wanting to push away the way he's making me feel as well as his physical presence. I cover my face with my hands, needing a moment with something between us, as if the skin and bones could shield me from his glare. "Perhaps we should tell them the truth." I speak into my palms, but he can still hear me.

"Are you out of your fucking gourd?" I can feel his breath on the backs of my hands. "This place would collapse. We can't tell them anything, about the seed or about his"—he jerks a thumb toward the living room—"bloody father or any of it."

"You're just afraid."

"Of course I fucking am! They'd kill us, Ren."

I lower my hands.

"Yes. *Us.* We just have to get through the ceremony, settle Sung-Soo in and it'll quiet down again. You have to help me keep all this together."

He looks frightened. I wonder if I look the same. Would they kill us? I don't know; it's impossible to predict, but he's right about everything falling apart.

I sag. "You'll have to show me where to go and how to get there without going inside."

He breathes out at the sound of my implicit agreement. "Of

course. I'll do everything I can." He pulls me into a tight embrace and even though I didn't invite it, I accept it, resting my head against his shoulder.

"Is everything okay?"

Sung-Soo's voice at the doorway makes me jump and instinctively I move to break the embrace, but Mack keeps hold of me.

"Ren had a nightmare last night," he says. "She was just telling me about it and needed a hug. We all do, sometimes."

He kisses the top of my head and lets me go. Sung-Soo's sympathetic expression makes me feel sick with nerves and self-hate.

"I know what kind of house I want," he says after a beat. "Can we start now?"

At last, something practical I can lose myself in! "Of course we can." I smile. Perhaps building something real is the answer.

15

I GUIDE SUNG-SOO through a rudimentary visengineering process to knock up a rough plan for the main structure of his new house. He chooses a dome structure with spokes, a lot like Mack's, but with a deeper floor like mine. Of course, only a portion of my house's layout is on the server: the sections that needed to be printed at the communal manufacturing center. The additions and changes I've made over the years are known only to me.

"I'll take you to the place where we print out the main struts for construction," I say to him as I save the file in the right place on the cloud. "We can talk about the next bits on the way."

"Next bits?"

"Yeah—how you want to create the energy your house will use. Each one has to be fully self-sufficient and have a zero-waste footprint."

He frowns with concentration. "The houses tread lightly, like my father talked about."

The door out of Mack's place opens and we wave good-bye to him. He seems relieved to be left at home.

"He used to say it was the best way to live," Sung-Soo continued. "We shouldn't take more than we needed and stay longer than we had to. Then we could be sure the food would be there the next time we stayed in that place."

It doesn't sound like Hak-Kun to me. But I knew him only as a pampered man, cosseted by technology in the way we all are here. I'm amazed he survived long enough to teach his son anything.

"We're keen to live lightly here, yes," I reply. "But not in the same sense as you're used to. There are rules about energy production versus consumption, water collection and processing waste. Most of that is handled by the materials we make our walls from."

"I want to be able to see the stars at night," he says after a pause. "Can you make the walls so that I can see out but no one can see in?"

"I can, but not one hundred percent—you need special soils between the membranes to process the waste. But most of the ceiling could be made like that, if you're happy to collect sunlight from cells around the edge of the house instead of across the roof. That's how mine works, and why I can grow stuff on the outside."

"But some of the plants on your house are dying."

I shove my hands in my pockets. "Oh . . . well, that's because I test new strains and new soil compositions on my house before rolling them out to the colony." I give him as confident a smile as I can. "Sometimes they just don't take. I'll replace them soon."

We walk through the colony to the side farthest from God's city and there still isn't a soul on the streets. I'm glad; I wouldn't want anyone else to come and stick their nose in and bombard him with options. "Can I have fish in my windows like Mack does?"

"Of course. You could get some energy from the algae too."

"Did his fish come from Earth?"

"No. We didn't bring any of the animals down to the planet. We couldn't predict their impact on the ecosystem."

He looks up. "Bring them down . . . Was the ship you came here on somewhere up there?" He points up at the sky, now a pale blue in the early morning.

"It's still up there. It's called Atlas."

"Could we go back up to it?"

"Theoretically." I look back to where we're heading. "We had to strip the shuttle for parts when the printer broke down, so that would have to be rebuilt."

"Is that why you didn't come and look for my father and the others? Because the shuttle was broken?"

I almost miss a step. "We thought they were dead," I say quietly. "We used Atlas to look for you, with satellites we'd sent out to scan the planet before we came down. But by the time we found the crash site, there were no signs of life."

It's only partly true. Mack sabotaged the satellite data as it was received by Atlas. By the time anyone else in the colony had gotten themselves together enough after Planetfall to look for the missing pods, they were actually looking at old footage of the crash site. Mack updated the pictures only after he'd screened them first.

Sung-Soo is staring at me and I realize I've fallen silent. "At least you looked," he says.

"We almost built something to go and search, but with nothing to go on, we couldn't risk critical people—" I shut my mouth.

After a moment I add, "I don't want you to think we didn't believe those we'd lost weren't critical too—they were—it's just that the early days were so hard. We needed every single person working at full capacity."

Sung-Soo just nods. "If you'd known where we were, would you have come to get us?"

"Of course we would!" I clench my fists inside my pockets. Sadly, that isn't a lie. Once things had settled down and everyone else had given up on the search and a formal memorial service was held, Mack had another look at the site. There were no signs of life—they must have moved on by then. But I know that if they'd stayed in the place they crashed, Mack would have built a craft and gone to get them. To kill them.

Would I have let him do that too?

"Why did their pods crash?"

His question makes me fear I'll be sick, or at the very least give something away. "We don't know exactly." Did my voice tremble? Can he hear the lie slathered on top? "There was always a risk; the pod technology was relatively untested."

We walk in silence for the rest of the journey. It must be so hard for him and I can't think of anything to say that will make it better. There is nothing to say.

When we reach the communal printers, I'm grateful for the change in topic. He watches closely as I run a check on the largest printer and recalibrate it. "It's not used so often now," I explain. He waits as I send the files to it and begin the printing, unable to see anything without a chip of his own. "We can start off the foundation preparations while that first batch is printing. It'll only take a few hours. The soil we take out will be put into the cavity between the wall membranes, after we've added in the correct biocultures and protocells to process the waste. There's a few other bits and pieces that need to happen, to manage water and stuff, but I'll take care of all that. It'll only take a couple of days at the most."

"Then I can live inside it?"

"Yep. And grow your furniture and stuff. Ready to pick a spot?"

16

WE PRINT. WE dig. We design. We construct. It's a glorious day of finite tasks with optimum ways to execute them. Every single one of them is within my comfort zone and none causes guilt or panic.

When the rest of the colony wakes, our construction project turns into a bizarre party, with people bringing food and drink and blankets or chairs to sit on and chat with one another and Sung-Soo as we work. I end up giving impromptu lessons to the children who were born after most of the colony's construction was completed, or are too young to remember.

Gilmour, our resident cultural history expert, tells us about barn raising as we eat our lunch and for the first time in years I feel part of this place. I actually chat with people instead of scurrying away like a rat to my nest, and by the end of the first day the rudimentary structure is up and the excavated soil is almost ready to be put between the membranes.

So many people ask Sung-Soo to dinner he suggests a

communal meal in the Dome around a fire pit and half the colony goes to hear the tales he learned as a child around a fire. I nod off partway through, only to be awoken by Sung-Soo, who is laughing at me affectionately. I'm forgiven, and the assembled applaud me as I make my good-byes and leave. It isn't until I get outside that I realize Kay has followed me.

"You look shattered," she says, slipping her arm around mine and squeezing it.

"It's been a busy day."

"I've never seen you look so happy."

I stop and look at her eyes, bright against the sky dusted with stars. "I like building things."

Even now, that statement is tainted. I recall my mother saying the same to a friend when they thought I was in another room. "She never decorates them; she just says she likes building things." She was waving a wineglass at the latest construction project taking up most of the living room. "I don't even know what they're supposed to be."

"Have you asked her?" Her friend, a man who thought he might fit into the gap my father left, stooped to inspect it.

"She says all kinds of stupid things; one minute it's a city and the next it's a tree. She can't settle on anything. And they're so ugly."

I saw something in the way he looked at her, something to suggest he might be an ally. "You don't see this as art?"

"Art?" She laughed and downed the rest of the wine. "I just wish she'd make something beautiful. Like the other little girls do. Or at least try."

Kay kisses my cheek. "And you're bloody good at it. I won't keep you—I know you're off to bed—but I haven't had a chance to talk to you about Sung-Soo's"—she pats her stomach—"guest."

"I assumed it wasn't anything bad, or else you would have told me or Mack."

"Oh, it's nothing bad at all. In fact, it's really useful. It's unlocked a whole new line of research into digesting some of the proteins in the native plants here. I'm just going to leave it be. It's not harming him; in fact, it's kept him alive this long. I'll keep a close eye on him, see if our germs and viruses give him a hard time, but his immune system is pretty damn robust."

"Have you talked to him about it?"

"Briefly. He's distracted, understandably."

We pause outside his partially constructed house. "I think it's sweet that he wanted to live near to you," she says.

I don't tell her that he wanted to live even closer, nor that I've planned his windows and doors to look out over all the directions except my house.

"He wanted to be near Mack's place at first," I say. "But it would mean extending the formal boundary, and he couldn't bear to wait for that to be approved by the council."

"At least there's room on this side."

There's room because I put my house as close to the edge as possible. The front door opens out onto the boundary instead of the rest of the colony and I don't use the back door anymore. Only the grass and the animals see into my house when I go inside.

Of course, we have more room than we need here, and space aplenty outside the boundary. We just don't want to sprawl unnecessarily, like so many places did on Earth. We're all too aware we're at the foot of a holy place. It would be wrong to dominate the landscape here.

"Well, I'll see you tomorrow, probably," I say and kiss her cheek.

"You are okay, aren't you, Ren?" She holds my hand, stopping me from leaving. "You've looked so stressed lately. Are you eating properly?"

"I'm fine." I pull my hand free and wave with it, leaving her to watch a moment before going her own way.

For a moment I wonder if I should follow her. Initiate something. But I'm tired and need to rest rather than stir up something that's finally settled. In minutes I'm curled up, nestled in my own little nook. Not even the thought of that metal artifact and the mystery it brings with it can keep me awake.

AS I'm walking to the communal printers early the next morning I realize I haven't been down to the Masher for a couple of days. The thought of what could have been lost already makes me clench my teeth with worry. I stop and consider turning back, but then I see Sung-Soo waving from inside the skeleton of his home and I know my only chance has passed.

"I've been looking at some more things on Mack's projector," he says as I arrive.

"Good morning."

He smiles. "Yes, sorry, good morning. And I wanted to ask you about the pipe that goes here. You said all my waste goes into the walls and gets filtered by the soil. So what's the pipe for?"

"The walls process human waste," I reply. "The pipe will connect your house to the Masher."

He listens, enraptured, like the perfect student. I answer his questions, surprised by how much detail he wants. Most people just want to know that their house will be functional, not how.

When the first lines of inquiry are exhausted, he comes with me to the printer I've left working overnight. The membrane is ready and already rolled onto a bolt so we can carry it over.

When we go back outside, the first tendrils are starting to emerge from the pods on God's city, nothing more than nubbins at this time of day.

"People are getting excited about the seed ceremony," Sung-Soo says. "Are you?"

Oh shit. What a question. I'm dreading it, but I can't tell him why, just as much as I can't pretend to be excited. He's too tuned in to people. "Sort of," I say. "It makes me miss Suh more." I look at him. "Messages only go so far, you know?"

"What is she like? My grandmother?"

Oh, he speaks of her in the present tense. We rarely talk about Suh in the colony, day to day, and not like this.

"She's the most amazing woman I know."

"How did you meet her?"

"At university. We ended up viewing an apartment at the same time and decided to share." I can't help but smile at the memory. "It was so hard finding somewhere to live in Paris then; the university had sold off its student accommodation and the only places most of us could afford were in dangerous parts of the city."

"Paris?"

"The capital of France and the European Union." Neither of which would mean anything to him. "Millions of people lived there. It wasn't a nice place, really."

"Was that where the food was? Is that why you had to live there?"

It strikes me then, more than it ever has with the children of the colony, that Earth is an alien planet to him. We have no shared reference for what life was like there. How can I convey the sheer number of people, the ancient infrastructure or the emphasis on money and prestige? He's a product of a life intimately connected with the environment, whereas the society I grew up in did everything it could to divorce us from that connection.

If he was chipped, it would be easier; there are exabytes of history archives on the cloud, a lot recorded with full immersion. I make a mental note to see what could be interpreted by the projector to remove this barrier between him and our technology.

"We were in Paris because it was the last independent university in Europe." I pause. I need to stop referencing things that have no meaning or context for him. "It was the only place we could learn without more powerful people . . . using it as a chance to control us."

He looks lost. I shrug. "It doesn't matter anymore. Suh changed everything. We live here now—that's the important thing."

We reach the house skeleton and he helps me fix the first layer of the membrane. Every single thing I do is accompanied by a question. At the first chance he's given, he does the work himself.

The more time I spend with him, the less he reminds me of Suh. When I think back to the Suh I met that day at the apartment though, she's nothing like the woman I followed here.

We stood in the lobby with the awkwardness of two people sharing a space without knowing why the other was there. I assumed she was meeting someone else who lived there. In fact, she was waiting for another agent marketing the property. Both parties were unaware of the other and their brief argument when both turned up pushed Suh and me together into a shared social role of innocent but involved bystanders.

As phone calls were made and bosses consulted, she held out a hand to me. "I'm Lee Suh-Mi," she said. "But call me Suh."

"Renata Ghali," I replied, but didn't invite her to call me Ren.

"Lee is my family name," she said, dumping her bag on the floor and leaning against the wall. "Unfortunately, my parents didn't realize that my 'very pretty' name sounds like an invitation for litigation in English."

I think I laughed. I was fascinated by the fact that she spoke to me in English, rather than French. It was a bit of a faux pas, in France, with so many of the natives infuriated by the sheer number of immigrants squeezed into their capital. Whether economic or intellectual, it didn't matter. We didn't belong. Did I give something away in my interaction with the agent? My French was flawless—I'd been speaking it all my life as it was my father's first language. Perhaps my accent wasn't Parisian enough.

"Are you at the university?" she asked and I nodded. "I thought I recognized you. I've seen you on campus. I'm studying synthetic biology. You?"

"Engineering, architecture and mathematics."

She looked impressed. "Which is your main subject?"

"Engineering, but the other two count as a full degree."

"Are you some sort of genius, then?"

I shrugged. I'd learned by then to not advertise the fact that I was gifted. It was only my first year and I was still working out who to be and where I fit in.

Suh's agent got off the phone first. "I'm so sorry about this; it really shouldn't have happened," he said in French. "We're just waiting to hear back from the landlord and our booking people to see who made the appointment to view first."

"Pas de problème," she replied, sounding Parisian as hell. "We'll share, right, Ren? If we like the apartment, that is?"

I realize now that I was always following her. Nothing but a little cork caught in her eddies and swirls, happy to bob along the river.

Soon after we moved in, I asked her why she offered to share with someone she'd just met.

"It made sense," she said. "And it was fate, us being there at the same time like that. But I wouldn't have suggested it if you were a philosophy major. They're so miserable."

17

SUNG-SOO'S HOUSE IS complete by the end of the day. We finish just after sunset and an impromptu housewarming party takes place in his empty house. He must think that's all we do here, but before he arrived, there weren't many celebrations in the colony on this scale.

When it's over, I help him clean up and then we end up sitting beneath the central dome's ceiling, looking up at the stars. The design works well.

"Come on," he says, jumping to his feet.

"Where are you going?" I ask, unwilling to get back up. I'm tired.

"I want to find something that's outside the colony. Now is the perfect time."

"It'll be easier in daylight."

"No, it won't. Come on."

I follow him out of his house and then out of the colony. He's heading away from God's city, back toward the mountains in the direction he came from. It's after midnight and very few lights are on in the houses we pass.

I'm used to sneaking out after dark, but doing so with someone else lends it an edge of excitement. It feels strange to be heading in the opposite direction of God's city.

Sung-Soo moves with grace and confidence through the tall grasses. He's sure-footed in a way that I'm not; he's naturally poised whereas I have to pay attention to where I'm going. I stumble a couple of times on rocks hidden among the tall stalks and it makes me irritable.

"Where are we going?"

"I saw one on the way here. I'm sure of it."

I haven't told anyone that I'm striking out into the wilderness with him. Then I wonder why that thought bothers me. He won't hurt me or lead me to my death. I put it down to the unfamiliarity of being with someone else on an excursion and decide to go down to the Masher in the morning, no matter what time I get to bed. The decision calms me.

"Yes, over there—look!" I can barely make out his pointing finger in the pale starlight. "Come on."

I do my best to look where he pointed but can see nothing except shades of black. I follow and he's moving faster now. The stalks of the grasses snap on my shoes and I lose my footing. Thankfully he doesn't notice. Just as I'm about to ask what the hell we're doing again, I catch sight of something ahead, a shift in the gray and black fabric of the landscape. I speed up in my eagerness to see what it is.

As I get closer, the shimmer I detected farther back resolves into the shape of leaves clustered tight together. They're reflecting the starlight, like the leaves are dusted with glitter. It's too soft to see from a distance but up close it looks quite magical.

"This is it," Sung-Soo says with delight. "They're easier to see at night."

I pluck one of the leaves and put it in a pocket to study at another time. Then I remember the botanists and pick leaves for them too. I turn back to the colony in an effort to get a bearing so that I might be able to lead them back to the bush later. It makes me wonder at his ability to have spotted this small plant, mostly obscured by the grasses, while dehydrated and exhausted, and remember it well enough to find it again.

He's scrabbling about in the dirt below the bush and I wonder if he's hidden something there.

"I want to carve again," he says. "This is the best stuff for it."

"The roots?"

"No." He grunts with effort but I can't see clearly enough to know why. I can hear the dirt landing on the grasses nearby as he excavates. "This."

He stands and holds out his prize: a large lump of . . . something. A natural deposit by the look of it, with the same iridescence of the pendant he wears around his neck. There isn't enough light to make out the colors properly, but I can see they range from light to dark, swirling through the material.

"It's hard, but still soft enough to work with the knife," he says. "You can always find it underneath this kind of bush. I don't know why. It doesn't kill the plant. If we leave it alone for a few months, another one will grow."

"Perhaps the root system attracts a mineral . . . or perhaps it's a by-product of some kind of exchange between the roots and the soil," I suggest. I know ten different people who will want to study it.

"We can go back now," he says and I see his teeth glint as he smiles.

We return to the colony and say good-bye. Even though my body is so tired, I have no desire to sleep. Perhaps the thrill of discovery has made me too wired or perhaps the mysterious deposit has reminded me of my own mystery left to solve.

Seeing as it seems to be the evening to go excavating, I return to the space beneath the tendril buttress and dig out my coveralls and the hinged metal artifact. I resist a moment of temptation to go on another excursion into the city and instead return home. The clothes no longer smell of the gunk they were covered in, thankfully, and are dry to the touch. I can't be bothered to tidy away the things in front of the Masher chute, so I stuff the coveralls away beneath the pile of stuff waiting to be thrown out when I've got a minute.

Once I'm as comfortable as I can get, I twist the object over and over, working the hinge and feeling the smoothness of the metal pieces. I know it's not part of something printed here or on Atlas, nor a relic left from any of the equipment we took with us on that first expedition. But it was made for some purpose and used by someone who went into that place and left it behind. Was it discarded because it broke? Was it a piece of wreckage left behind after someone else succumbed to that hellish place unprotected?

I call up the virtual replica I created and play around with some additions, but it's like pissing into the dark. Nothing feels right and I don't even know what I'm heading toward with each variation of the design.

Then I decide to go hunting. I access the cloud and start searching in the archives taken from Earth, stashed away like a Noah's ark of data before we left. I create a search algorithm, take a portion of Atlas's processing capacity that's barely used now, and work with the AI to refine the parameters. Then I leave it to scour photos and film for anything that might resemble the artifact. I instruct it to shortlist candidates and create a 3-D model of each one that I can manipulate in my visengineering software, sending me a daily digest of results, knowing that I'll only get distracted if it pings me throughout the day.

That done, I tuck the metal artifact under my makeshift pillow (I've no idea where my usual one has got to) and invite sleep in.

18

"WHERE IS GOD in all this?"

I rest my head against the plasglass as the memory of my mother's disapproval comes to its natural end. Why do I have to think about that every fucking time I come down in the Masher room?

Sometimes I barely notice it, but today my mother's words seem horribly loud. She's probably dead now. I'll never know how or where or when she died and the thought of that makes my throat tight. Was she alone? Was it sudden or slow? Was she even herself at the time or had dementia taken her like so many others?

I pull back from the plasglass and look at the reflected red mark on my forehead before spotting something on the other side of the door. A bundle of wool attached by a length to a half-knitted doll seizes my attention. I knew someone was planning to create something like wool with a plant fiber of the same consistency, but I didn't realize they'd achieved it.

I open the door, retrieve the doll and the unused thread, and untangle them from the rest of the rubbish. The maker must have treated it in such a way to stop it being processed as an organic material, and I'm so glad they did.

The doll is bald and has eyes that are slightly different sizes made of a few tiny stitches. Judging by the blue dress, I assume it's a girl, with brown woolen skin and black shoes. She has only one arm and the second one is nothing more than a few rows of knitting that seem uneven. She was abandoned, unfinished.

"I'll finish you," I say to her even though I don't have a clue how to knit. But I can learn; no doubt there are thousands of instructional recordings on the cloud. I'll print some needles and finish her arm and make her some hair.

I clutch the doll to my chest with one hand and rummage through the rest of the discarded items with the other. There's another vase with that same printer defect running through it, only worse than it was before. Surely the owner can see it? Why not ping me to come and sort it out?

Perhaps he or she doesn't like me.

I dig deeper and pull out a hair comb with two broken teeth. I could use that. I put it on top of the Masher. And there's a cracked bioplastic wallet that could still hold all sorts of things. That comes out too, along with a mug with a broken handle that could easily have a new one printed and attached. It's not one of the standard patterns. Why throw away something that's clearly been visengineered? Do these people not know how to fix things?

Nothing else appeals to me, so I close the door and try to pick up the collection on top of the Masher with my free hand as I don't want to let the doll go. Just when I think I have a grip on it all, the mug slips from my hand and smashes on the floor.

I stare at the tiny chips and the white chunks, the curved

slivers rolling back and forth. I made it worse. I could have fixed that, but all I've done is destroy it.

For a while I'm just tears and self-hatred. Then there's nothing to do but gather up the pieces—not caring about the stabs and tiny cuts they cause—and dump them in the Masher again. I activate the machine, scoop up the things I've rescued and go home, sniffling.

I'VE barely had time to find somewhere to stash my new finds and untangle the spare wool when I get a private encrypted message from Mack.

Carmen is at Sung-Soo's house.

I look up at a crack in the ceiling—has that got bigger?—and groan. Everyone in the colony has been in that house over the last two days.

She's there with the ones who're supporting her in this seed business.

Look, I don't agree with her reasoning, but is it such a big deal if they get the colony to vote on this? It's within their rights. You're not a dictator, are you, Mack?

I sound horrible. I feel horrible. I can't be his emotional Masher chute right now.

I read Kay's report on that thing in his gut. I have no idea if the seed would work properly on him. I don't have time to

test it—I've barely had enough time to build in a mention of
his arrival. And I don't have a profile for Sung-Soo; he's not
chipped and his life has been too different for me to just
make guesses on which messages he'll pick up from
environmental cues. If it doesn't work on him at all, we're
even more fucked.

He's panicking. The seed ceremony is the central pole that
keeps the circus tent up. If Mack's manipulation doesn't work
on Sung-Soo, it could all come crashing down. He's perfected
the technique over many years, a frighteningly powerful combination of alien chemicals and the exploitation of human
neediness, designed to shore up the lies he's been telling since
Planetfall. I see his point, but don't share his terror. Should I?
Do I just have nothing left in me right now?

I don't know how to respond. It's uncomfortable using the
v-keyboard in here and I just want him to go away—I want all
of it to go away! I just want to learn how to knit so I can fix
this poor—

So you need to go over there and get Sung-Soo away from
them. If they convince him he should be the one, there's no
way I can go against that. You need to make sure he
understands that it has to be Marco.

Is there no other person on this fucking planet who can be
your bitch today?

No.

A pause.

And I'm sorry I keep dragging you into this, Ren, but you're the only person I can trust.

I tip my head back and let a guttural cry burst out in the hope it will release some of the pressure inside. I see an image of him on that day, with Lois's gun in his hand and Suh's blood on his helmet, staring at me. "Are you with me, Ren?"

"Oh for fuck's sake!" I yell at that crack and I get up and I leave the house and I know I'm just shoveling another pile of shit for Mack. For decades I've been keeping it all shut away and there's a part of me that just wants to grab him and stand up in front of the colony and say, "This is what we did, and we're sorry and now you know the truth," but I'm a coward and a failure and there's no way I could do anything that—

I'm at Sung-Soo's door. I slap my hand against the sensor and then realize I have no idea what to say.

The valve opens and Sung-Soo beams at me. Behind him, Carmen peers around to see who it is, and there are a handful of others there, all sitting on the new moss floor.

"Ren! I forgot—I'm so sorry!"

His words throw me. "Um . . ."

He winks. "I'm coming, right now." He turns around to his guests. "I'm sorry, everyone; I was supposed to go to Ren's house and I totally forgot. How about we see each other another time?"

My God, he's actually using me as an excuse to get away from them! Not the most plausible excuse in the world, but they're not going to call him out on it.

"See you soon," Carmen says. "And please, do think about what we talked over this morning."

"Yes, I will," he says and I walk away a few paces, not wanting to interact with more people than I need to. I give Carmen a smile and she returns it. I can't tell if it's genuine or not. As long as she doesn't come over and talk to me, I don't care.

When the last guest leaves, Sung-Soo closes up his home and strolls over, waving the group off. He heads toward my house and I rush to his side.

"You don't mind me saying that, do you?" he asks, moving relentlessly closer to my front door.

"No. But you're acting as if it was true instead of a way to get away from them."

"They're watching us," he says and waves in their direction. Several wave back. Fuck.

"Once we go around to the front door, we'll be out of sight," I say. "You don't have to follow through." When he says nothing, I carry on, fear squeezing words from me. "They were trying to persuade you to take the seed, weren't they?"

"Yes. They really want it to happen." He shrugs. "They look at me very strangely. Like I'm more special than I am."

"Carmen can be a bit . . . full-on. Do you agree with her?"

His face crumples with concentration. "I don't know. She says me arriving when I did is a sign. But I decided to come here because of the storm. Does that mean God killed everyone I knew to make me do that?"

The proximity alarm activates and I look away from him so I can select the icon and cancel it.

"Carmen doesn't think things through," I say. I don't want to bad-mouth her; it doesn't seem right. "And she's not thinking about Marco and what it would mean for him."

"Do you think I should take the seed?"

"No," I say. Don't ask me why, I think.

"You don't trust her," he says as we circle my house to get to the front door.

"Not on this, no."

And then we're there, right in front of my door, and the conversation halts. "You don't trust me," he says. "That's why you don't want me to go inside your house."

Not this, not today, not now. "Mack told you, I'm very private."

"Everyone else here lets other people into their homes. Why don't you?"

Can he see the sweat on my forehead? I can feel it on my palms.

His eyes—Suh's eyes—watch me, and I can't speak. This is the first time that I've been in this situation. Everyone else learned to be respectful of boundaries on Atlas, when there was so little private space and the need not to kill one another. He hasn't had to embed that in his thinking like we did.

"You want me to trust you more than Carmen," he says. His voice is gentle and soft, barely louder than the grasses behind us being swished by the wind. "And yet you won't trust me. Where I grew up, if you kept someone out of your home, you were telling everyone they must be a bad person."

Is that true or is he just saying it to make me feel guilty? Either way, I can't respond. No sensible answer is presenting itself to me.

"I'll tell Carmen that Marco should take the seed, if you let me into your house."

"What the fuck have those two things got to do with each other?"

"I'll trust your judgment if you trust me."

I shake my head. He's more manipulative than I'd credited him for. "That's emotional blackmail."

The look of confusion seems genuine enough. "What does that mean?"

"Making someone do something they don't want to by making them feel bad . . . threatening them if they don't do it."

The confusion lingers. "I haven't threatened you. And I don't want you to feel bad. I just want you to feel you can trust me. I don't want to hurt you."

"Then back off."

"But . . . you being like this . . . it isn't . . ." He looks up as he struggles to express himself. "If you're my friend, like I feel you are, then something must be wrong for you to be like this. You look scared. Why be scared of letting me into your house?"

The impulse to run out into the grasses seizes me and I actually take a step backward before I realize that I can't do that. I can't run away from this, or the colony. There have been so many times that I've wanted to and it always comes down to the fact that there's nowhere else to go. No new town to settle in, no other culture to go and lose myself within. There is only this place and these people and this man standing outside my house.

If I say no, he could turn on me, go to Carmen and pander to her wishes, just to spite me. Would he? I don't know! I don't really know this man!

"Ren—" Now his hand is reaching toward me. "It's okay. Nothing bad will happen. Just open the door. It doesn't have to be a big thing. Just open it and you'll see it isn't as bad as you think."

If I don't, he'll go to Mack and tell him. Or Kay. He'll tell them how much I freaked out and then they'll come and ask to come inside and I won't let them and then they'll override the lock with the emergency code and go in and they'll see they'll see they'll see—

His hand catches mine. "Please. You've helped me. I want to help you."

This isn't—he isn't—going to go away.

"Just promise me you won't talk to anyone else about this."

"I promise."

It feels like it takes an age to move again and then it seems like I cover the distance between myself and the house in an instant. My hand is over the sensor, like my body is moving in rebellion against my wishes.

The valve opens.

I know what's in there. I'm expecting it and still it feels like a part of me is seeing it for the first time and oh sweet Lord I want to die.

19

I CAN SEE only a few centimeters of moss near the door and that's brown and mostly dead now. Everywhere else is filled from floor to ceiling with . . . stuff. My stuff. My life. Exposed.

There's no way to see past it all. There's a tunnel through it into the far end of the hallway and the light only penetrates so far into it. Every time I come home I crawl into my house, like some supplicant, some unworthy sinner.

The comb with the two broken teeth that I rescued from the Masher slides down and lands at the entrance to the tunnel. I thought I'd wedged it in but clearly not well enough. I hold my breath, fearful a little avalanche will begin there as well as in my heart. But nothing else falls.

I had forgotten that his hand is still holding mine and I only recall when his slips away. I feel like I've been cast adrift suddenly, that I was unknowingly tethered but now I could just drift away, spiral into myself and never come out.

"Ren," Sung-Soo whispers and I look at him to make sure

he's real. He took his hand away because he needed to cover both his mouth and nose. "Oh, Ren, what is . . . Why is all that there? Do you actually live here?"

His voice is strained with disgust and disbelief. I can't reply. I look back at the pile and the entrance to the tunnel and then put my hand over the sensor to close the valve.

"Do you really live in there?"

I look at the closed door. Other people live in their houses. I don't. I cram myself in. I don't want to say that though. I just nod.

"It's not . . ."

"Normal?" I ask.

"Well . . . it's not—" He finally lowers his hands. "I can see why you don't let people in. Ren, don't you think you need help?"

"No," I say. "I just collect things, that's all. Just because I have a lot of stuff doesn't mean it's a problem."

"But the smell . . ."

The shame and embarrassment devour me. I start to shake more violently. "Just leave it. Leave me alone. You got what you asked for; now I really have to trust you. That's what you wanted, isn't it?"

I've no idea why he looks hurt. "I won't tell anyone," he says. "I'll leave you alone, if that's what you want."

He turns and walks away a few paces, far enough for me to feel better, and then he stops.

"Oh. I forgot. I made you something." He pulls something out of his pocket, threaded onto a thong. He comes back to me and holds it out on his palm.

A tiny fist holding a stylized mallet has been carved from that iridescent deposit. In the daylight I can see it's a pearlescent blue. It's ready to wear.

I take it. It's beautiful and still holds his warmth. "Thank you," I say but he's already walking away.

I hang the pendant around my neck and tuck it beneath my shirt. I don't want to lose it.

For a few moments I just stand still, paralyzed. I want to go inside and find a nook to nestle in and find something to take me away from myself. But if I do that and Sung-Soo calls Mack and Kay, they'll break in if I refuse to come out. If I'm not in there, however, they'll have to leave it be.

I need to be somewhere else.

I turn and strike out into the grasses, walking swiftly and purposefully away from my house and the rest of the colony. I don't have supplies, not even any water, but right now I just need to get away.

Each step is accompanied by a new stab of worry. I can hear imagined conversations between Sung-Soo and Mack, sometimes Kay, about what he saw.

"*But . . . the smell.*" I close my eyes at the memory of his words. He thinks I'm an animal. He thinks I'm broken in some way, like that printer with the defect.

Why hasn't that person asked me to fix it? Do they not want me in their home or haven't they realized there's something wrong? How long will they wait until they act? Are they hoping it will just correct itself if they leave it alone?

These people . . . they don't think about the things that underpin the life we have here. They just assume I'll be there to fix it. What if I wasn't?

There are two other people who can fix printers in the colony—or at least who were trained. It was a core policy of the trip: all critical skills had to be held by a minimum of three people, who would make Planetfall in separate pods to ensure that if anything catastrophic happened on the way down, the colony wouldn't be left with a skills gap. But the other two haven't kept those skills up since we arrived; they know I'm faster and that I've always been happy to fix and build. It was one of my primary roles after all, but secondary for them.

The colony would struggle without me for a while, but there are so many immersive tutorials, they would soon be up to speed.

Mack might miss me as confidante, but he'd probably be relieved. He wouldn't have to worry about me telling anyone about what happened back then and what's happening right now. Kay would miss me, maybe.

No one else though.

I could leave.

I look across the plain to the low hills beyond, the edge of the mountain range that curves around the grassland. Diamond Peak is behind me, the colony between us. The weather will be gentler ahead, without the mountains to affect it. I could download the maps and do some climate forecasting to pick a spot that would be sheltered and safe all year round.

I'd have to get hold of seeds and download instructions on how to grow and care for the plants. I'd need something to eat in the interim, and shelter that I could build without a large printer. I could make a small portable one that could make simple structures but nothing that would be fast enough to protect me from the elements quickly.

What else would I need to take?

The moment I think of all the things in my house, I know this flimsy plan is an absurdity. I couldn't leave all that behind. There are holy relics in there, the last connections to my daughter, the book my father wrote, my mother's art. Too much to carry.

My legs give out from under me and with an unceremonious rustling thud I land in the grasses, disappearing beneath the tops of the stalks. I cry and swear at myself for falling into Sung-Soo's social trap. I was right; he will destroy the balance here. The balance inside myself.

I sit there and sob long enough for my back to ache. I'd curl up like a cat but I'm afraid of putting my face near the dirt and the microscopic organisms within it.

A message arrives and the "urgent" tag makes me almost vomit with fear. What has Sung-Soo said? Is this it? After all these years of hiding, am I about to be exposed?

I bring my knees up and rest my head on their bony hardness, wrapping my arms around my legs and squeezing them as tight as I clutched my dying child.

The smell of her hair, her tiny frame that I'm afraid I'll crush, her limp, doll-like limbs. She's barely there and no matter how much I want it and how hard I press her against my chest, my body can't give hers life again.

Then I'm outside of myself looking at a grim tableau. It's a study in futility: my face distorted and inhuman with grief, the sound of my animal roar slamming into the walls of the tiny hospital room. The doctor standing a meter or so away, her face the picture of sadness within permitted professional parameters and the nurse staring at me, his eyes wide at such a display of raw, brutal, ineffectual love.

Countless machines beeping and flashing impending death with cold impartiality. All of them useless. My maternal instincts equally so.

A second urgent message brings me back into my body, now wretched with tension. This one could be from Kay, saying she's at my house and has seen inside, that they're coming to find me and put me into treatment of some kind. There will be an emergency council session addressing how to deal with someone like me. They'll vote to destroy my house and take my things away.

They'll force me to live in an empty shell and I'll rattle around inside with nothing to hold me tight.

Eventually, the tears stop and I begin to ache too much to keep sitting so still and tight. The sound of the wind in the grasses becomes comforting, as does my little dell walled by the thick green stalks. I feel safer, sitting down here with only the sky above me, and it eases the panic.

I twist onto my hands and knees, turn around like a timid dog and raise my head slowly until I can peep over the top of the grasses. I expect to see a small posse heading straight for me, ready to cart me off for some sort of inquisition, but there's nothing between me and the colony except the grass and the bugs lurking within it. I can't see anyone near my house, but I can't zoom in to see if the door has been forced. What am I thinking? No one has been near it; otherwise my alarms would have gone off. I lost sight of that in the panic.

I sit back on my heels. The stalks are squashed flat below my legs and pressing uncomfortably against them. Everything looks peaceful there. Slowly, reluctantly, I accept that I have to open these messages and face whatever is within.

They are both from Mack. I select the first, and after opening and closing my fisted hands a few times, I blink twice.

I don't know what you said to him, but it worked—look at Carmen's discussion group. Thanks, Ren—that's a massive weight off me.

I read it three times, to be sure. Sung-Soo did what he said he would.

Then I remember the second message and the anxiety spikes. That could be the one about my house.

There's nothing to do but open it.

I still need you to place the seed for me though. Carmen's not done with this yet and I can't take the risk. She's sent me a message about wanting to revise the ceremony and questioning why things are done the way they are and all sorts of bullshit. I suppose she's worked herself up so much she doesn't want to see it all go to waste. Maybe she just wants to see me squirm for the fun of it. What a pain in the arse. You're quiet, are you OK?

I flop backward, my shoulders, neck and head pushing back more of the stalks until they hold me at a fairly comfortable angle. Sung-Soo kept his promise.

I clasp hold of the pendant, which is slick with my sweat from where it's rested against my chest. I don't like him knowing about this, but I can cope if that's all it's going to be. I think I can, anyway.

A tickle on the back of my neck makes me leap up onto my feet and brush it frantically. Dozens of itches creep across my skin as I imagine some creature crawling around on me from the grass. After satisfying myself I haven't been bitten and nothing is trying to hitch a ride, I head back toward the colony.

There's nowhere else to go.

20

I MANAGE TO get back to the house without anyone seeing me. At least, no one calls my name or waves or comes over. I open the door, crawl in and sink into a pile of clothes, exhausted. It isn't even lunchtime and I could sleep for hours.

I'm woken by something falling on my head. It happens sometimes. I pull it from my cheek and see that it's the top I wore to Sung-Soo's welcome party. It has wine spilled down the front. I didn't notice that at the time. I ball it up and toss it away from my little nook. I'll deal with it later.

With trepidation I check my messages. There's one about a list that's been set up by Nick to coordinate the colony's desire to shower housewarming gifts upon Sung-Soo. Everyone is free to open it and see what hasn't been made for his house yet and then tick off the item they've decided to give him. It's a nice idea, like an old-fashioned wedding list.

All the basics have been given already, and even as I scan the list, items are being grayed out as someone makes their choice. By the end of the day Sung-Soo will have everything he could possibly need and significantly more than he'd ever want.

I see that a projector unit hasn't been picked yet, probably because it requires assembly. It intimidates most people, despite there being so many construction guides on the public server. I built the house and the water filtration unit, basic kitchen and waste management system, but I still feel like I should take him a gift. Something to calm the waters between us again, perhaps. Or just an excuse to go and see him and determine whether he still wants to talk to me. No, it's more than that; I want to see if he's going to hold this over me. I need to see if he's a threat.

I mark the projector as my choice and see if there are any time slots available on the colony's midsize communal printer. It will be faster to split the component manufacture between that and my home one. I book a slot later in the day, select the model I want to make and check that the base metals and minerals needed for it are available in the communal feed. Levels are lower than they would normally be, thanks to the current high demand, but there's enough. We need to either recycle some things or make an expedition again if the levels get much lower. I'd rather the former, seeing as we've managed for the last ten years or so to keep fairly balanced without the need to mine for more base materials.

There's probably a thing or two I could chuck in the Masher to help replenish some of the rarer elements. Then I remember I can't actually reach any of the three Masher chutes in my home anymore.

Sitting up, I resolve to clear the pile in front of the one in my bedroom. But when I see it all stacked so high, the desire disappears, like a tiny water spillage sucked up by dry, cracked earth. Where do I start?

The one in the hallway might be easier to reach. I squeeze

and twist my way out of my room and into the corridor with its valleylike route leading toward the printer. I don't really think of it as a living room anymore, seeing as I stopped using it as anywhere other than the place I collect my printables from some years ago.

Now that I'm looking at the stuff stacked in front of me, I'm struggling to recall exactly where the Masher chute door is. By the time I've found the right spot, it's clear there's far too much work to be done to access the chute considering I want to build a projector today too. It's a job for another time when there's less going on.

I was so distracted by the list for Sung-Soo that I neglected to check the rest of my messages. I clamber my way back to the nook in my bedroom and open them up. There's one from Kay with a report on the parasite's genetic makeup that I almost open before seeing the subject of the message below. It's from the program I created on the Atlas server to find potential matches for the metal artifact.

The first batch of results is in.

I open the report and select the first match that leaps out at me with its evidence score of photo and film matches in the high thousands.

The potential match is for "glasses," or "spectacles," to use an older word pulled from the archive. I ask the AI to provide a visual summary of one hundred randomly selected examples it's found to come up with the suggestion, just to be certain it's the kind of object I have in mind.

I watch the pictures, each one displayed for five seconds before being replaced by the next. There's one of a woman on a beach (oh God, to go to the beach again!) and she's wearing a pair of sunglasses like my grandfather used to wear. There's one of a child hunched over a paper book in what could be a schoolroom but I'm not certain, having never been in one myself. Image after image of the past, across multiple countries, people of multiple ages and races all with defective vision. They're from the days before it was routinely fixed by crude laser surgery in the time of my grandfather. Once basic lenses formed computer interfaces, they were used to correct vision instead.

Memories of people wearing glasses in Paris when I was a student come to mind. They lived in the poorer areas, had the worst jobs and were the people society did its best to ignore. Some still wore them because they distrusted the lens technology and tried to persuade everyone else it was another way for the gov-corps to track your movements and exploit your data. I ended up arguing with one of them in a bar one night until we realized we agreed; I just accepted that all the data he feared would be harvested by the lens was already being captured by a dozen other devices and techniques. One more data source wasn't going to alter the fact that I was already in the system. We ended up drinking so much I passed out in the stairwell outside the flat. The man died a week later in the first wave of violent protests that marked the beginning of the "bloody summer" that the press reveled in reporting. All those protests achieved was raising the profiles of several citizen journalists. Nothing changed, of course.

I pause the images, minimize the interface and fish out the artifact from the little crevice I tucked it into for safekeeping. Could this be part of a pair of glasses?

I run my finger along the lengths and feel patches of roughness on one of them. There are two, separated by a smooth portion. The ends of the two pieces look broken, but one of them has a slightly bulbous edge, suggesting a second hinge used to be there. Am I trying to fit it to the suggested pattern? It's what human beings are far too good at, after all.

I hold the length with the rough patches up to my face. It's certainly long enough to form the front part of the frame. The rough patches correspond with my eyes—perhaps the large external lenses were attached there. The hinge makes the second piece bend in the right direction to form the arm over my ear.

No. This is madness. How would a pair of glasses end up in God's city? If others did travel here before us and explored . . . and even died in there . . . why would they be wearing such primitive devices? Surely they'd have technology comparable to ours to travel here and—

That's an assumption. Several, in fact. Aside from the one about physical similarity, who am I to think I know the technological development of all species and cultures? Besides, the glasses could just be an earlier form of interface, just like they experimented with before integral retinal lenses.

The program provides other potential matches, which I scroll through, but none have as much visual evidence from the archive. The search is far from complete though. I have to keep an open mind.

Mack pings me, asking if I'm free. It makes me groan and curl up on my side. Hasn't today been enough? Do I have to go outside again? I allow myself one minute of indulgent self-pity and then reply with a promise to be over right away. I can't let anyone think something is wrong with me. I can't risk the attention.

EVEN though there are dark circles beneath his eyes, Mack looks happier than I've seen him in days. He offers me a drink and I ask for Turkish coffee. He's the only person on this planet who makes it just the way I like it. I can't tell the difference with printed versus cooked food, but I can with that.

I flop onto his sofa and cradle my head in my hands as he clinks and thuds away in the kitchen. If someone left the glasses behind, where are they now? Did they leave? I imagine a body rotting and decomposing in the tunnel and it makes me nauseous, so I tune back in to what Mack is saying.

"So I'm thinking when she sees how much it means to everyone, she'll simmer down. And Sung-Soo's been brilliant. Hasn't fazed him at all."

He brings in two steaming cups and hands one to me. I let the aroma waft up and try to focus on the simple pleasure, but it isn't enough to still my thoughts.

"Do you think anyone came here before us?"

He frowns at my question. "Where the hell did that come from?"

"Theoretically, it's possible," I continue. "We found a way, right?"

The frown doesn't lift. "We haven't found any signs of anyone else. Atlas didn't detect any old structures or wreckage or—"

"But they might have come to God's city and left again. Not settled, like we did."

"Like tourists?" He sniffs. "Who knows? There are more important things to think about now, Ren, remember?"

I sip the coffee and let it soothe the flicker of fear that I've just let myself blather on without thinking. I'm not usually so careless, but after the upset with Sung-Soo earlier and the ramifications of this damn artifact, I'm not at my best. Thank goodness he's too distracted to wonder why I asked. I refocus myself.

"I suppose you wanted to see me about the seed," I say and when he nods, a little pocket of dread blooms within me.

"It's got to be done," he says. "How's the coffee?"

I don't let him divert my attention in the way he wants. "I'm really not comfortable with this."

"I'll show you the best route. Just make sure you wear all the protective gear, don't take out the seed until the last minute and make sure that—"

"I mean, I'm not sure this is the right thing to do."

He sighs. "Do we really need to go through this again?"

I turn my attention inward. Do I have the courage to stand up to him? It's not like I'm afraid of him. But I keep going along with what he wants. Why?

"You know there's no better way to keep this colony going," he says softly. And he's almost right; I don't challenge the way he does things because I can't think of a better way, but that doesn't mean there isn't one. "If there is," he continues, "tell me; we'll talk about it. But just flatly refusing to help when there's only days to go isn't good enough."

"I haven't 'flatly refused,'" I say before I realize the trap he's led me into. Shit.

He smiles. "Glad to hear it."

"But I'm not happy about it."

"I don't exactly skip there every year either," he says, a harsh edge creeping into his management voice.

"I know. I just . . . don't think this can go on forever. They have to find out one day. I think this should be the last year."

"It can't be. I haven't put anything into the message about that. We have to plan further in advance."

I want to be the kind of person who would stand up now and declare that there is a better way, or that I'll stand by my principles in this as all things and not do it. But what is the alternative? And I'm just as afraid of what will happen if the transition from lies to truth isn't handled carefully. I should have spoken up over twenty years ago.

But if I had, I would be dead.

"You'd better show me how you do it, then," I say, without bothering to hide the defeat in my voice. He isn't the victor. Fear is. And cowardice.

21

AFTER A COUPLE of hours at Mack's place, being actively taught by another human being for the first time in years, I decide to go to God's city via the proper entrance. I won't go inside—I can't from this direction—but I want to embed some of the details he showed me via the projector and an immersive gaming platform adapted for that purpose.

I walk through the eastern gate, one I usually avoid, and follow the only path that crosses the boundary out of the colony. The crystal is laid right up to the outer edge of God's city. The path stops about three meters away from where the first tendrils of the city rise up from the ground. Its end point is just in front of the city's natural entrance through the outer perimeter, formed by the space between two of the thickest tendrils, which make an organic pointed archway.

I still pause, even after all these years and the twenty-odd times I've been forced to parade into here with everyone else for the annual circus. Those times within the crowd, among their excitement and anticipation, haven't been enough to scrub away the very first time we walked through this alien archway.

I retrace the steps I took then. This time I'm not looking up at God's city with wonder and apprehension; instead I'm mapping what Mack showed me onto the structure looming ahead of me and reinforcing the route I'll need to take tonight. It helps to look at it this way. It distances me from that time before.

I cross the central courtyard—a grand name for nothing more than an area of compacted earth between the archway in and the entrance to the main city. I avoid looking at that as long as I can. It always makes me feel sick and I don't want to engage with the people on duty today unless I have to.

I'm used to them being there now. At first I hated it and voted against the motion to post people at the entrance, when it was debated in the early months of the colony. Once people had got the essentials of colony life in place, they had time to think about Suh's return. Nick was worried she would emerge from God's city and think no one cared about her return if she wasn't greeted immediately. I argued that she wouldn't mind, but this wasn't good enough and Mack spotted an opportunity to start growing the mythos that fed into the seed ceremony. He backed the people who wanted to maintain a vigil around the clock. A senseless waste of time and energy, but the majority worked its magic again and now no one wants to be the one to say it was a mistake.

This is why I don't come here. It always makes me bad-tempered.

The courtyard is large enough for us all to fit in, standing room only, and it's a bit of a crush toward the front. In only four days we'll all be packed in here, staring at Marco as he climbs the slope to the entrance. It's the time I feel the most lonely.

"Hello, Ren!" Pasha calls from his post near the entrance. I try to hide my reluctance to engage as he jumps down from the platform that holds him level with the door without touching God's city.

I wave and mumble a greeting as the other person on duty—Dr. Lincoln, as my luck would have it—complains to Pasha for abandoning his post.

Pasha ignores him. "This is a nice surprise," he says, enveloping me in one of his giant, loving embraces that even the most surly of citizens are subjected to on a regular basis. Even the doctor will have had one at the start of their shift.

"Just wanted to make sure everything was in order before the ceremony," I say, having prepared the lie beforehand. "I was thinking about the rain we had last week and the ground here . . ."

"It's all good," he says, tugging gently at his thick black beard as he looks around the courtyard with me. "It's so sheltered and the ground is so compacted it would take a lot more than that to cause any problems." He tilts his head. "Anxious?"

I shrug and he smiles.

"Dear Ren," he says, sucking me back into his bear hug. "Always worrying for everyone else." He kisses the top of my head as I return the embrace. His size and bulk make me feel childlike again, held in the security of a paternal hug.

The silk of his salwar kameez feels as soft as its shade of peach and he smells faintly of cinnamon. "Has Neela been baking?" My voice is muffled, but he can still hear me.

"Cinnamon rolls," he says and I hear his stomach rumble at the thought of them. "She's a true artist."

I wish I could be more like them. They are so . . . light and easily contented. They laugh and work together, are dependent on each other but not dangerously so. Could I have something like that with Kay, if I tried?

Dr. Lincoln is calling him back and Pasha releases me. "I'd better go back. He'd have my head if the Pathfinder chose this moment to come back and not be greeted properly." He starts off, then turns to face me, walking backward. "And come for dinner, for goodness' sake—you look like you need a good meal."

"Soon," I say. Perhaps when all this is over, that would be good. They're both excellent cooks and good company, when I'm in a state to handle that.

I watch him climb back up onto the platform and stand with his chest puffed out. His long black hair is being teased away from his shoulders by the breeze coming through the archway. I have to stop myself from going over and saying, "You should go home; there's no point in your being here." I can't allow myself to give in to that need to tell the truth. It's one of the pillars that supports Mack's elaborate ruse. If I destroyed it, the rest would come crashing down and we'd be crushed beneath it.

I spend the rest of the day making Sung-Soo's projector. It's just absorbing enough to put the last task of the day out of my mind. If only everything else could be as straightforward as this.

I check whether anyone else is at his place when it's ready. No one with their location settings set to public is there at the moment, so there's a risk, but I decide to take it. If someone else is there, I can just drop it off and leave.

Cradling the unit in my arms, I leave the communal work-shop and make my way over. The sun is setting behind God's city, creating long shadows across the path. Now that I'm not building, I'm worrying again, so I walk faster.

I press the sensor beside his door and cast my critical eye

over the exterior of the house. It looks good: the lower portion of the dome running around the bottom edge is made of shiny black solar cells; then there's a layer of aquarium windows with the rest of the dome covered by partially reflective plasglass windows. They're less harsh on the eyes than a mirrored surface and just as good at maintaining privacy.

The door opens and he grins at me. "I was hoping you'd come," he says, beckoning me in.

The room is warm and there's a fire in the pit at the center of it. He invites me to take off my shoes and I do so, seeing that he's barefoot. The new moss has a superb springy softness to it.

The room feels completely different from the last time I was here just after completion. It has a homeyness to it and a cozy, inviting security as well. There are several pieces of furniture and I recognize a couple of Neela's pieces displayed in pride of place against one of the walls. There's a circular sofa, which Pasha probably made or at least contributed to, that reaches most of the way around the fire pit.

"What do you think?" he asks.

"It's lovely."

"Really?"

"Yes! I made you a projector. I'll hook it up to the network if you want?"

"Thank you. And yes, please; I'd like that."

I unroll my tool wrap and get to work. He stands nearby, curious as always, but I think it's also a reluctance to relax while I work.

"It feels strange," he says after a couple of minutes of silent industry. "Like it's someone else's home."

"You'll settle in."

"And it will stay here and not be moved. That's strange too."

"It'll be fine," I say and realize I'm trotting out the same old shit that people say without thinking. I put down the screwdriver and look at him properly for the first time since I arrived. "I can only imagine how weird it must be. But don't worry. If there's one thing human beings are good at, it's adaptation."

I don't think I'm very good at reassuring people. His expression doesn't change anyway. I go back to what I am good at.

"Have you ever been to Korea?" he asks.

"No."

"My father says that's where my family came from."

"A fair way back," I reply. "Your great-grandparents were born there, but they left when they were pretty young. Suh only went there once, when she was a teenager, and she hated it."

"Why?"

I smile. "The humidity, mostly. She said it was okay to visit, but she couldn't live there. It was too different from what she was used to."

"Father said it was a wonderful place."

I raise an eyebrow. "I don't think he ever went there."

"Then why say that?"

I shrug. I stop myself from saying the first thing that comes to mind: that he was probably half mad with grief and nostalgia when he said it. "Well . . . it was a wonderful place. But he was just as European as Suh and I were." I've lost him again. "On Earth, people often lived a long way from where they were born, or their parents or grandparents. Lots of places couldn't cope with the number of people there and the demand for water. So people moved on."

"Like I used to?"

"Yes, I suppose so. But on a much bigger scale. Sometimes it was because of war; sometimes it was to find work or avoid persecution. It was pretty chaotic there."

He seems interested. "Go on."

"My dad's family came from Ghana and we lived there a while. My mum came from England, but she lived in France. So did my dad, for a few years, but he moved all over the place because of his job. So I ended up speaking different languages and feeling part of lots of places, rather than just one. That was the same for Suh. She spoke Korean at home but English and French everywhere else. She used to laugh that I liked Korean food more than she did when we both went to visit her parents."

"Do you miss Earth?"

"Sometimes."

"Can you go back?"

"It's complicated." I don't want to go into the details; none of it will make sense and it will only confuse him and make me miserable. It would take years of preparation and the efforts of the entire colony, there would be risk—and what would we return to? Would there even be anything recognizable left?

It hits me that everyone I knew on Earth will be dead now. And not only the people I knew, but the music and the games and all the other transient cultural references that used to make the world familiar. Technology would have evolved along different routes; the omnipresent threat of war might have finally been realized. It would be like going back to an alien planet, in many ways.

"This is home now," I say, hearing Suh's echo.

The conversation ebbs as I focus on connecting the projector to the network and testing its interface with the dozens of sensors embedded in his home. He laughs as I ask him to stand in different places and try to hit a virtual ball so I can calibrate it.

When it's done, I slide the tools back into their places and roll the container up.

"Ren," he says, coming over. "I know you don't want to talk about your house, but I think we should."

Just when I thought it was going to be glossed over for the sake of least resistance, he brings it up. I clutch the tool roll to my chest.

"There's no need." I head toward the door.

"But don't you want to be able to live somewhere like this?" I don't reply. "It just doesn't seem right for me to be somewhere so nice—that you made for me—and for you to go back to that . . . place."

I make it to the door and open it. "It's all fine," I say, too stupid with panic to think of anything more intelligent. The only thing that stops me from losing it completely is the fact that he doesn't follow me out.

22

FOUR HOURS LATER, when the majority of the colony is asleep and I'm kitted out with another protective coverall, my smart-goggles and freshly cleaned filter mask, I leave the house.

Initially it feels like I'm headed for my secret hollow, only with more fear mixed into the excitement than usual. Now that it's time to actually plant the seed, I'm more focused on the practicalities of what I need to achieve, rather than the ethics tangled up in it all. I just hope everything goes as smoothly as Mack thinks it should.

I pass the curved tendrils hiding my secret entrance and walk farther around to the back of the city.

We argued when I practiced this climb at his house. It has to be one of the most difficult and inefficient routes to the front entrance, but, as Mack said, it isn't about efficiency; it's about not being seen by the people holding the vigil outside the entrance. Climbing over the top from the back of the city means no one will see me as I make my ascent, and once I'm at the top, my descent down the other side will be masked by the lower tendrils and the darkness. Mack showed me various simulations he'd run, proving that, thanks to the angles involved, the route makes it very unlikely that I'll be seen by either the people on duty or a random passerby who happens to look up at the wrong time. Like he said, he's been doing this for years. It's still inefficient as hell though.

God's city towers above me, directly between me and the colony now, the grasslands at my back. I don't have any filters or enhancements active on the goggles at the moment, but my eyes have dark-adapted sufficiently during the walk to pick out more details at the base of the tendril I'm standing in front of. I shrug the pack off my back and kneel down to sort the contents. Inside there are three climbing ropes, clips and a climbing harness. Underneath those are crampons that I can strap over my boots, capped with the roughened surface of ultra-velcro instead of the metal spikes we'd use on the mountain, and a small box with the seed inside. I had to smuggle it out of Mack's house once he was finished with it, for fear of Carmen's watchful gaze spotting him delivering something to me.

I resist the temptation to open the box and check that it's in there. I put it in there less than an hour ago. I have to redirect that nervous energy toward getting my climbing gear on and checking the harness straps, buckles and crampons. Twice.

Once I'm satisfied, I kick the tendril I'm standing next to very gently and don't pull my foot away after contact. Instead, I move as if that foot is on the first rung of a ladder, to see if the friction provided by the u-velcro is good enough to prevent my foot from sliding down to the ground.

It holds. With a twist and bit of effort I detach, satisfied they'll do the job. I won't be depending on them anyway if Mack's securing hexes are where he said they are.

I heft the rucksack into place and feel the hard edge of the box inside dig into my lower back. After a slight readjustment I fasten the security straps over my chest and waist so it doesn't slide off at just the wrong moment. Then two of the coiled ropes go over my head and shoulders, with the third just slung onto one shoulder for ready access. I won't need it yet, but soon I will.

I check all the clasps. Twice. When I start the third round of checking, I realize I just need to get started.

I fumble for the handholds I felt in the game version and they're only millimeters from where I think they should be. A good sign. My right foot finds the place where the tendril butts against another, forming a V shape about a meter off the ground. It stretches my leg uncomfortably as I manage to lift myself onto the structure. Now that I've left the ground, I've committed myself.

I climb, but there's no exhilaration or sense of adventure that usually accompanies the activity. I curse myself for forgetting to enhance the data coming into the goggles and resort to whispered voice commands to boost the signal. In the enhanced view the two tendrils I'm climbing between are like obsidian tree trunks against a pale gray sky. There isn't much for the goggles to work with here; the starlight seems to be absorbed more than reflected by the surface. It's like climbing with my eyes closed when I try to look for the hand- and footholds. There's no way I could have done this without the training at Mack's place beforehand.

It's slow progress and the shaking doesn't help, but I finally reach the first hex. I'm relieved and appalled in equal measure. It will get easier now, but the fact that Mack sullied the surface of God's city with semipermanent climbing gear makes me angry. Still, I connect my rope to it with a carabiner and test the strength as the sensor inside it acknowledges the presence of the rope and beeps softly in response.

An unfamiliar icon pops up, bright and garish at the edge of my vision, and I open it, checking that the interface between me and the first hex is working as it should.

"Climbing route Mack006a is available for use. Would you like help with your climb today?"

I select "yes" and look back up toward the next part of the climb. The next hex is shining out into the darkness, thanks to the climbing software's enhanced-reality mode. I can see a route for the first time since I began and my movements become more confident.

The first ten meters or so is practically a vertical climb between the tendrils until I reach the bottom of the first nodule. There's a clip that helps me scrabble onto the top of it with a combination of swinging (which leaves my heart in my throat) and then gripping the surface with the u-velcro crampons at its widest point. By the time I've maneuvered myself onto the top of it, I'm panting with fear and exertion. What the fuck am I doing?

A message arrives from Mack. That's the hardest bit done now.

I should have known he'd be following along through the climbing software. I lie flat on top of the pod, its top directly below my stomach. Even though the rope and harness and the carabiners are uncomfortable to lie on, it's all I can do for a moment.

Keep going, Ren. It's easier from there. I promise.

Fuck off, Mack.

A picture of a laughing face pops up and I swipe it away with a sharp leftward glance. Bastard.

A prompt for voice contact appears and after a few moments of intending to snub him for the entirety of this sorry affair, I accept. I might need him.

"Are you okay?"

"What the fuck do you think?" I keep my voice to a whisper. Even on the other side of God's city I'm scared someone will hear me.

"Catch your breath. All the climbing gear is working as it should. I can guide you over any tricky bits."

"You said it would be easier now."

"It's going to be fine. You're a better climber than you think."

"If you're going to pep talk me, I'll cut off now."

He laughs again, and as much as I don't want to, I smile. It's a nice sound. It almost makes me feel like we're doing something normal.

"Ready to carry on?"

"I suppose so," I reply.

"Before you do, make sure you sit on top and look away from God's city, goggles off."

My thigh muscles complain and twitch as I shift my position, moving first onto hands and knees, then twisting to plop unceremoniously on top of the nodule.

I lift the goggles to rest them against my forehead and take in the view. Even though I'm only a few meters above the ground, the vista is transformed.

The sky is just as it always is: crowded with stars, swathes of the sky as pale as milk in patches, and obscenely beautiful. My new vantage point has nothing to add to its majesty.

The pure blackness created by the edge of the mountain range to my right and the ground below looks like it's been caused by someone tearing off a piece of creation and revealing the void beyond. But not even that is the reason why he told me to do this.

It's the river in the distance, one that I've walked along several times. On this peaceful night it looks like a crack in the world, exposing a planetary interior of stars rather than molten rock and metal. It makes everything else feel like a scene cut out of black paper. Being the only one who can see it makes me feel simultaneously magnificent and insignificant.

How did I get to this point? How can I be climbing the outside of a holy place like a criminal, perpetuating this absurd cycle of lies? Where did I go wrong?

"Are you with me, Ren?"

The gun wasn't pointing at me when he said that. But it might as well have been.

"Ready to carry on?" His voice, here in the present, makes me jump.

"Do you regret it?" I'm able to ask the question without him in front of me.

There's a pause. "Which part?"

What a question. There's so much to choose from.

"Yes. And no." Evidently there's no need to distinguish between different items in the reprehensible list. "I wish none of it had happened."

"Do you wish we never left Earth?"

I've never asked anyone that, not even myself. It's such a pointless question, but something about the torn sky and cracked earth in front of me is making me want to prod that despair and see if it wakes or turns out to be nothing.

"Only once. You?"

I look up at the stars. "I don't think so. I can't imagine knowing Suh and staying behind."

"Do you wish you'd never met her?"

The breath catches in my chest. I can barely imagine what life would have been like had I missed that appointment to view the flat. I ran to catch the train. If I'd missed it, would I be in some research facility now? Would I have been a better daughter? Would I have saved thousands of lives like my father predicted?

The guilt stirs inside me like a slumbering snake needing to feed soon. I see my father's face from the window after I said good-bye for the last time, how his hand came up to cover his eyes, how he crumpled when the taxi pulled away and I watched him sob. Because of me.

I almost told the driver to stop. But the words never quite made it out of my heart. I try to remember what it was like to think it was more important to find God than to console the man who, in many ways more than my mother did, gave me life.

Do I wish I'd never met Suh? "Yes," I reply, but my voice doesn't sound like my own.

23

I CLIMB AND the focus required puts me right back in my body instead of in the past. Even though this is the last thing I wanted to do, it's exactly what I needed.

Between the climbing software and Mack's reminders, I manage each of the new obstacles without incident. I climb higher, over progressively larger nodules, all spherical in their nighttime state. They would be easier to climb in the day—assuming the spokes that emerge from them are solid—but I need the darkness to hide me.

When I reach the highest point of the climb and the colony first comes into view, it's no longer about which handhold or foothold comes next. I feel exposed for the first time and the risk of discovery sharpens into a point pressing on my chest rather than being a nebulous thought at the back of my mind.

"How did you do this every year and not get caught?" I whisper to Mack.

"By being careful."

"I can't believe it works."

"Well, it won't if you don't get a move on."

It's no easier to climb down than it is to go up. It just torments a different set of muscles. My knees are starting to ache and I make a note in my reminders to get the cartilage checked out. It might need a top-up. We've no idea how long we'll live; no one dares to make a serious prediction when there's practically zero data available and a pathetically small sample size, but I think I'll be getting along fine for at least another fifty years or so. Maybe more. I might see two hundred and be one of the oldest human beings alive. Does that mean anything when we're millions of miles away from the people who keep those kinds of records?

I slip and the rope goes taut, jerking me violently against the harness as I lose my center of gravity and end up flipping over. I gasp and grip the rope as I sway away from the pod I was trying to climb down from without sound. My skin flushes with heat against the coverall and the box containing the seed bangs the back of my neck as I scrabble to right myself.

"Would you like to resume the climb?" the climbing software asks. My heart is still pounding and all I can manage for a few moments is righting myself and clinging on, terrified the hex and carabiner supporting my weight will give out. Then I remember that it will be distributed across several of them and that the software would tell me if that were about to happen.

"Would you like to resume the climb?"

I'm closer to the pod below me than the one I fell from, so I lower myself down slowly by letting out the rope fed into my harness a few centimeters at a time. Once my feet touch the spongy surface I breathe out again.

"Fuck," I whisper.

"Would you like to—"

"Yes," I snap.

"Keep your voice down," Mack says. "The sound can travel farther than you think."

I revoke the voice contact authorization and sit on top of the pod, shaking until the adrenaline surge subsides. I could abort now, damn this sordid business and let it all play out in the open for once.

Surely they suspect? Surely they know she's never coming back?

Are you okay? Mack doesn't understand I broke contact to shut him out, rather than just shift to text.

I don't answer. I don't want to say what's on my mind.

Ren?

It's ridiculous. All of it: from my clambering over the top of the bloody city to the way they believe Mack's lies. These are intelligent, rational people and they just absorb all this shit without even thinking about it. Are they so desperate to hold on to something that they'll ignore the facts? How long can they do that?

But if someone told me what I wanted to hear, I'd believe it too. What alternative is there? I'm envious of them and their comfort and their faith. I don't have the right to look down on them for believing Mack when I'd rather be one of them.

Ren, are you hurt?

A movement below makes me duck my head down and then flatten myself out on top of the pod. I'm certain it was one of the people on duty; it was definitely inside the courtyard.

I could stand up and shout and give myself away. I could

rappel down there in a matter of seconds and show them the contents of the box. And yet I remain pressed against the black sponge as if someone were holding me down.

I'd have to tell them I've known the truth all these years. It hasn't just been Mack lying to them. It's been me too. And I don't have the right to be angry with him when I've been just as guilty.

I send him a simple ping, hoping he'll realize what's going on and stop freaking out. I wait a few minutes and check the network for any comments from the ones on duty. Nothing.

There's a terrible self-awareness that creeps up on me in the dark. There are two people down there waiting. I have no idea if they really believe Suh could come out the doors at any moment. They could just be standing there because it's their turn to and they don't want to be the ones to question it. There may be only a thousand or so people here, but it's easy enough to make the pressure of conformity irresistible. Hell, sometimes we only need one other person to make us fall into line.

And I'm up here, above them, waiting until I can go down there and break into a holy place and plant a lie. A lie that will make people happy to stand there over the next year, one shift each, hoping that when Suh comes back, they will be the one she sees first.

We're locked in this lie's orbit together, none of us able to break its gravitational pull.

So I check my gear and ping the next hex location that's gone dormant while I've been waiting and I climb down. Mack remains silent. I suppose he can see I'm moving again and is letting me concentrate. But the closer I get, the less I can lose myself in the climb.

The last hex is right next to the point I need to cut in. Just the thought of it makes me feel nauseous. I'm not sure I can do it.

It's only about ten meters from where the greeters stand

guard, farther along the tendril that ends in the entrance to the city. It's glowing in my enhanced vision, like a landing pad for a shuttle. To reach it, I need to lower myself down on the rope from the last pod above and land in the right place the first time. If I miss the spot and move about too much, it increases the risk that my movements will be detected at the end of the tendril.

Lowering myself down takes the last of the strength in my arms, but I manage to hit the right spot. It's like landing on a giant tree root just large enough to enable me to stand on the top without falling off. I'm down to the last coil of rope now and it's all a bit easier without having to carry the other lengths too.

Well done, Ren. Let me talk to you again—it'll be easier. We can talk about what happened up there later.

I accept the request but I don't say anything. I'm too close to the greeters now.

"Okay," Mack says. I can hear a tremble in his voice. It sounds like this is just as stressful for him. "Remember, you'll be able to feel the scar but not see it. It's exactly fifty centimeters in front of your toes."

I let out a bit more slack in the rope and tie it off carefully— I don't want to be trapped down there—and crouch down to brush the surface of the tendril in the place I expect the scar to be. For a moment I doubt whether I can feel it through the gloves, even though they're designed to minimize the loss of sensation at the fingertips. But then I feel something like a wrinkle in the smooth surface.

With the v-keyboard I tell him I've found it.

"Good. Get out the cutter and don't touch the settings; I've already programmed it. Hold it five centimeters above the surface and move slowly."

I clench my teeth. I know how to use a fucking cutter. I've used them more than he has! I pull it out from the pack along with the headlamp, which I slip into place over my forehead and tighten into a snug fit. It will give me a headache but at least it won't come off.

"Wait!" he says as I'm about to start. "Put the filter on now, and make sure your skin is covered. It's best to drop down and get it done as soon as you can so you don't have to recut to get out."

It heals that quickly? I type back.

"Yeah. I was sealed in after I planted the seed the first time. I nearly cut the rope when I had to reopen it. You don't want to have to do that, trust me."

I pull the filter mask down and check it's working. I check the coverall opening at the neck and make sure the collar is rolled right up to cover my skin where it joins to the filter mask and the edges of my gloves. Then I cut.

The laser is silent and doesn't emit enough light to be a problem; I'm between the laser and the greeters anyway. The black surface of the tendril splits below the red pinprick like the skin of a ripe plum and I can see deep purple tissue below. It's disturbingly fleshy and my gullet burns as bile rises suddenly from my stomach. The way it parts and oozes a dark sap like blood makes me feel like I'm cutting into an animal.

Oh God, this is so wrong. If I believed in hell, I would be convinced I'd just earned my place there. Forgive me, I silently plead. Please forgive me.

"Done it?" Mack asks. I send a yes and he breathes out. "Drop the rope through first, then climb in. Once you're a few paces from the cut, you can use the headlamp."

I have to push the rope through and battle the nausea as I do so. The tendril trembles beneath my feet, so I push the rest in with greater care. Then I untie the knot and make sure it's running smoothly enough through the clasps to enable me to rappel again.

It's time to go in, but my foot hovers over the wound, and then I lower myself through it, wanting to get this over with as fast as possible. I try not to think too hard about the feeling of compression as I squeeze myself in, but then my hateful brain starts thinking about a reverse cesarean and I have to swallow down a sour mouthful that bursts up my throat for fear of vomiting into the filter.

There's a disconcerting—yet horribly familiar—squelch when I land at the bottom of the tunnel formed by the tendril. A brief glance up at the rope and the stars not obscured by the pods above and then I'm trudging, feeding the rope through the clasp with neurotic control. As soon as it's safe to do so, I switch on the headlamp and bathe the tunnel in light. It brings shadows with it and those bring memories.

Memories of hushed awe and speculation. The sight of Suh's back as she strode ahead, fearless. This tunnel was stable and things didn't go wrong until we were trying to get up to the first pod. How many times did we try to get up to that room from the inside? Ten? Twenty? I can remember only the exhaustion and the sinking despair. I felt like we were missing something, but Suh wouldn't have it. "There's a place at the top and we're supposed to get to it," she kept saying, every time I tried to suggest slowing down or at least reconsidering our approach.

She had to listen eventually. We resorted to using ropes and clips then, but the higher inside we got, the more violently the city affected us. I can still hear Winston screaming at Mack to keep his helmet on after he'd vomited the first time. We all threw up—some of us multiple times—most of us had migraines, and Lois had a seizure at one point, which could have been much worse if Winston hadn't medicated her so fast.

It was like it was trying to kill us.

But Suh wouldn't accept it. We ended up scaling most of the city on the outside after we'd been squeezed out like waste from one of the tubes and refused to go back in. Hak-Kun pleaded with his mother to reconsider, but it was like she didn't hear us anymore. We'd already lost her by then.

I haven't been in this tunnel since that day. In here, when we were walking in the other direction, we were clueless. Still innocent, then. In so many ways.

The light falls on the thick stalk growing a couple of meters behind the closed entrance. There are people on the other side, oblivious to my presence, and I feel a childish thrill at the prospect of getting away with this.

After tying off the rope in two places on my harness, I open the pack as quietly as possible and pull the box out. It's made of thick bioplastic and locked with a simple combination key-pad. Very old-school but I suppose Mack wants it to look as innocuous as possible. By putting something so precious inside something so easily hackable, it reduces the incentive to peep.

Mack's been quiet for a while. He must know I'm about to plant it. I send a ping, unwilling to speak so close to the others even though we're divided by a thick, living wall.

"I'm here. I didn't want to interrupt you. I'm here if you need me."

He's backing off. It's then that I appreciate how hard this must have been for him. He knows that I'm struggling because he has struggled every year. I need to be kinder to him. I don't know a better way to handle this and I don't like what he's doing, but it doesn't change the fact that it has a cost for him too.

His hands were shaking the day the lie was born, when he spoke to the crowd just after second Planetfall. Hundreds of people weeping with relief and shock, some staring up at the sky and some terrified to look up at it. We gathered at the rendezvous a kilometer from God's city, halfway across the grasslands toward Diamond Peak. No one realized three pods were missing at that point, but it didn't take long for them to notice Suh's absence.

"Where's the Pathfinder?" someone shouted at Mack as he stood on top of a crate he'd dragged out from his pod. The panic was visible, spreading across the crowd like a gust of wind upon water.

"She's in God's city," he said once the crowd had fallen silent. "She's . . . communing with the creator."

"God is in there?" I think that was Carmen. It was a woman at least.

"Yes," he said and the crowd's silence was smashed upon the rocks of vindication and joyous rapture. But I was silent. I stared at the back of Mack's head, thinking of the gun, of the blood, of her body. Abandoned. She was still in there, but there was no communion.

"Mack," I said and tugged the back of his coverall to try to pull him down and think about what he was saying.

He covered his mouth by pretending to wipe away a speck from his helmet and subvocalized a private message to me. "Shut up, Ren, and go with it. I know what I'm doing."

I looked out into the crowd of people cheering and weeping and praying. Helmets banging against one another as people tried to get as close as they could to loved ones. Each sealed in their own microenvironment, trying to connect. None of them were looking at me.

Gradually people looked back to Mack for more. And he gave it to them. Promises that Suh would contact us when she could, promises that she would get a message to us soon. The declaration of the city as a holy place, out of bounds until Suh's work was done. Reassurance, comfort, support. All built with false scaffolding.

And they all believed him. He was the Ringmaster. I doubt it even occurred to them to question him. And by the time people realized the three pods were missing, the lie about Suh returning had become so firmly embedded, such a key part of the foundation upon which the new colony was being built, no one linked them.

I open the box, take out the seed and then look at the plant. When we saw it here that day we made first Planetfall, growing seedless inside the tunnel, Suh said it was a sign we were near the end of our journey. How else could there be the same plant growing in an alien structure on a distant planet that Suh found on Earth? And now I was about to twist that miracle into something base.

I cut into the stem at the top and wedge the seed into the sticky, oozing sap, desperate to get it over with. The growth stimulants coating the seed will force the plant to make a casing around it by the time Marco arrives. To him and anyone else who sees it, it will look like that was the way the plant had grown.

I've renewed the scaffolding that Mack built and his lies will endure at least another year. I don't know if I can.

24

THE CLIMB BACK out of the tunnel is as uneventful as the way in and just as nerve-racking. Every one of my steps is dogged by a seething, oily mess of unfocused anger. Mack pings me and I send a terse confirmation that the deed is done before cutting off all comms. I trap my finger in a carabiner before I winch myself up to the partially healed cut in the roof of the tunnel, and when I reopen it the anger spikes into a sharp point of the purest rage at myself. The self-loathing builds as I climb until, at the top of the city, I have to stop and press my temples with my fingertips. I want them to penetrate my skull until they pierce my brain and just end this.

I can't stop thinking about the seed, but not the one I've just planted—the first one, the one I saw in Suh's lab on Atlas. We were due to have dinner, but she hadn't turned up. We were ten days out from our destination and she'd been less reliable the closer we got. When I found her in the lab, she was crying.

"They're happy tears," she said as I rushed over. She laughed as we embraced and I tried to reframe the sobs I'd heard on the way in as nothing to worry about. "I worked it out, that's all," she said, wiping her cheeks, only for new tears to fall.

"Worked what out?"

"How it happened. Why I changed." She pointed at the plant behind the plasglass in front of her. I knew the shape of its leaves and its thick, hairy stem far too well. She'd grown hundreds of them since we left Earth. But this one had a fat seed pod growing out of the top.

"Is that what you saw that day at the nature reserve?"

She nodded and I went closer, noting the sealed container now and the pipe running off it into an analyzer. The seed pod was round and veined, like an uglier version of a poppy ready to scatter its seeds everywhere. I had thought about it so many times over the years since her coma—it was what had caused it after all—and finally seeing it was strangely anticlimactic. How could so much have been started by such a small thing?

"It's not the first one I've managed to grow," she confessed. "I didn't want to show anyone else. Not until I was sure. Now that I am, I still don't want this to go on the network."

That was contrary to everything else she researched. "Why?"

"Because it could be abused. I don't think my reaction to it was unique. I think I was more susceptible than most, but it could work on someone else."

She was skipping ahead, having forgotten how little I knew about this line of inquiry. I'd given her guidance on various aspects of the genetics—it was trying to solve the puzzle of her coma and subsequent change that inspired me to study a new discipline on Atlas—but she'd been joining the dots alone. I couldn't see how it all fit together.

"Have you isolated a poison?"

"It's more elegant than that. Look at this."

Moments later a share invite arrived and I opened the link. It was raw footage from her lab notes. The seed behind the sealed plasglass, then her face coming into view until her nose touched the glass. Just as I was about to ask if I should speed it up, the footage slowed and zoomed in to the seed pod. A puff of what looked like pollen sprayed the screen between her face and the plant.

"It's not pollen," she said before I could ask. "It's closer to a pheromone, but not like anything else I've studied. It's not to attract insects—it's not for attraction at all, in fact. It's only released when a person gets close enough to it to trigger the mechanism."

"Only an animal? Not an insect?"

"No, you misunderstand me—it's designed to be breathed in by a human."

I folded my arms. "How could you know that? We don't have any animals on board, so how could you test the theory?"

"Ren, that footage was taken two years ago. I've been working on it ever since. Like I said, I didn't tell anyone."

She must have seen the hurt on my face. "But we talk about everything."

"I had to keep this just for me. While I was working it out." I knew there was more to it than that. Whatever happened to her that day brought us together in many ways, but also separated us. And not just us: it separated her from the rest of humanity.

She beckoned me over to one of the chairs set up in front of a projector and taught me everything she'd learned. Slowly, I fit the pieces into my own narrative.

It started the day we went hiking in the foothills of the Alps just over a decade before. For months she'd battled with the authorities to gain permission to enter a nature reserve and in the end my father pulled strings to get it for her and one assistant.

I wanted to see wildflowers and a place untouched by advertising executives, so Suh made me her assistant for the day.

I was recording some crap for my dad as a sort of postcard, which was why I wasn't looking when she saw the plant. She called out something about a unique plant that wasn't in the reserve's database. It wasn't until she said something about it tasting so good that I stopped what I was doing and paid attention. By the time I got back to her she was convulsing violently. She was unconscious long before the paramedics arrived.

I wrenched the plant from the ground and stuffed it in a bag, not caring about the possible prosecution I faced. The hospital had it tested by the right people, but no one could identify it. Its genetic profile wasn't listed on the universal genome database and hit the headlines for all of five minutes, which was pretty remarkable at the time.

When Suh woke and wrote that string of numbers, she couldn't even remember going to the reserve. Then slowly the memories re-formed and she recalled the plant and the urge to eat a seed that had just unfurled from its protective casing before her eyes.

"We knew there was something wrong about it all," Suh said. "Now I know it wasn't just me being stupid. It's a drug keyed to human beings. It compels the person who has found it to eat the seed."

I thought about the endless questions from the hospital staff, from the reserve keepers, from the universal genome office and her family. At one point I was accused of engineering the plant myself and putting it there to poison her. It was madness. All of it. It was only the testimony and pictures of the reserve staff proving the plant had been there several days before our arrival that cooled the attention on me.

There was speculation about genetic sabotage—a serious

problem for specialist crop growers—but when it was revealed that the plant had no identifiable system of pollination, the theory was thrown out. It became a mystery, something for the scientists and academics to publish papers about while I sat at her bedside. By the time Suh was out of the hospital, it was relegated to the annals of genetic history, something only a handful of botanists and specialists continued to be in a frenzy about. The most popular conclusion was that the plant was designed by some wayward genius and planted in the reserve as a prank.

I didn't believe that for a moment. Someone would have claimed it if nothing else—why do something so difficult if not to gain fame or to prove a point? And if it wasn't engineered, how did it spontaneously grow there, completely divorced genetically from the local ecosystem? Plants didn't just spring out of nowhere, not in France anyway. Every square inch of Europe had been cataloged. There wasn't a living organism that hadn't been analyzed and put in the UGD. If we'd been hiking in some obscure part of the Amazon—and it would have to be something like a previously undiscovered cave network—I'd have entertained it as an idea. But only because it's more comforting to accept that than the alternative of not ever knowing.

I looked through the plasglass at the seed. "If I ate this, would . . . would I be like you?"

She came over and put a hand on my shoulder. "No. It's inert. It's as useful as a Brussels sprout."

A spark of anger behind my breastbone. "Did you engineer it that way?"

"No. Of course not. I've tried so many times but each one is just . . . plant fiber. They taste like sprouts too." Seeing my disapproval, she added: "Oh, I tested each one thoroughly first, obviously. I don't know what I'm missing, but none of them can do anything like the one I ate on Earth. I have learned a lot though. The plant is insanely adaptable. I've been able to grow it in vastly different environments and conditions. I haven't seen any other species able to survive just about anywhere with such success."

"Weird," I agreed. "Most plants adapt to fit a particular environment. Which one do you think it would be most successful in?"

She shrugged. "Equally successful in all of them. Or perhaps I should say one hundred percent successful in an environment with humans in it. If an animal ate it, I'm pretty certain it would have no effect on them. You saw the scans of my neocortex just a few months after the coma. I suppose there might be an effect on a primate, but even so, it wouldn't have the same impact. I'm certain it was artificially made. It doesn't have any of the features needed to propagate itself, for one thing. We call it a seed, but I don't think that's what it really is. Nor a fruit. You want to know something crazy? I'm starting to think it was made by the one I think we'll find at those coordinates. I think it's like a . . . biological message in a bottle. It could be that the seeds were cast out across all sorts of places—planets even—waiting for someone to eat one and change, like I did."

I nodded, used to just letting her speculate aloud. She spoke so fast it was hard to converse with her like we used to. Many mornings I would wake up to essays thousands of words long that the AI had transcribed for her, full of thoughts she'd had while I'd been asleep. Sometimes she'd get frustrated with speech and the time it took for her thoughts to emerge from her lips and be processed by us slow normal people.

If she was right about the seed on Earth being one of many scattered in the hope of finding someone like her, the natural question that followed was, by who? But we'd already talked that out. I had my faith; she had her hope, "untainted," as she put it, by religion. Even though I'd tried to explain that I could have faith without the dogma and historical baggage of organized religion, she just couldn't get it, despite that densely populated neocortex of hers. The only thing we truly agreed upon was that Suh had been changed in order to lead us to our destination. It seemed that faith wasn't required in order to do that. "Do you think it would have changed me in the same way if I'd eaten it instead of you?"

"It might have killed you. It nearly killed me."

I tried to imagine her having succeeded in replicating the original. Would we take the risk to choose between death or superintelligence? Would we still be able to function as a fledgling society if we were all like her?

"You said it could be abused," I said. "I don't see how, if the seed is inert."

"Not the seed, the pheromone. It compels you to eat the seed, but not just that. It puts you into another state, one that makes you highly suggestible. In the wrong hands, it could be used for all kinds of dark shit." She took hold of my hands. "That's why you mustn't tell anyone about this."

"Even Mack?"

"Especially Mack."

"Don't you trust him?"

"Of course I do! I just don't think that someone who knows how people work in the way he does should have access to something this potent. He's been fantastic to us, and we wouldn't be here without him, but don't forget how he made his fortune before I came along."

I hadn't thought about it for a long time. I'd forgotten what most people did in their previous lives before Suh happened to them. He was the most successful advertising specialist in Europe, arguably the world. The press called him the "desire hacker."

"There's nothing that counteracts its effects and it disappears from our system in seconds," Suh continued. "It doesn't even leave a synaptic signature like other psychoactive drugs. No. You're the only person I trust completely, Ren. You wouldn't use this for yourself like he would, given the chance."

I think about the tunnel far below me and the plant inside. With a seed in place—even an inert one—the plant is tricked to reproduce the pheromone Suh discovered and confided in me. Mack may have decided to trick everyone, but I gave him the tools to do it. Only I could have made this whole circus sideshow happen.

My fingers play over the knots in the ropes keeping me safe. I imagine untying them and leaping from the topmost pod, experiencing a few seconds of total freedom before oblivion, ending all this here and now. But then I think of Kay examining my broken body and I know I can't do it. I breathe in and out until I accept that there's nothing more to do than go home. But something has changed, even though the lies will go on; all the anger I'd focused on Mack I now direct toward myself.

25

ONCE I GET home I don't even attempt to fall asleep naturally. I'm too wired mentally and too exhausted physically to be able to cope with being curled up, awake and caught between the Scylla and Charybdis of guilt and reminiscence. I choose a drug that Kay would never recommend—one that doesn't just help me to drop off, but will keep me under. I don't want to remember any dreams tonight. I'm still shaking as the tiny pill is printed, even though the job is done and the coveralls and climbing gear are stashed away in my secret nook beneath the tendrils, too filthy to stuff back into my pack without contaminating it. No one saw or heard me. No one knows what I've done. But I won't stop worrying about that until the ceremony is over.

I shift from lying there, worrying the dose wasn't enough, to a sinking blackness. The neural alarm still punches through it though. It takes my body a horribly long time to respond. Groggy and confused, I realize someone is coming toward my house only when the second band of sensors triggers another neural blast.

Battling heavy eyelids, I call up the camera feed and see Sung-Soo striding toward my front door. It's a little after nine in the morning and I simply cannot handle this shit right now.

My usual panic is dulled by the heavy sedative that hasn't had enough hours to work through my system. I shut my eyes again, thinking with only a fraction of my usual capacity. Hopefully he'll go away if I don't answer the door.

He doesn't.

Sung-Soo resorts to knocking loudly. That is enough to spark a bigger spurt of adrenaline; if other people hear that, they may come over and see what's wrong.

I stagger and then crawl to the door, grateful that it opens automatically when I press my forehead against it.

A combination of the sunlight and Sung-Soo's disgust as I emerge on hands and knees gives me another wretched kick-start and I get to my feet as quick as I can.

"I'd rather you left a message with Mack than come and bang on my door."

"You'd rather I disturb Mack every time I can't find you?" Now he looks even more unimpressed.

"Has something broken?"

"Yes. You."

I groan. "This isn't a good time."

"I have the feeling there won't ever be a good time." He stares at the door that's closed behind me and hidden the interior. "Let's walk."

I'm in the grubby, sweat-stained clothes I wore under the coveralls during the climb. I can barely stand up straight, thanks to the muscles I pulled last night, and I need to either sleep this off or take a stimulant to counteract its effects.

"I don't . . ." I manage to stop myself saying something acerbic. "Look, normally I'd be happy to, but I didn't sleep well."

He shakes his head. "I've been thinking about this. A lot. It's just like what happened to my friend a couple of years ago. It wouldn't be right for me to just ignore it."

I lean against a patch of dying grass next to the door and hope that if I talk to him for a few minutes, his need to interfere will pass. "Your friend collected things?" It didn't make any sense to me—they would have to travel light. Was this some crap made up to try to get me talking?

"No, he stopped eating properly. He'd only eat one plant after it had been boiled to mush. It wasn't good for him."

I scratch my head, wondering if I could get my chip to give me a direct adrenal blast without Kay being notified. I have no idea how much stimulation would be safe though.

"We didn't say anything for a while, even though we could see it was making him weak. We were in a good place with fish and stuff and he didn't have to walk much. We thought he was just recovering from a bad stomach or something."

"Umm, how about we meet later and—"

"The thing is, Ren," he cuts in, ignoring me, "we should have spoken to him about it right away. By the time we had to move on he could barely handle it. He got sick and it hit him harder. When we did talk to him, we realized it was all in his head. He'd decided that only eating that one thing was safer than eating other stuff we caught. It all got mixed up in his brain or something."

I fold my arms and look out across the grassland. It's cloudier today and the tops of the mountains are hidden. I think it will rain.

"That's what's happened to you." Sung-Soo touches my arm and I flinch. He pulls away. "No one's said anything, or even noticed though. And because you don't move around like we did, it'll probably go on like this until it kills you."

"Don't be ridiculous."

"If all that stuff fell on you, it could kill you."

I haven't got time for this shit and I take a breath to tell him as much, but there's no point. We'd devolve into a childish back-and-forth until one of us lost our temper. He's trying to get me to confess some fictional problem to him and I won't fall for it.

"Sung-Soo, I collect things and I'm a bit untidy. There's nothing—"

"You have to crawl into your own house!"

I hold up my hands, miming for him to keep his voice down. "That's no one's business but mine."

"If you don't think it's a problem, prove it to me."

I narrow my eyes, folding my arms again and tucking my hands tight underneath. What do I need to do to get rid of him and go back to sleep?

"I don't need to prove anything to you. That would only be necessary if I cared about your opinion in this, which I don't."

"Just get one thing from that pile behind the door and give it to me for the Masher. Mack said we were getting low in some metals, so something made of metal would be good."

Shit. I've been so distracted by the seed debacle I forgot to fiddle the communal feed's stock report.

"There isn't anything I want to recycle."

"Just one thing, Ren, and then I'll leave you alone."

We stare at each other, his hands palm up and his face open and expectant. I feel like a child given one of those utterly shit choices parents offer to trick the child into thinking it has a say in anything: *Do you want to record that thank-you vid for Aunt Jasmine now or after dinner?*

"Just one," he repeats.

"Oh for fuck's sake!" I say and twist around to slap the door sensor.

Is there something here I can sacrifice in return for sleep and peace?

As always, a couple of items slip down when the door opens. One is a chunk of pink crystal, the other a deformed fork.

"What about that?" Sung-Soo points at the fork and I clench it tighter in my fist.

"I need this."

"Need it? Don't you have a fork that would actually work? No one would use that."

It has three prongs and they all point in different directions. The steel is scratched and dull. "I'm going to fix it."

"When?"

"When I get a minute."

"But why fix it when you can chuck it in the Masher and print a perfect one?"

"Because it isn't just any old fork. This is the first one that Kay designed and printed herself. I taught her how to do it."

That evening was full of wine and laughter. She wanted to understand why I loved printers so much and asked for a lesson. By the time she wanted to do it by herself she was too drunk to make a good design. She ignored the software's warning that it wasn't viable and printed anyway. When she pulled it out and held it out to me triumphantly, we laughed so much I fell off the sofa. That was the first night we kissed.

"When was that?"

I shrug. "A few years ago."

"And all it's done is sit there in your hallway? You couldn't find a minute in all those years?"

"Is there a point to this?"

"What about that?" Now he's pointing at the crystal chunk. "That's not even a thing! It's just junk!"

"It's not! This is a piece of history. This was one of the samples we rejected for the path."

Sung-Soo's jaw drops open. "But . . . wasn't that made, like, twenty years ago?"

"Yes. And it's just as well I kept it because Pasha deleted the files and I wanted to compare it to the structure we chose a couple of years ago when we were—"

"Ren!" Sung-Soo puts his hands on his head. He looks annoyed. No . . . frustrated? I can't tell. I just want him to go away. "It's trash. And so is the fork."

"That's not for you to judge."

"Give me the fork." When I continue to hold it tight against my chest, he holds his hand out again. "If you can't give it to me, you've got a problem."

"That's not actually an infallible way to prove that; it's—"

"Give me the fork and I'll leave you alone. I know you hate me right now, but I'm doing this for you, Ren."

"Like fuck you are," I mutter. But he's standing there, that palm open, like a gaping yaw waiting to be filled.

I look at the fork. If I give it to him, I might forget that night. He just doesn't understand how important it is. It's not just metal. And it can be fixed.

"No."

His hand drops to his side. "I'm going to ask you again tomorrow. And then the day after that and the day after if I have to. You have a problem, Ren. Let me help you."

I turn and drop down to crawl inside, wedging the hunk of crystal into a crevice partway in and instructing the door to close by voice command as I go. One of the fork prongs digs into my chest as I squeeze through at the end but I don't care. I won.

I wake three hours later, hungry and stiff. The fork is the first thing I see when I open my eyes. It doesn't make me feel triumphant now.

I wash in the usual way, using a cup of water, flannel and powdered soap that I scrub onto my skin and wipe off. It takes too long, this brainless task, and by the time I'm clean and in newly printed clothes I'm tense and desperate to get away from myself.

Fiddling the stock levels doesn't take very long. I've been doing it for years. I doubt many people take any notice of them anyway, but with the demand created by Sung-Soo's arrival the levels are low enough to start triggering warning notices. I can see that someone has been chucking metal down their chute in response, but it's not enough to resolve the problem.

I look at the things in my bedroom, most of it clothing. There are a few things made of metal containing small amounts of the materials that are critically low.

I try to pick one thing that I could return to the communal stock, but every time I pluck something out and think of chucking it down the chute, my chest gets tight and I reconsider. Slowly, I realize that there's nothing here I'm willing to give up. It's all too important.

I make my way through to the un–living room and see more objects that would be fit for purpose. I break into a sweat at the thought of there being a solution to the low levels here, in my own house, coming into direct conflict with my needs. I should recycle some of this; it would solve the problem in a more sustainable way than me having to monitor the levels every hour and certainly preferable to more costly solutions such as a mining expedition or commandeering the molecular printers from people who'd booked them weeks in advance. Using them to print gold and copper would be insanely inefficient.

I stand in the doorway, chewing my thumbnail for what seems like a horribly long time. Unable to act, I check my in-box and the network, but all the while I know I'm merely trying to divert my attention away from this paralysis.

Snippets of the confrontation with Sung-Soo slither in at the edges of my artificial concentration and not even the latest digest of possible matches for the artifact sent by the Atlas AI is enough to keep them out. None of them look as good as the first suggestion anyway. Even though I'm aware of the inherent bias of getting attached to the first explanation of a mystery, I can't shake it. Just as I can't shake the feeling that Sung-Soo is set on interfering.

It makes sense. He's come from a life with little leisure time. Now he has luxurious comforts, safe food and drink available with no effort twenty-six hours a day, and no fears about his own safety. Of course he needs something to fill his time. I just don't want to be his project.

He said he would come back. I can't bear the thought of it. I need to reassure him there's no problem and then give him something to do. Everyone here has a role, after all.

I send Mack a note saying he needs to think about how Sung-Soo could contribute. There hasn't been any contact between us since he acknowledged my safe return home. I think he's giving me space. Or is too busy setting up the rest of the side-show. It's only two days until Marco comes out of isolation and takes the seed after all. My stomach clenches at the thought of it.

A reply arrives and I open it. He's already asked. He wants to learn how to maintain and repair the printers. Looks like you have an apprentice at last ;]

Fuck.

IT takes over an hour but I finally manage to find something I'm prepared to give up in return for an end to Sung-Soo's ultimatum. It's an aluminum pot with a nice finish to it, banded with copper and gold. It's dented and one of the copper bands is loose as a result. I must have found it in the Masher as I'd never have made something like it. I hate the thought of letting it go, but stocks of all three metals are low and I'm not particularly attached to it.

That's what I keep telling myself as I wait for Sung-Soo to come to the door. I turn the pot over and over in my hands, seeing its potential. It could hold all sorts of things and it would take only two minutes to repair.

The door opens and my grip on the pot tightens so much that the edge of the loose copper band digs into my palm painfully.

He smiles, but the usual warmth and delight is guarded now. I'm not the person he thought I was. I have no idea who that was supposed to be. Now he knows what I'm really like. A sour thought, if there ever was one.

"Mack says you want to learn about printers."

"If you're happy to teach me. I think I could be useful. Come in."

I step inside and breathe in the scent of fresh moss. It's pristine in here, almost as if he hasn't lived in it since I last visited.

"What's that?" He points at the pot and my heart races. I don't want to give it up. I want to take it home. "Is it from your house?"

"You said that if I didn't give up one thing you'd come back tomorrow and hassle me, so here, that's the thing."

I thrust it out at him, wanting him to take it and put it away somewhere so I don't have to see it and think about it a moment longer. But he doesn't.

"I said that if you couldn't give up just one thing you have a problem."

"Well, this is that thing, so no problem. Good, let's move on."

He looks at me for an unbearably long moment and then points to the nearest Masher chute. "Put it in the chute and we'll get started."

It feels like I'm walking through thigh-deep mud rather than on new moss. Then I remember that the Masher won't pass it on for rendering down for at least four hours. As long as I get out of here before dinner, I can go and get it. I push the flap open, throw it in the chute and turn to him with a smile. "See? No problem."

He nods but doesn't smile. "Okay. So. Where do we start?"

IT takes some time for me to find the right place to begin. He's never grown up with technology in the way we have, but he was raised by people who were dependent on it. It's clear some bits of tech lasted into Sung-Soo's childhood, but it's left him with a patchy and rather strange impression of how it all fits together. Some of the terminology is familiar and about three-quarters of the time it means what he thinks it does.

He learns fast though and is the perfect student. Once I know he's got the fundamentals, we cover a lot of ground and I actually enjoy it. There's something nourishing about teaching. It reminds me that I'm capable and useful. Enough to keep the darker thoughts at bay while we're engrossed.

But it eats the day and the evening too. Making dinner turns into a lesson on how to print in the kitchen. I demonstrate how different ratios of water and oils, mixed with base proteins farmed from algae grown in the upper levels of the Dome, can create a huge variety of textures. We experiment with taste additives and create some truly awful things, but each one is illustrative.

It's only when Nick calls over to collect Sung-Soo for a gaming night that I realize it's dark outside.

I make a hurried good-bye, not wanting Nick to feel he has to extend an awkward invitation to me out of good manners. I prefer solo games anyway.

I don't have to look up the time to know I've left it too late to rescue the pot from the Masher. Furious with myself, I go and dig out the protective gear I wore to plant the seed. The thought of going back inside the city tonight on my terms, to go where I want, soothes me. I'll find another pot, a holy one, and then I won't miss the mundane one I accidentally trashed at all.

26

BACK IN THE tunnel I know best, dressed and prepped for the usual migraine-inducing light show, I pick up the rope and give it a tug to see if it's still firm. My gloves are covered in the same slimy gunk that makes my boots squelch as I walk, but my sense of purpose outweighs any disgust.

It's been a year since I found a room inside one of the pods that contained more than just air. I've found three in total. The first time I found a small cluster of rocks. They were rough and didn't seem to serve any purpose. I wondered if they'd somehow been caught up in the city's growth and left, indigestible, like boulders swept up and moved by glaciers on Earth.

It wasn't until I found the second room that I began to suspect they had been placed there. That one was discovered at the end of a particularly arduous climb up the interior of one of the thick stalks. There were rocks in there too, but they were shaped.

Some were crude bowls; others were rudimentary tools. That's a theory, of course, a product of my very human brain shaped by experience on Earth. In this place they could have been made or used for anything. But it was clear to me that they had been shaped by someone wielding a tool. The one I took home has spectacularly even gouges forming the depression of the bowl.

It was so hard not showing it to anyone. So difficult to keep the endless speculation about my find within my own ears. I'm convinced people lived here once, perhaps an underclass scraping a life at the bottom of the city. Certainly the rooms I've found things in are nothing compared to the beauty and craftsmanship we saw at the top of the structure. But something about that doesn't add up for me. I saw things up there requiring technology vastly more advanced than hand-carved stone bowls. Why would there be such a wide gulf between a single city's inhabitants?

I'm still not even sure anyone actually lived here anyway. It's so hard to tell when there's no common cultural reference point. I can look around this place and think habitation is impossible because there are no windows, no signs of water or food storage, no furniture or places that are dry enough to sleep. But that's the wrong way to look at it. Perhaps the ones who used to live here needed damp conditions and constant dark. Maybe they licked the walls to sustain themselves and knew ways to shape the rooms here according to transient needs. My gut instinct still says this wasn't a city in the sense of a densely populated place. That's just what we call it. The only person who might have been able to tell us is dead now.

The third room contained things that looked like weapons to me, reminiscent of the flint arrowheads and stone axe heads I'd peered at in museums on Earth. Perhaps that's what this place really is: a museum. I shake my head at myself. Yet another human concept I'm desperately trying to impose on my surroundings.

Those times, I didn't come here with the intention of taking something. I just wanted to explore, and if I stumbled across something, I'd take it home. After the first time, I'd be lying if I said I didn't hope to find something. But right now, I need to, in a way I haven't before. I'm not leaving this place until I have something I can hold and look at and love in a way Sung-Soo will never understand. I'm never going to let him bully me into losing something ever again.

The floor of the tunnel bucks beneath my feet and I tumble, my grip on the rope made ineffectual by the slime coating my gloves. I'm falling again, in the direction I did before, but this time my feet don't hit a ledge. I twist away from the tunnel so my mask doesn't get clogged, which sends me into a spinning, rougher tumble that wrenches my left arm. I hear a sickening pop from my shoulder and then there's nothing but pain. It crowds out the panic and the desire to try to brace myself. All I can do is swear until I finally land at the bottom of the tunnel.

The emergency icon is flashing over my vision as I try to look up and see how far I've fallen. There are more valve ridges than I can count and no rope in reach.

"You have had an accident," the MyPhys software says. "Do you require rescue or assistance?"

"No."

"You are injured. Would you like your physician to be notified?"

"No."

"Initial diagnosis from neural feedback suggests you will be able to walk. You are at high risk of shock. Recommended action: seek medical advice immediately."

"Shut up."

"Do you require further advice?"

"No, go away."

It's small consolation, but if I'd been knocked out, the chip would have notified Mack and Kay immediately and my excursion would be all over the colony in minutes. I realize I've made an error in dismissing the software.

"Open MyPhys," I say, puffing my breath in and out to try to manage the pain. I choose voice interface, unable to focus well enough on a visual one. Somehow keeping my eyes screwed shut is helping.

"Welcome to MyPhys. Would you like assis—"

"Do something about the pain. Reduce it."

"Are you aware that artificial reduction of pain at the neural level increases the risk of further injury?"

"Yes."

"Safety parameters recommend dampening of the parieto-insular cortex for no longer than fifteen minutes. Would you like to proceed?"

"Yes, for fuck's sake."

The effect is instant. Before I was nothing more than an unbearable throbbing pain with a mind and voice. Now I feel other parts of my body. The fall less than twenty-six hours after all that climbing has left my limbs strained and aching. I start to laugh and then violent shivering begins. I need to get home. No, I need to get to Kay. I can't move my left arm.

I open my eyes and look around the area in which I've landed. The beam from my headlamp is shining from a place beside my feet. Carefully I stoop to retrieve it and notice what it's illuminating. The floor here is carpeted with thousands of cilia, each a few centimeters long. I've never seen anything like it here before.

The beam moves as one of the cilia at the edge of the area sticks to the headlamp and pulls it away from me. Before I fully realize what's happening, several other cilia push it along too with what seems to be a reflexive movement. I swipe the head-lamp away from them, pulling long strands of sticky mucus with it, and put it back on. It's tricky to do so with only one hand.

Once I can direct the light, its sweep across the floor and up the curved sides of the tunnel reveals that this entire portion is covered with cilia. Nervously, I cast the beam in the direction they were sweeping my lamp.

There's an open valve, just another of the many I've fallen past, its circular edge clearly visible. But beyond it there's no more tunnel.

It's a room. A new one and it's full of . . . stuff. Hundreds of objects made of metal, plastic, glass maybe. All artificially made and all in one great jumble. Things that must have been swept in there by the cilia.

There's a tremble at the edge of the valve and I can see it's about to close. "Open, camera!" I yell and the relevant icon from my lens software appears translucent across my vision. "Record vision and audio only, no immersion."

I stare into the room and, as slowly as I can, scan the contents with the sweeping movements of my eyes as the valve closes. I can analyze it at my leisure once I get home.

Once it's shut, I leave the recording running, taking in the band of cilia and end it when I'm satisfied I've got it all. The rest of the tunnel remains infuriatingly vertical above me and impossible to climb. I'm stuck.

It's the longest length of tunnel that's moved—in my experience anyway—and I'm struggling to map it to what it must look like outside. Has one of the tendrils that twisted in a curve around the lower edge of the back of the city straightened, thrusting the end of itself higher into the air? Is there a chance someone has noticed? It's unlikely; most of them will be asleep by now and there are no scheduled expeditions this close to the seed ceremony.

I'm desperate to go to the closed valve and force it open, but there's no way I could walk to it without crushing the cilia. Would I have been swept in there had I landed unconscious just a meter farther toward the door?

It's reminiscent of tiny organisms that use cilia to move microscopic particles into their mouths, but none of the things in that room showed any signs of being digested. Is it just a store for rubbish swept out of the tunnels? Why not dump it all outside, like we were dumped several times? And where did it all come from anyway?

My head is pounding. I can't stop shaking and my left hand is tingling. I need to get out of here.

There's no sign of the tunnel moving back to its original orientation. Usually it returns to normal fairly quickly, but even when it has, it will take time to reach the rope and my usual exit point. The pain suppression will stop way before I can get to Kay and if I try to override the safety parameters she'll be notified anyway.

There's a knife in my pack. Mack said the tunnel walls heal themselves very fast. Could I cut my way out? But if I did that, where would I come out? I don't even know which side of the city I'm in now. I could emerge from the tunnel wall in plain view of the greeters, for all I know.

I close my eyes and take a moment to suppress the panic that's rising within. Losing my shit is not going to help.

It would be easy to ping the network for a geolocation and from that I could work out where I am in relation to the colony. But the ping would be registered. If someone went scouting for that kind of information, they'd know I've been inside the city. I've never had to fiddle with that data set before; it would take a bit of time to work out how to cover my tracks, but it isn't impossible. Short of waiting until I can walk out, the latter part of the journey in terrible pain, I don't have a choice.

There's a rendering of God's city on the server. From the outside it's been studied a great deal, thankfully, and the structure has a 3-D representation modeled from the external appearance. There was a plan to add in more detail from the original trip into the city at first Planetfall, which was quickly shelved. Mack doesn't have the skills and I couldn't face processing the data from our multiple failed attempts to navigate the inner areas. Now I wish I had.

But between the external map, the point of entry into the city and my current coordinates, it's possible to work out that I've fallen about ten meters. It felt like much more. If I cut through where my feet are, I should drop out close enough to where I came in to not be noticed.

Cutting from the inside is so much worse. It feels more visceral. I listen for any accompanying howls from inside the city but there are none. It's been very quiet tonight. I try not to think about it too much, knowing it will close itself fast enough and that the alternative is much worse. For me anyway.

There's a drop of a couple of meters down to the ground and my landing is rough, jarring my body and probably making my injury worse. The neural dampening is still in effect, so I don't cry out.

The coverall is easy enough to undo and climb out of, but my shoulder feels horribly wrong when my other hand guides the fabric off it. Dislocated, I reckon. I rattle off every expletive I know in English, French and the ones in Akan that my grandfather taught me when he was drunk.

I make my way back to the colony. The fifteen minutes are up by the time I get home, stash my gear and get back out of the house again. The software gives me a handy countdown of the last minute so I have plenty of time to build myself up into a tense, gut-clenching wreck of anticipation before the pain returns. It brings me to my knees a couple of meters away from my door, even though I tried to be ready for it. I suck air through the gaps in my teeth to fuel the expletives. Unsurprisingly, the emergency icon returns.

"Would you like assistance?"

"Ping . . . Kay . . . Dr. Reed," I say between panting breaths.

"Dr. Lincoln is the current emergency physician on duty."

"Ping Dr. Reed, you fucking piece of shit AI, or I'll delete you from the fucking server."

"Pinging Dr. Reed."

27

"SO, ARE YOU going to tell me how you did this now?"

Kay is standing with her arms folded, giving me her best impression of a disappointed mother.

Whatever she gave me for the pain has made me relaxed and dozy too. Perhaps that's just the post-panic comedown. I close my eyes, lying on the same bed she scanned Sung-Soo's intestinal guest from, my left arm snugly held in a sling and the shoulder joint back in the correct position. There's an ice pack over it.

"I told you, I fell."

"In your house?"

"No, outside."

"You fell off a path?"

"No, outside the colony." Shit, I shouldn't have said that. "Can I go to sleep here?"

"Ren, what have you been doing? Your body looks like it's

been put through some pretty intense exertion. By the look of your muscles, I'd say you've been trying to climb Diamond Peak if I didn't know better. Your knees are ropy as hell and you've been sedating yourself. You know that's not recommended without advice."

I sit up, knowing she won't let me sleep yet. "I went for a climb; I got back later than I should have. I tripped and tried to grab something and it wrenched my shoulder. I'm fine."

"You buggered your knees up a couple of days ago, judging by—"

"I went climbing twice."

"At night. Alone."

I offer an uncertain smile. "I didn't go very high up. I like to look at the stars. I haven't been sleeping . . . It helps if I go for a long walk out of the colony."

She pulls a chair over and sits in front of me. "I could tell something was up. You've looked strung out the last few days."

I wonder if others have thought the same. No, she's the only one, apart from Mack, who would take any notice.

"It's Sung-Soo, isn't it?"

What to say? My thoughts are sluggish and I struggle to think of a way to deflect her concern.

"It's perfectly natural," she continues. "It's shaken everyone up. You're not the first person I've spoken to about it and you're certainly not the only person who's been losing sleep since he arrived."

"I'm not?"

She takes my right hand and cups hers over it protectively. It's hard to see where the concerned doctor ends and the ex-lover begins. "He's reminded us of the people we lost, people we'd lived with for years. It stirs up guilt too. It has for me."

"Why would you feel guilty?" There are only two people in this colony who can rightfully shoulder that and she isn't one of them.

"Winston and I got drunk the night before Planetfall. I never told you that, did I?"

I shake my head. Of course, she and Winston were close. He was nervous about the trip, having drawn lots with her and Lincoln for the privilege of coming with us on that first trip down here. They were all equally qualified and equally keen.

"He was angry about Hak-Kun making the pick. He said the Pathfinder had a blind spot when it came to her son and that he didn't deserve a place. They really didn't get along."

"They didn't?"

"No. I hate to speak ill of the dead, but Hak-Kun was a bit of an asshole, let's face it. Winston asked me to swap places with him in his pod for main Planetfall. I was supposed to meet with him once you guys got back, but there was just so much to do, so much excitement and people freaking out that I was too busy and forgot what we'd agreed. There wasn't time to meet up and swap. I should have been in his pod with Hak-Kun. He should be here now. And I haven't stopped thinking about that since Sung-Soo came."

All I can do is stare at her. She's sitting there, thinking that a forgotten rendezvous saved her from death in a terrible accident, whereas I'm filled with the awful thought that Mack and I almost murdered her.

"I feel sick," I say and she grabs a bowl positioned nearby in readiness.

She rubs my back as I vomit. "It's just a bit of shock," she says after checking her interface, now linked with my chip and its physiological software. "Some people sleep, some people laugh too much, some people throw up. Want me to give you something for it?"

I shake my head. I deserve to feel this wretched. There's a bit of dry heaving and then it passes, leaving a heavy lump of guilt in my stomach instead. I have to tell her. I can't keep this all inside a moment longer. I take a breath to confess our crimes and then just as swiftly the instinct to preserve what I have resumes its dominance. I can't tell her that Mack and I killed her friend. I can't bear the thought of her hating me. Hating myself, alone, is preferable to that.

"Do you want to stay at my place tonight?" she asks and then adds, "I can sleep on the sofa. You've had a tough evening and I'd worry about you less."

I nod. I can't go back home and sleep in that nook with my shoulder like this. "Thanks," I whisper.

WAKING alone in her bed disorients me briefly before the pain in my shoulder pushes all of that away. She hears me swear and comes in with her medkit and soothing words. I doze as she makes me breakfast and she leaves soon after, saying I can stay as long as I want.

I drift off again and dream of God's city trying to eat me. Mack is in the room, among the rubbish, and I'm swept in there with him. "I got it wrong," I say to him as it fills with stomach acid. "All of this place is God. This is his body. I cut God open and now we're going to die."

It's impossible to go back to sleep after that, so I get up and strip off for a shower. The only times I shower are after I play squash in the court beneath the Dome, my own bathroom being a tiny bit too cluttered to use this way.

Before stepping behind the screen, I ease the sling off, keeping my arm in the position but unsupported. I examine the bruising that's flourishing in a lurid burst of purple. Even after treatment I need to take care not to move it too much. At least I got the seed planted before this happened.

The shower feels so good I moan with pleasure until I forget to keep the pummeled spray away from my shoulder. Then I finish up as quick as I can, keen to get it back in the sling before I do more damage.

Kay has printed me a clean set of clothes, knowing my size and taste well. I record a thank-you message for the house to play to her when she gets home and leave for Sung-Soo's house. I'd rather start analyzing the footage of the room I discovered past the cilia, but I slept too late and Sung-Soo is expecting me.

I hurry, hoping I won't have to explain it to anyone. Fortunately the only other people I see are engrossed in conversation and don't even notice me pass.

I have my story ready for Sung-Soo, who is predictably shocked when he answers the door. But he doesn't accept it as readily as Kay did. He can probably tell I'm lying and thinks I did it at home, but I don't let his doubt and blatant mistrust bother me.

"There's work to do," I say to break the silence after he asks me to explain exactly how I did it.

"Before we start," he says when he realizes I'm not going to be drawn into a discussion, "I want you to stay with me while you're healing."

"Oh, I couldn't possibly—"

"No, please. I want you to stay. You gave me a home. You're teaching me so much. It's the least I can do. And you won't be able to . . . get in with that sling on. It would mean a lot to me to be able to repay your kindness."

I can understand his desire to rebalance things between us. I don't like feeling indebted to people either. "Okay," I say.

"You can have my bedroom. I can't sleep on the bed anyway."

"We can change how hard or soft it is pretty easily, you know."

He shakes his head. "It's not that. It's sleeping so high up. I kept worrying I'd fall off when I dreamed. Anyway, I like the moss."

"We can work on a redesign of your room and change it once I'm better," I suggest, thinking of a sunken bed design that would make the room seem even more spacious. "It'll only be a week or so."

"No, a few weeks, surely?"

I smile. "Kay is very, very good at treating this sort of injury. She injected some of my stem cells into the area last night. They'll repair it ten times faster than if it were just left to heal by itself."

"Kay can do that?" He looks distant for a moment. I wonder if he's thinking back to injuries he or the others suffered and had to recover from without anything more than basic medical assistance. How terrifying to live without these things we take for granted. If I lived a life like he's had to, I'd be a drain upon the group for weeks, unable to hunt or look after myself properly and in terrible pain. Here, I'll have a week of discomfort, then a month of specialized exercises to make sure I don't lose any strength or mobility in the long term. I wonder what he makes of it all but I don't want to ask. I don't want to focus on all the things his people were denied, thanks to my actions. And my inaction too.

We work throughout the day and I nap in the afternoon, the strain and patchy sleep of the last few days catching up with me. I let Kay know I'm staying with Sung-Soo, adding an explanation for fear she'll be offended, and she pops over to check on me in the early evening.

After she leaves Sung-Soo builds a fire with a few sticks of clean fuel he's printed, some dried grass and a couple of stones he strikes to create the spark. It couldn't be more different from Mack's approach of dousing a pile of fuel sticks in accelerant and then chucking a piece of lit paper onto it.

There's a beauty in Sung-Soo's technique. Each stick is positioned artfully to ensure the right amount of contact between them and a clear airflow beneath and through them. He lies on his stomach to strike the stones next to a clump of grass, nurturing the first tendril of smoke that appears with cupped hands and gentle puffs of air until a flame flickers into life.

He brushes the edge of the arranged grass with the new flame until there are several licking the bases of fuel sticks.

Even then, he doesn't move away from it until he's blown on it a few times, treating the fuel sticks like those made of wood. I stop myself from telling him there's no need, that they're designed to light much more easily than anything he would have found out in the wild. I don't want to steal the sense of achievement the fire gives him, a primal satisfaction that dances across his features as he pulls himself up and away from the fire.

I look up to check that the ceiling above the fire pit has detected the heat and that the protocells are making the plasglass panel shift into its permeable state. The clean fuel gives off only a tiny fraction of carbon dioxide compared to wood, but it's still important to vent it. When it turns a deep black, I know it's working and I relax, even though I tested it in my final build checks.

"My father taught me how to do that," he says, flopping onto the sofa.

I wonder where Hak-Kun learned it. Maybe from Lois, who

was into all that survival stuff. Then I notice Sung-Soo frowning at me.

"Did you like my father?"

I fidget. Trying to get comfortable with the sling is not easy. "I didn't know him very well."

"But it sounded like he knew you well. He talked about you a lot."

"What did he say?"

"That you were Grandmother's best friend. That you were very clever and did a lot for the project."

I wonder if that was all he said about me. I can't ask for more though. At best I'd seem narcissistic and at worst I'd seem too concerned about it. Then I think about what Sung-Soo said. Anyone on Atlas would know those things about me; they're hardly personal. Does he just want to talk about his dad with someone who knew him before it happened?

"Your dad and I worked in different disciplines," I begin, working hard to think ahead as I speak so I don't paint myself into a corner. "He was very serious and I think he saw me as your grandmother's friend, not really his. I watched him grow up too . . . That can make things weird. You know—knew— him better than I did. How would you describe him?"

Sung-Soo stares into the flames. "Angry," he says in a low voice that makes me shudder. He looks at me. "I suppose it was because of Grandmother. But he said she lied and God's city wasn't here. He was wrong. So why be angry all the time?"

I shake my head, pretending not to know. I don't trust myself to come up with another reason without giving something away. I have no idea why he lied to his son. But then I realize there's an easy answer. "He was probably angry because he was supposed to be here with us."

Sung-Soo nods, accepting that. "He would have known what it would be like here, I suppose," he replies. He sinks into silence and I make no effort to break it with clumsy small talk. "He should have had a house like this," he says after a while.

I remain silent. He's right. All of them should have had this life.

Sung-Soo looks away from the fire and straight at me, a sudden passion in his eyes. "That's why I can't stand you living the way you do. We all lived in the dirt, not knowing where our next meal would come from, and you're wasting that place, being so unhappy and—"

I stand and he jumps up too, holding his hands out toward me as if he's trying to calm a snarling dog.

"I'm sorry—I'm sorry! I just want you to have this too, don't you see? Dad couldn't have it, but you can!"

I feel like I've been punched in the chest. The air flies out of me and I sit back down.

He comes around to sit next to me.

"Have you always lived like that?"

I don't speak, looking at the fire instead, hoping this will just pass. But the pressure of him staring at me is too much. I should talk or leave. "Only since Planetfall." I'm surprised to hear my own voice and feel detached from myself, uncertain of what I'll do next. I should go to Kay's house instead, but I'm not moving. I'm just staring at the fire.

"So when you lived on the ship and on Earth, you lived like everyone else?"

I nod.

"Did something happen? What made you change?"

I laugh. I don't know where it comes from but it sounds horrible. I smack my lips shut and avoid looking at him for fear of what else would slip from them.

"I'm just trying to understand." His voice is gentle and he looks like Suh again, more than his father. "I can't just ignore it."

"Why not? It's not your house."

He's close enough to touch me but he doesn't, thank God. "What if it was where I lived?" he begins. "What if we were the other way around and you saw me living that way. Would you be happy?"

"I'd leave you to it. It wouldn't be any of my business."

"When you came home and sat here, would you be able to enjoy it, knowing that I was crammed in between piles of garbage? Wouldn't you worry about whether I was safe?"

I go to fold my arms and the movement makes my shoulder twinge. Instead, my right hand goes to my throat and I cover the skin there, feeling my pulse beneath the skin. "I know what you're trying to do. You're trying to make me see how I live differently."

His laugh fades quickly. "You're too clever for me, Ren. You're so clever you'll die in that place."

There's a bitterness in his voice. I focus on the fire, trapped, wanting to get away from him but unable to run to my usual hideout. I can't look after myself. I would have been fine if my house was like his. I'm stuck here, under scrutiny and unable to review that footage of the room past the cilia, just because I'm untidy.

"You must hate yourself," he says. "To live like that. You must think you're garbage too."

"Don't tell me what I think I am!" The shriek rings off one of Neela's sculptures and I'm amazed at how loud I was.

It doesn't seem to bother him. "But it must be true," he says with the same maddeningly gentle voice. "Otherwise you would do something about it. The house is dying, Ren. The moss I saw, the plants on the outside . . . there's no way you can look after it. It can't be working properly. How can you teach me all these things about efficiency and 'environmentally responsible' living when you have the most broken house on this planet! It's all backward!"

The crack in my bedroom ceiling floats up out of my memory.

"It can't go on forever," he presses. "Other people are going to notice soon enough. Why don't we fix it now, together, before it turns into something worse?"

The simple truth emerges like a bubble of swamp gas and just as foul. I can't live like that forever. It's a wonder I've managed to keep it secret for so long. But just the thought of pulling things out and throwing them down the chute makes my palms sweat. There are things in there I might not want to see again. The mud has settled at the bottom of my lake. I don't want to churn it all back up again.

"We'll do it slowly," he says. "We won't get rid of anything you want to keep."

"I want to keep all of it."

There's a flash of exasperation . . . impatience? Or pity? I can't tell. "Some of it needs to go down the chute. You said today that you'd show me how that all works and where the garbage goes. Maybe . . . maybe it could be part of a lesson. I want to understand it, and if it helps you at the same time, even better."

"We could learn with *your* stuff that *you* want to throw away." I sound like a grumpy child.

He waves his hands at the room. "There's nothing to get rid of here! And anyway, people are saying we need to clear out things we don't need anymore, because they made all this stuff for me. There's so much in your house, Ren. Other people shouldn't have to worry when you've got all that—"

"All right! All right, for God's sake we'll start tomorrow, okay? If you'll just shut up about it!"

"Okay." He leans back, satisfied now. "Want to watch something on the projector?"

It seems absurd to say yes, but I do. Anything to take his attention away from me.

28

ONCE I'M IN bed with some privacy at last, I call up the footage I took from inside God's city. It's easy enough to increase the definition of the shapes inside that room with some simple adjustments. There's only a few seconds' worth that's any use, but it's enough to be able to define particular objects, separate them out from the others in the room and then use my visengineering program to help me extrapolate three-dimensional models of them.

It's slower work with only one hand, but after an hour or so I have wire-framed models of six objects, three of which are just different-sized canisters that appear to be made of metal. The smallest is the size of a toothbrush and the largest is closer to an old-fashioned oxygen tank they used to have in the university labs. There's a crumpled sheet of plastic about the size of a double bed, a small oval pebble of plastic with something sticking out the end of it that looks very similar to one of the probes we took into the city, and something that looks like it's part of a wing.

I run a match on the pebble probe against the equipment manifest for our team, and sure enough it belonged to Winston. It wasn't checked back in after our trip down and was listed as lost.

There are three other items listed as missing and two of them match more models I've made from the objects in that room. On one of the many occasions we fell or were thrown about, we must have dropped them and then they must have fallen down that tunnel. That was why we couldn't find them; the city had swept them away into that room.

I go back to the object that looks like it's part of a wing. It would be for a very small craft but still too big to fly inside the tunnels of the city. There's a chance it isn't part of a wing, of course, but the fact that it's an airfoil shape in cross section and has all the hallmarks of something designed to be aerodynamic makes the theory too compelling to discard immediately.

There are markings on it that seemed random at first glance but now that I'm examining it I can't help but think there's more to them. The edges of the shapes are too crisp to have been made by scratches and there are a couple of symbols that are repeated.

I sit up, the fatigue that had been creeping up on me shrugged off in an instant. I connect to the Atlas AI and request an analysis of the shapes using any linguistic programs it has on file.

"No known matches," the AI reports after a couple of seconds.

"Could it be a language?"

"Define parameters of language for comparison."

I tut. I'm not a linguist. "Did Hak-Kun Lee have definitions of language in the program he designed for Planetfall?"

"Yes. Would you like me to import those parameters for this analysis?"

"Yes."

"Likelihood of language: ninety-five percent."

Oh. Fuck. I rub my hand over my face as I try to process that. "But . . . you said it didn't match . . . Which language is it derived from?"

"No known matches."

"Check against . . . fictional languages . . . ancient dialects."

"Sample has been compared to all known languages. No matches."

"So where the fuck does it come from?"

"Unknown origin."

I lie back down. My poor heart doesn't know what it is to beat a normal rhythm anymore. My thoughts are a tumbling landslide of questions as my curiosity surges. Who made that and painted their words onto it? Where did that person come from?

Not from Earth.

The sight of God's city and what we saw in the topmost room ended any vestiges of mankind's childish belief that we were the only intelligent species in existence. But to think there were other civilizations with their own Pathfinders who had been led here too . . .

But where are they now?

And where are the ships they landed in? Did they need ships? Did they teleport down here with vastly advanced technology?

There's too much in my head. I need to talk to someone about this. It has to be Mack—he's the only one who won't freak out about my excursions and he'll know the best way to tell everyone.

I look up his status. It's set as "busy." He's either working or shagging someone. I ping him. Neither could be more important than this.

A standard "Sorry, I'm busy, I'll get back to you as soon as I can" message comes back instantly. I open the v-keyboard.

Mack, I need to talk to you. I send it with an "urgent" tag and in less than a minute I receive a text back.

> Is it really urgent or can it wait till after the ceremony? I've got a to-do list the length of Italy here.

> I've got evidence of people visiting God's city before us.

> Aliens?

> Well, they weren't from Earth.

> Bloody hell. Okay, come over for lunch tomorrow. No, scratch that—the ceremony is the day after. Come for lunch on Friday, when it's all over.

I'm astounded. If our places were reversed, I'd be asking for the evidence, demanding to meet right away, desperate to know more. You don't want me to send you some stuff over now?

> Talk me through it on Friday. I've got too much to do. Carmen's paying too much attention, I have to be extra careful. I just don't have the head space for anything else.

> You're seriously telling me that your sideshow is more important than this? There's a room in God's city full of stuff swept out of the tunnels that other people have left behind. We have to work out why!

Give me three days. You can work on it in the meantime.
Don't talk to anyone about it.

Obviously.

I heard you were hurt. You OK?

I'm fine. Good night, Mack.

I lie in the dark for a while, churning through the possibilities. Of course, the AI could be wrong about the language, but there's no refuting those things in that room, swept in there by the cilia. Our party's lost instruments are in there, so it's not a huge leap to hypothesize that the other objects belonged to other expeditions.

Am I getting carried away? Could those things just have been thrown away by the city's former inhabitants?

There's not enough data to work with and the only way to get more is to go back. But the memory of the cilia brings back the thought that I'd crush them if I stomped across to the room. And even if I decided not to care about that and went inside it, what if there was no way to reopen the valve from the other side?

The solution presents itself in a flash, fully formed, like a firework being set off in my head. A CrawlerCam! I've got one at home, somewhere in my bedroom; I'm sure of it. Or maybe the hallway. I last used it a couple of years ago to clear a blocked chute, so it has to be relatively easy to find.

I built several of them on Atlas to help service the miles of ventilation ducts and pipework in the habitable areas. A camera, light and robotic legs with little retractable hooks at the ends for crawling in difficult spaces. All the legs can be retracted too, making it into a ball shape that can be rolled into a pipe or used by the device itself to return faster.

When I started to explore the city again, once I could bear the thought of going back in there, I did consider using the cams then. But something about that seemed disrespectful. Suh wouldn't let us use them, saying it should be seen only with human eyes and shouting down arguments we all had when planning the first expedition into the city. I couldn't bear to go against her wishes, even though she'd never know I had. I shake my head at myself. If I hadn't been so sentimental, I might have found that room sooner; I might have understood the city by now. But I used it as my private escape, a source for secret trophies to take home and make me feel better. What kind of scientist am I?

But my find has changed everything. I have to understand its function now and I'll use every tool available. I could put a CrawlerCam in through the valve I usually enter to explore and then leave it recording. If it is swept into that room, as I think it will be, I'll be able to look at everything in there and map out all the objects without damaging anything.

Once I've run them by Mack, I'll share my findings with the colony. They need to stop seeing it as something so holy it can't be understood. They are not incompatible.

The solution gives me a brief respite, but the endless speculation about what the CrawlerCam will find in there is as loud in my head as a crowd outside my window, and just as effective at keeping me awake. It's so late and I'm so tired. I'm going to be useless tomorrow if I don't get some rest.

Then I remember Sung-Soo talking me into starting on my house tomorrow and dread creeps in, spreading its cold fingers through my chest. Will I be able to find the cam and hide it in a pocket without him noticing?

I can't handle all this at once. I just want some stillness, some time alone with normal daily tasks. The way it was before he came. But he's here now, and there's no way he's going to let this go. Perhaps if we clear the doorway a bit he'll be satisfied.

A message arrives from Kay and I open it.

> You're welcome back anytime, if you need time away from Sung-Soo. And if you can't sleep, there's a sedative in the medkit I left in his kitchen for you. It's a safe one and you can take them for a few days if you need to, just until the discomfort eases in your shoulder. I'm here if you need me and I'll pop back tomorrow evening. Kay x

I send back my thanks, fetch the sedative and some water, and take the pill. There has to be some peace soon. Surely.

DESPITE my best efforts to delay and distract him the following morning, Sung-Soo is at the door and ready to go to my house before eight. Even though I slept heavily, I'm exhausted already. I've spent the last hour imagining him inside my house and a hundred different ways that he'll react. None of them are good.

My body feels like a wrung-out rag. It's taking everything in me just to hold it together enough to get dressed and eat breakfast. I have to force the food down, not wanting him to see how much this is upsetting me. If he notices, he'll only use it as evidence of my having a problem and I simply don't have the resources to argue with him today.

At least he wants to go early. Used to waking with the dawn, he's been up long enough to do a tiny carving and practice a few designs using the printer. I can see from the way he moves that he needs to get out there and do something.

He bounces on his tiptoes as he waits for me to finish my coffee. "Perhaps you should take up running," I suggest.

"Where?"

"Outside. Or in the gym. There's one under the Dome."

"What would I chase?"

"No, I mean run for the sake of running." He looks at me like I'm an idiot. "Actually, maybe you should get Nick to teach you how to play squash. I think you'd like that."

"What do you squash?"

"Look it up," I say, too tense to explain it to him. "There's all sorts of stuff on the cloud."

"Let's go," he says, evidently disinterested in anything other than tormenting me.

The walk seems both epically long and far too short and we're back in front of the door into my house again.

"I'll follow you in," he says, looking at me expectantly.

"I could just pass—"

"Ren." He takes a step closer and lowers his voice further. "I need to come inside. We need to face this."

I press my palm to the sensor, trying to manage the swarm in my chest with a few breaths in and out. I glance back at him and he gives what he must think is a reassuring smile. It does nothing to help. He has no idea how this feels. No one here does. No one on this planet does!

I crawl in, one hand on the ground, the other pressed against my body, held by the sling. It's much harder than usual and the movement makes my shoulder complain, but I press on.

Some part of myself is surprised this is happening. Is that the real me? I feel like I'm watching my actions through gaps in my skull, like I'm trapped inside my body and things are unfolding around me that I can't quite hold together in my mind. Why did I give in to him last night? Am I weak? Or does another part of me agree with him? Where am I among all these parts? Am I just a mosaic of myself, held in the shape of a whole person? Perhaps the cracks are too tiny for people to notice. Perhaps I only let them see the mosaic from a distance, still looking Ren-like.

He's following me and the thought of someone else coming into my house crushes me with shame and embarrassment. He's making me feel this. I would be fine if I were by myself.

The door closes behind us as I emerge into the hallway. The sides of the valley are as I remember them, the route between them the same as ever.

"Be careful where you stand when you come out," I say, moving back to make way for him.

He straightens as soon as he emerges, wiping his hands on his clothes swiftly. He covers his nose and mouth with the back of his hand, then looks at me, dropping the hand away. Perhaps he doesn't want to hurt my feelings.

"Can we open a window?"

"They're all covered up," I say, looking up at the lights in the ceiling, which have come on now that we've entered. I can't remember the last time there was natural light in here.

His eyes are darting around, flitting from one object to the next, getting wider as they go. "There's so . . . much," he whispers. Then, a bit louder, he says, "Where do you sleep?"

"In there."

He starts to walk toward the doorway and I hear something crunch beneath his shoes. The panic spikes again. "Watch where you're stepping! You're breaking my things!"

Sung-Soo freezes and looks down. "Where can I walk? There's stuff everywhere!"

"Just stay still, then."

His face is pure disbelief. "I'm not going to just stand here."

"You could go and I'll pick some things off the floor."

He folds his arms. "No. I'm not leaving until we make some progress. Is everywhere in the house like this?"

I nod and the way his eyes widen makes my cheeks flush with shame again.

"And you printed all of this . . . over what, twenty years?"

"Not all of it. Some of it I brought with me from Earth. Some of it I printed and the rest is . . . recycled."

"I don't understand. I thought the Masher does that."

I fiddle with the edge of the sling. "People throw too much away. They don't fix things. I . . . I save them from the Masher."

"You can go inside it?"

"It's a big room; all the machinery has to be accessible. I'm the only one who goes down there. No one else thinks about it and they just chuck stuff down the chute without even bothering to try to—"

"But I thought that was what they were supposed to do. You told me that all the base materials for the printers are served by the communal feeds and they get filled back up again each time someone recycles something." He gestures at one of the piles closest to him. "This should have been recycled by the Masher. Then the stocks wouldn't be low. Or am I missing something?"

I can't answer. It's all I can do to stop myself pushing him back toward the tunnel. I turn away and head toward the living room doorway, not wanting to see his face or let him see mine.

"And how can it work . . . with the levels, I mean," he asks, following me. "Surely someone has noticed that there isn't enough stuff going back into the feeds?"

I can hear more things cracking beneath his shoes. "You're breaking my stuff!" I yell and he stops again.

"If it's fragile and precious, why is it on the floor?" he shouts back. "There's broken shit everywhere, Ren—look at it! It's trash and it needs to go back to the feeds."

My teeth are chattering and there are waves of shivering radiating out from my core. I keep my back turned to him and stare at the printer ahead, trying to focus on anything but him.

"You're faking the feed levels, aren't you?" His voice is quiet again. "You know how it all works—you built it . . . That's why no one knows what you're doing."

It's impossible to do anything but stand there, trembling, holding a lungful of air inside myself as I wait to hear him say that he's going to report what I've been doing to the colony. There's no point denying it—it's obvious.

He sighs loudly. "I'm not going to say anything. If you let me help you."

"If?" It sounds like a threat.

"Let's . . . let's get started." I hear him moving again, not far. "Where are your Masher chutes?"

". . . Covered up." I damn myself with my own words.

"That's the first job, then. We need access to a chute, so we need to clear the hallway. Is there one in here?"

I go and join him in the hallway again but avoid looking at him. I point to the drift that conceals the nearest chute.

"Jeez . . . We need to take some stuff outside. There's no room in here to—"

"No! Don't be stupid. Everyone will see."

"Perhaps that would be for the best."

"Shut up!" I press my temples with my thumb and forefinger,

trying to ease the headache that's building steadily. "We can move things into the living room. There's space there."

He peers through that doorway and there's the telltale pause as he struggles to take in the sight of it all. "Ren . . . we have very different ideas about space."

29

THREE HOURS LATER the flap covering the Masher chute in the hallway has been uncovered. I'm standing in front of it for the first time in years and Sung-Soo's cheeks are pink with anger.

I'm exhausted, but I'm not going to move. I've seen the way he's tried to make a new pile behind him, ready to throw in the chute as soon as it was accessible. He won't let me look at things properly as we find them, always wanting to rush me. He doesn't understand that I haven't seen some of the things at the bottom of the pile for months—years in some cases. I have to be certain I don't miss the CrawlerCam—easy to do as it's so small—and each object pulled free brings a memory with it. None of it has been suitable for throwing away, and at the start there was no option but to take things into the other room once I checked them. When I saw that pile growing behind him each time I got back to the hallway, I knew his plan. Now he's holding a mug in his left hand and a scarf in his right and he wants to throw them away.

"What is the point of clearing all that stuff if we're not going to use the damn chute!"

"I need those."

He looks up at the ceiling and makes a guttural moan. "No, you don't, Ren. This is chipped and this is full of holes. You have to throw something away—that's the point!"

"Not those." I'm standing my ground now. The threat of losing them has tapped a new well of strength inside me. I let him bully me into coming here, but I won't let him throw my stuff away.

"What, then? Show me something I *can* throw away."

"You're rushing me."

"It's not difficult. How can you build a house in two days and then look at a pile of garbage and not find one thing to throw out?"

"It's not garbage! How many times do I have to tell you?" My throat is raw and I feel sick. I need another dose of pain meds, but I don't dare leave him alone in here. He doesn't respect my things.

He puts the scarf and mug back on the pile behind him and wipes his face with his sleeve. He looks tired too.

"It's lunchtime," I say. "Why don't we take a break?"

His scowl is answer enough. "We've been here all morning and all we've done is move one pile of stuff to another room. You can't get to the printer in there now, can you?" When I shake my head, he throws his hands into the air. "That's why we have to start using the chute!"

"I'll go through it in my own time."

"When? How long have you been telling yourself that?"

"I can't do any of it when you're angry with me!" I've shouted at him so many times today. I never raise my voice usually. This isn't good for me. None of this is. It's turning me into something else.

"I'm . . ." He breathes in deeply and starts again, his voice more calm. "I'm not angry with you. I just don't . . . I don't get it. I don't get how you can be so clever about everything else and so stupid about your house. No—" He pats the air, fearing he's upset me. "That came out wrong. I don't mean stupid. I mean—"

"Mad?" I say for him. "Crazy? Insane, perhaps? That's what you think. Isn't it?"

He doesn't reply. I close my eyes and lean against the wall. I can't remember the last time I saw the floor here. I can't remember the last time I felt at peace. I don't think I ever have on this planet. For a moment, the valley of my belongings feels like it's closing in on me and I'm so painfully aware of how much there is between myself and the door. That tunnel out could collapse at any moment. I could be trapped under it.

I pick up a ball lying at my feet, something thrown into the Masher chute by a parent whose child has got too old for something spongy and pastel colored. I twist, intending to put it in the chute, but then I feel such a crushing wave of sadness for it, for something once so loved now being discarded without thought. My thoughts spin on to this house being empty and me lost within it, nothing to hold me, no cocoon, and all the things I've rescued and loved when no one else wanted them being lost forever.

I press the ball to my chest and then tuck it under the edge of the sling, protecting it from Sung-Soo's glare. "No. There's nothing to throw away here. We're done."

HE leaves after that, without saying a word. I sit, resting my head against the chute flap, and cry. I don't know where the tears are coming from, or feel any particular grief or sadness.

It's just the end of hours of terrible tension. I don't know if he's going to try to come back. If he does, I won't let him in. This morning is just more proof that I was right to keep people out.

The ball is uncomfortable, so I pull it out and place it next to me. It was pressing my pendant into my skin. I pluck it out from under my top and then pull the thong over my head. The desire to wear Sung-Soo's gift has been burned away by the day's events.

The carving is so warm it's pleasant to keep held in my palm a while. I take a moment to admire his skill and decide that, once the heat has faded, I'll find a nook for it. It will remind me to keep people at a safe distance. I don't need to keep it that close to me; the lesson is too raw right now to be forgettable.

The heat remains for a good couple of minutes. That material has interesting properties as well as being beautiful. It should be studied. I see a gap in the pile opposite me, about halfway up that side of the hallway valley, and lean over to tuck it in. That's when I spot the CrawlerCam.

I can still access the printer in my kitchen; it just takes a while to get to it. Once I've made and drunk a shake and taken some painkillers, I dig out my tool roll and run a set of tests on the cam to make sure it's fully functional. The logical tests and tweaks I make as a result soothe me.

There are twenty-two hours before the seed ceremony. I can't risk placing the CrawlerCam inside God's city until tonight. It leaves the whole afternoon stretching ahead of me and the anxiety seeps back in without practical tasks to keep it at bay.

I look at the flap covering the chute and then at the tunnel between myself and the door. Is there anything I could bear to part with? I scan the edges, the makeshift walls, the unlikely roof of it. I see a patch of fabric from a dress woven in and around keepsakes that I wore to Kay's house for dinner. She cooked everything from scratch, based on old recipes saved from her grandmother's archived blog. We made love afterward and lay tangled up in each other and the sheets for hours talking about games and music.

Was I at peace then? Maybe. I think she helped push everything further away. I recall the message she sent last night, her thoughtfulness and the way she let me stay over without any fuss. Should I go to her place tonight? I send her a message letting her know that I'm fine and back home again. I promise to come and see her soon.

A strand of brown wool catches my eye and I remember the doll I rescued. I pluck her from the top of the tunnel and diligently untangle the remainder wool while the printer makes a pair of knitting needles for me. I call up knitting tutorials on the cloud and am filled with the thrill of potential. I ease my arm out of the sling and experiment with keeping my upper arm still and in position while using my hand to knit. As long as I keep my elbow tucked in, there are only occasional twinges. A quick search uncovers a new pattern for wool that can be printed with minimal resource cost and I download it to print while I practice with virtual wool in a gaming platform built to teach newbies.

It absorbs the afternoon and the early evening. I never make anything like this with my hands. I work in solids, metals and ceramics and the creative process is speeded up and distanced by the printers. I'm enthralled by the sight of something cloth-like appearing one row at a time beneath the needles. There is an intimacy with this creation that my usual work lacks.

My back and shoulder are aching by the time the doll has a new arm. I feel so much better and so fulfilled by the sight of her whole. I want to show her to Sung-Soo and say, "This is what I meant!," but I don't want to open myself up to any more of his judgment. I position her next to my sleeping space so she's the first thing I'll see when I wake up, and after more food and painkillers I clear some of the things cluttering the bed. There's room to lie down now and no need to stay anywhere except here. I can't access the bedroom printer anymore. I'll sort that out another time. Now I need to take the Crawler-Cam to God's city and gather some evidence. I'm back on track now. Soon I'll have some answers. No more distractions. No more skulking around the edges of these lies and holy fears. I will learn that city's secret, and when the time is right, I'll take that knowledge and serve it up to the rest of the colony like a beautiful feast that will nourish us all.

30

WHEN I WAKE late the next morning, my stream is full of comments and excitement about the seed ceremony and one notification from my CrawlerCam. It's the only one I'm interested in.

It's been swept into that room and has already been recording for two hours, having been programmed to begin as soon as it was moved from the place I left it last night. I resist the desire to open the file and begin analysis, knowing that if I do so I'll miss the ceremony. It will take me longer than usual to get ready. I can't resist setting up a connection between the data from the recording and my visengineering software though, meaning that the next time I review the results, it will have already pulled out things that can be defined as distinct objects and wire-framed them at least.

I have to be disciplined and turn my attention to what everyone else here feels is the focus of today. I can only imagine that Mack is out of his mind with stress and decide not to bother him. No doubt he's been spending hours setting up all the subtle visual cues in the environment and getting the subliminal messages set up for Marco's chip. He'll have already set up the private connection to Marco's lens, the illegal (as if that's relevant now) hack into his comms software, and it will all be ready to go once he's breathed in the pheromones from the plant.

Like every year for over two decades, I'll stand there and pretend to be awed. I'll remain hushed at the right point. I'll maintain a respectful silence as he opens the door to God's city and enters a space considered holy. I'm not sure I see it that way anymore. It's just an entrance, like a porchway into a church rather than the inner sanctum. I know that is a holy place.

But unlike everyone else, Mack and I won't be uplifted. In fact, the party after the seed ceremony is the lowest point of the year for me and the hardest to get through. The people who know me more than most—Kay, Pasha, Neela—they all think it's because it reminds me of Suh and how much I miss her. Mack handles the fakery so much better than I. He's a showman and so used to tricking people into thinking they want things that it's not a big deal to him anymore. But I've seen how stressed he's been since Sung-Soo arrived. I send him a quick note checking in and, unexpectedly, get an immediate request for voice chat. I accept.

"Just wondered how you are," he says. He sounds cheerful. Relaxed even.

"Not looking forward to it," I reply.

"Everything's done now. Try to focus on the positives. Everyone will feel better."

He and I are so different. I can't see past the lie.

"And in a few days," he continues, "we can talk about how to handle this in the longer term. I don't want to go through this again."

"Neither do I. And they'll all want it to be Sung-Soo next year."

"I know. I'll have profiled him by then; it won't be such a big deal. Especially if I can persuade him to get chipped."

Not for the first time, I wonder if he's ever used his techniques on me. "If we were on Earth, you'd be locked up."

"Only if I worked for anyone but the gov-corps."

He laughs, but I don't. We left some terrible things behind. I don't want anything like them to take root here. "I'll see you later," I say, wanting to have as much time truly alone as I can before the madness starts.

Eventually I'm in a newly printed outfit, smart enough to show I've made an effort, as is expected. I'm sure half the reason this has caught on over the years is the excuse to dress up and have a party.

People still celebrate Eid and Christmas and Thanksgiving and the like in small groups on days calculated to be as close to the appropriate one in the new calendar, but this day has become a universal celebration. It doesn't make sense to me—why celebrate the fact that Suh still isn't back? But they see it differently, celebrating it as a moment of connection with her.

When I leave the house, I have a momentary anxiety spike. It's the first time I've been outside since leaving Sung-Soo's place. He'll be there today. We didn't part on the best terms and I'm certain he's pissed off with me. I need to avoid him. I don't want anyone else to pick up on there being something wrong between us.

His house seems empty as I pass it and I can see most people are already much farther along the path than I am. The gentle bubbling noise of the crowd gathering within the courtyard of God's city grows louder and I shove my free hand in my pocket to clench my fist.

Kay is waiting next to the eastern gate and waves when she sees me. She's wearing a bright red aso-oke wrapped around her head in luxurious folds and then fanning out high and wide like a crown. It matches the wrapper set she's wearing; both were her grandmother's and one of the most precious things she brought with her from Earth. It makes her look bigger, taller, and lends a proud tilt to her chin. I want to pull her away from the crowd gathering close by and unwrap her in private, lay her down among the folds of rich satin and kiss her everywhere. But I just wave back and feel underdressed as she comes to meet me, the glorious red drowning out my pale blue trousers and long-sleeved top.

As she approaches I notice something hanging at her throat from a leather thong. It's a new pendant, one shaped like a hand cupping a face, carved from the same chunk of that strange deposit as mine. It makes me stop and so she closes the distance between us, kissing my cheek when she reaches me.

"Sung-Soo gave you that?" It's half question, half statement.

She nods and smiles, brushing it with her fingertips. "Isn't it beautiful? He carved it himself. I was wearing the ruby necklace you like, but he gave this to me while I was waiting for you and it's just too nice to stay in my pocket. Do you like it?"

I nod, unimpressed with the animal response that flared up inside as she spoke about it. As if I would be the only person he would give such a gift. I don't deserve to be singled out for his affection anyway.

"You shouldn't have waited for me," I say to her, pointing at the entrance to the city's courtyard. "You'll be at the back now."

She shrugs. "I don't mind. I wanted to see if you're all right."

"I'm fine."

"I didn't think you'd last at Sung-Soo's."

"Why?"

"You like your own space too much."

"I'd like to . . . Can we . . . I've been missing you." I finally get the words past my lips.

"Come to my place after the party," she says before kissing me with her hand cupped around my cheek, like the one on her pendant.

Even as I nod I worry that I've made the wrong decision. Am I just seeking solace in the easiest place I can find it? Why can't I just be in the moment like she can? I bet she isn't worrying about what she said as she takes my hand and leads me through the gate.

We squeeze in at the back and there are hundreds of people between me and the entrance. Everyone looks their best, from children who have been coaxed into tidiness and ribboned hair to people I never see in anything but coveralls now wearing suits and dresses.

Some are chattering with one another; some are looking around and up at the city with the telltale slow movements of LensCam recording. When they look up at its heights, do they really think Suh is up there? Really? Or is this event now relegated to the status of "tradition" so established that people don't really think about it at all?

If Mack and I don't put an end to this, will it endure? Would the children here be content with a fantasy of the undying Pathfinder, waiting for the right time to return, kept alive by strange and unnatural means in that alien place? Four generations from now will there be twee stories of Suh and the colony founders? In eight generations will they be regarded as allegory and nothing more?

They all seem so happy. I search the faces I can see from the back for any signs of doubt or cynicism, and there's none.

They've all been sucked into the glorious sideshow and if they have any disbelief, they've willingly suspended it to make room for a good old-fashioned get-together.

Mack understands these people far too well. They may be scientists and experts and handpicked from thousands of hopefuls vying for every single place on Atlas, but they're just people. Just frightened, insecure little things millions of miles from home.

This is home now.

I look down at my feet. What would Suh make of this? Would she be appalled? Flattered? I think she would be bemused.

"Sung-Soo looks a bit freaked-out." Kay is pointing toward the entrance.

I follow her finger until I spot him next to Carmen, who is holding his arm and gushing animatedly at him. He's looking back over the crowd.

I don't think he looks freaked-out at all. I think he looks cynical. He looks like a man waiting for a magic show when he knows how the tricks are done.

"Shit, he looks like Suh," Kay says.

He's wearing his hair loose and it's shining like patent leather in the sunlight. Carmen just won't shut up, even though he's not replying or speaking at all. He's scanning the crowd, taking in the faces. Is he looking for me? For Mack?

He doesn't find whatever he's looking for and turns back to face the entrance.

"Marco's coming!"

The hushed whisper flies from the child by the gate, one who's been staring out the whole time, hoping to be the first one to see him. It's quickly propagated through the crowd, leaving silence in its wake as everyone turns around and looks toward the entrance expectantly.

Marco arrives soon after, dressed in black linen trousers and top, looking significantly leaner than the last time I saw him. He pauses at the sight of everyone, then fixes his eyes on the entrance to the tunnel at the top of the slope and strides on. The crowd parts ahead of him, pushing Kay and me farther to the side as it does so.

This is something he has worked so hard for. He's meditated, avoided all stimulants and any drugs, lived apart for months, all to be the star of Mack's show.

I look away again, fearful that if I watch too much more, the urge to break the social spell will be too great to resist. Instead, I reach for Kay's hand and focus on its softness and the way she squeezes mine back.

If I start something between us again, the same thing will come between us. Is it time to open up to her? I try to imagine telling her about the house, even showing her, but the thought rapidly dissolves into anxious slurry. She'd never want to be with me if she knew about that.

I glance at her and she's watching Marco's progress through the crowd just like everyone else. I want to talk to her, but it would be selfish to do so now.

She notices my attention and leans across to whisper "What?" in my ear.

I press my cheek against hers and whisper back: "I had a little girl. The father and I agreed we'd be better apart. She had a genetic disorder. She died when she was three."

She pulls back, still holding my hand tight, to look at me properly. At the edge of my vision I can see Marco walking up the slope to the entrance. She looks shocked, then full of pity, I think. Her eyes shine and she embraces me, taking care to avoid my hurt shoulder.

"You were right before," I whisper. "I didn't share much with you at all. I'm sorry."

"Why now?" she whispers back.

"Because I suck at timing," I reply and she stifles a laugh. "Because I was scared."

"We'll talk more later," she says and kisses me again, this time with the intimacy and tenderness of a lover.

We both focus on Marco as he reaches the door. I feel horribly separated from the crowd, united in their anticipation, but no longer totally alone. Kay is with them and holding her breath too, but there is a connection between us now. I feel like I've started to rebuild a bridge between us and even though it's a flimsy, rickety thing, it exists and that's enough for now.

Marco presses his hand against the join of the door and the valve opens, just like the ones inside the tunnels that I'm used to. He leans back slightly, nervous—as everyone is—of the air inside. We tested it in the first year in full environmental protective gear and it's nothing like the atmosphere farther inside. But still, he's understandably cautious.

He takes a moment to prepare himself and then enters the tunnel. Those closer and at a different angle will see him take a few steps inside, pluck the seed from the plant and eat it. They won't see the puff of pheromones in the dingy interior, nor will they see any sign that he's been affected when he emerges.

Like the others before him, he comes out to face the crowd with a huge smile. He begins to speak the same old stuff as the others before about how much we've achieved, how much there is still to do. I tune out when he starts to talk about impressions of connecting with Suh, uninterested in the drama thanks to my knowledge of the special effects Mack has used.

My attention drifts to Sung-Soo. I can see his face in profile, mere meters from Marco, and I'm disturbed by the frown on his face. Perhaps he's just concentrating, but I expected to see him . . . I don't know . . . enthralled like everyone else around him.

The frown leaves his face and he glances at the people around him, surreptitiously, like someone trying to find something interesting to look at during a sermon the rest of the congregation is attending to with diligence. It's as if he's checking their reactions. To compare them with his own perhaps?

I start to record, but it takes longer than I'd like, having to activate with eye movements rather than hand or speech interface. I don't trust my ability to read people. I've never been very good at it. I want to show Mack.

I'm left with a gnawing nervousness in the pit of my stomach and I want to leave. It rapidly escalates into a need to get away from here—away from all of it—as quickly as possible.

"I don't feel too well," I whisper to Kay. "I need to go and rest."

She gives a concerned glance. "Ping me if you need me," she whispers back, not tearing her attention away from Marco fully. She knows my chip will automatically inform her if there's something seriously wrong.

I push my way past the people between me and the gates, grateful that I'm so close to the back. No one cares about what I'm doing; they're all fixated on Marco and the drug-induced crap he's spouting like a transcendental experience.

My heart is pounding like there are dogs hunting me and by the time I'm through the gates and around the edge of the city I feel like I'm about to have a full-blown panic attack. I haven't had one for years.

Initially I head toward the colony, falling back on old techniques my father taught me when I suffered from them as a teenager. I focus on my breath and stop trying to work out why

I feel so panicky. All that matters is getting a steady inward-and-outward rhythm.

Soon they'll all come out and go to the Dome. There will be food and drink and laughter and all the things I can't face right now. I change direction and head for the southern gate. Maybe I'll find some peace between the grass and the sky.

31

ONCE I'M OUT of the colony and putting distance between myself and God's city behind me with every step, my heart steadies itself and it's easier to breathe again. I listen to the distant animal calls, the gentle wash of sound from the breeze through the grasses, and I can't understand why I felt so panicked. It's over now. It's done. The spectacle has given everyone the excuse to come together, to focus on the positive aspects of the past year and the perfect excuse to drink and eat far too much. All the worry about whether Carmen would derail it, all the concern over getting the props in place and whether the leading man would speak the right lines—all that is over now. Mack will be his usual self once more and won't demand anything of me over and above my usual duties.

I'm free to solve the puzzle of the city now. If people remark on my absence, Kay will explain. They saw the sling; they'll be primed for it.

I walk a little farther until I can't hear anything from the colony and then make a little patch to sit on by walking in a circle, easing the stalks flat with the toe of my boot. I'm like a slow, ungainly cat making a temporary place to sun myself. When there's a small circle of flattened grass, I plunge myself into a green well, lidded with nothing but the blue sky. It hasn't rained for over a week now, and it's not forecast for another three days.

Once I'm relatively comfortable, I pull the CrawlerCam data that's been processed through the visengineering software. An electric thrill shoots through my chest when I see it's already modeled fifty objects.

Looking through them one by one makes me feel like an archaeologist. There are tools and things clearly made for some function or other, made mysterious to me by the distance of time and culture. All the items listed as missing from our party's original manifest are there in remarkably good condition apart from a bent prong on one of the probes. I spot something with a similar piece of hinged metal to the artifact I found and put them together, forming something like a visor with a couple of attachments I can't explain. I find three lenses, their width matching the two roughened sections of the piece I have at home, the third matching a section of one of the attachments, perhaps for enhanced magnification.

After a couple of hours working through the individual models, I'm beginning to see a possible theme. I free my arm from the sling, too excited to be held back by working one-handed any longer. I open a new design project and import some of the objects in, piecing them into a whole until I can see a flight suit taking shape. The wing piece I saw before is now part of a larger whole with a mirror of it forming what seems to be a retractable pair that can be housed in something akin to a backpack.

The pilot would have been about five feet tall with longer fingers than that of the average human and an extra knuckle in each one, by the look of the gloves. There's nothing left of them, not even a skeleton, which makes me shiver.

I try to imagine that person from another world gliding down, probably from a ship in close orbit, landing and walking into God's city still wearing the very craft used to make Planetfall. There are only enough pieces for one suit. He or she came alone. Perhaps the pilot was also a Pathfinder, having had the same encounter with a mysterious plant and the same compulsion to eat it.

Suh said the pheromones from the plant—and the seed itself—would work only on humans. The city responds to human touch—at least on the outside; I've never dared touch anything in there without a glove. The flight suit was designed for a humanoid shape. I lie back on the stalks, unable to keep sitting now that my mind is so filled with the ramifications of this find. Could it be that humanity wasn't just an evolutionary quirk of Earth alone? Could it be that our existence was somehow engineered and the same process carried out across multiple solar systems in the galaxy? Could it be that God scattered our building blocks, then called us back when we were ready?

I'm getting ahead of myself—these are just conclusions I've leaped to in the moment, hardly backed up by rigorous testing and data. But I can't help but be snared in the jaws of the idea that we're one of many seedlings evolved in isolation but part of a larger project. I'm sweating. I'm too small and feeble to hold these ideas and questions inside without feeling strained at the seams. I start to laugh; then I want to weep; then I'm covering my eyes, unable to even look up at the clouds as all I believed about us as a species unravels within me.

Then I wish I didn't know about the room and the suit inside it. I wish I never came here. I should have stayed on Earth and let Suh go. How much easier to regret not leaving than being here now—knowing so much and yet so little—so very far from home. I could have saved those lives, been the person my father hoped I would be, been there for him as he became frail and protected him from a world leaving him and his values behind. I could have been there for my mother too, when her string of lovers finally came to an end and she was facing death alone.

Where Dad had wept and doused me in bitter regrets and drowning loss, Mum listened and nodded when I explained I was leaving on Atlas when it was ready. And for the first time there was no sense of exasperation or dismissive assumptions that what I was talking about was so unfathomable it wasn't even worthy of discussion. She just nodded as I rattled off the reasons that formed my preemptive defense.

She'd wept in front of her friend when I made my announcement. He hadn't wanted to be there, but she had insisted, thinking I was about to tell her I'd been nominated for some sort of award or that I was off to another country after being headhunted by some prestigious gov-corps. She could think that because she didn't understand I'd never work for something like that.

So I had to tell her I was leaving on Atlas in front of a stranger and that meant she had to put on the show of being distraught until she'd pushed him out the door. She made a passing attempt to make it look authentic by dabbing at her eyes as she came back to the living room, and I didn't call her out on it. Perhaps part of me wanted to believe the tears. Perhaps the rest of me thought I should let her do what she felt she needed to in order to maintain her facade. I don't remember as clearly as I do the sight of the old plane trees in the London square her flat overlooked. It was fenced off from people who couldn't afford to touch the peeling bark on the trees. Those were reserved for dogs owned by the wealthy to piss against three times a day when walked by the au pair.

She sat in her usual way in the antique chair, recently upholstered in the latest fashionable fabric, perched in a position that made her figure look perfect. She had been arranging herself to look her best for so long she didn't realize she did it anymore.

She didn't say a word until my unnecessary defense fizzled out. I should have known I wouldn't get the same response from her as from my father, but telling him had been so traumatic I'd readied myself anyway.

For a moment, I thought she just didn't care. Then I realized that she understood why I had to go. I didn't even have to justify it.

We looked at each other for what seemed like a long time. I met her gaze and she met mine without even a flicker of performance or social agenda. I fancied I could see someone real, looking out of her eyes like a lone woman looking out from a house on a hill.

"When do you go?"

"In about eighteen months, if everything goes according to schedule. I almost didn't tell you until just before I went, but one of the psychs on the project, Dr. Lincoln, said we should tell people when we're certain. To give us time to—"

"I'm glad you told me. I understand. It would kill you to be left behind, always wanting to know what they'll find. You wouldn't be living anymore, wishing yourself so far away."

I cried then. I cried like Dad did when I was in his house. I had known myself so much better by virtue of her being such a different creature from me. But the one time it meant the most, she understood.

She was right. I had to come. Just like I had to know what that bit of metal was and what was in that room, and what it could mean.

Who do I talk to now about the objects in God's city? Do

I want to inflict this on anyone else? Everyone here has a right to know about what I've found, but they could unravel too. Our little colony, huddled in the shadow of God's city, built on lies and hopes, could be shattered.

Or would it? Would it simply put the city into perspective? Would it make us study it more and keep one eye on the sky for the arrival of another Pathfinder? Would it help bring Suh down from her unique pedestal? Perhaps it would do some good.

My hand is pressing too hard on my eyes and bursts of ghostly light splash across my private darkness. I'm thrown back to a night as a child when I learned that I could still try to look even with my eyes closed. The thought plunged me into a panic when it felt like I could never rest again; my eyes didn't feel closed even when they were shut tight. I just couldn't help trying to pierce my own darkness.

Now I open them and watch a lone cloud, fearing I'll never rest again, but for a different reason. I'll never know who wore that suit. I could recover the pieces and see if any genetic material has been preserved, but even if I build a model of that person, I'll never know what they loved or feared or hoped for. Perhaps the pilot didn't die and then rot away, instead taking off the suit and abandoning it in one of the tunnels. Maybe he or she reached the top room too. Maybe . . .

An urgent message arrives from Mack and I'm tossed back into the fear that something terrible has come about because of that fake seed. I watch the icon flash insistently, unable to summon the courage to open it. I know it has something to do with Sung-Soo. Something to do with the way he looked as Marco spoke. My body knows it; it knew it back then and drove me out of the city.

Another icon begins to flash; over ten messages have arrived in the last minute. Then another. My stream is full of mentions of my name, but I don't dare open it and read what they're saying. I shut the notifications off, sit up and tuck my arm back into its sling as my heart feels like a ram trying to butt its way out of the cage formed by my ribs. I'm paralyzed by fear of what is happening back there. I imagine a fierce crowd baying for blood, having learned the seed is false and that I was the one who planted it.

But if they know that, they have to know about Mack.

Perhaps his urgent message is a call for help. A tight croak is squeezed through my throat as I realize I have to open it. He may need me.

I can feel my pulse in my throat as I blink twice at the icon and the text floats across my vision. I have to read it twice to get the meaning through the thick fog of anxiety.

Ren, you need to watch this. Sung-Soo is saying things about you and I don't know what to believe.

There's a share link below and my chest burns as I'm unable to take another breath. My cheeks are burning and my lips tingling. I can't handle this. I close the message box and curl into a ball, letting myself tip onto my side, holding my slinged arm tight against myself with the other.

It has to be about my house. He threatened me and now he's making good on his promise and I want to run. An urgent message from Kay arrives and my fear sucks in shame and guilt with it, like a black hole within my chest, pulling everything into itself. The fear and guilt are compressed as more images of people outside my house burst into my imagination, making a dense ball between my lungs, growing every second.

The MyPhys software pops up. "Your health care provider

is requesting access to your physical well-being files. Would you like to give permission?"

I can't speak. I tuck my head down until my chin is pressing against my chest.

"Your health care provider will access your current well-being files in ten seconds if you do not respond."

I can't breathe. My lungs are turning to stone inside me, my throat to iron, my skin to wet paper. I want to dissolve into the earth below me, to collapse into a pile of component parts, all the little pieces of my mosaic no longer held together.

The voice counts down. I'm unable to stop it. When it reaches zero a dialog box pops up, showing the things Kay is looking up right now. My heart rate, my blood pressure, my oxygen saturation, and then lines and lines of other data fly up the screen. I recognize neurotransmitters and find my voice. "Stop it," I yell. "MyPhys, stop access!"

The connection is broken and I curse myself for not acting sooner.

Another warning icon, just for a second it seems, and then I can hear Kay. It's her privilege, as my doctor and as one of the colony's emergency health care providers, to be able to speak to me via the chip without any need for permission to be established.

"Ren, you're having a panic attack. I want you to listen to my voice. You're going to be okay."

She doesn't know anything.

"This will pass. All you need to do is focus on something nearby. You're out in the grasses—find a cloud to watch; can you do that for me? I want you to look at the cloud and breathe in to the beat of three and then out again."

Even though I don't want to, even though I can't believe it

will do any good, I look up and find a cloud that's too rounded and generic to be imagined into the shape of anything else. I let her talk me down and my breathing eases.

Right up until another message arrives from Mack, tagged "urgent" again.

"I'm going to come out to you," Kay says.

"No."

"I want to help you back and make sure you're okay. You can come to mine if you don't want to go to the med center."

"No. I'll be okay."

"Has Mack pinged you? Is that what set this off?"

Her question confuses me briefly. She may have been with Mack and Sung-Soo. She may know too!

Know what? I don't even know what he's said yet.

"I'll come back when I'm ready." I say it without any idea when that will be, nor any desire to attempt to return.

I expect an immediate reply but there isn't one. Perhaps she's ignoring me and is coming anyway. I struggle to my knees so that I can peer across the top of the grass back at the colony. That's when my neural alarm sounds. Someone's heading toward my house. The second bang triggers seconds later and I open the data on who it is, expecting Mack's weight, or Sung-Soo's.

My stomach feels like it's dropped into the soil when I see the numbers. At least a dozen people are outside my house.

32

I STAND, MY legs feeling like they're going to collapse from under me at any moment. The panic within me shifts into something with purpose: stopping those people from entering my house. Instead of destroying me from the inside, it focuses my body and mind and I run, desperate to return and put myself between them and my door.

But the shoulder pain caused by the sudden exertion is too much and I have to slow down to an uneven jog. It's been hours since my last dose of painkillers and I'm feeling the extra movement I've been putting it through. The colony is farther away than I appreciated, slowly growing larger as I hurry toward it, wincing with each step. It feels like one of hundreds of nightmares I've had over the years in which I'm trying to get somewhere and things keep slowing me down. The despair yawns wide within me and I open the first message from Mack, hoping that if I arm myself with knowledge of what has happened in my absence, I'll be able to handle it better once I arrive.

I select the link and there's a few minutes of footage recorded through his own LensCam by the look of it. Sung-Soo, Kay, Pasha and a handful of other people are there; Carmen too. Mack is one of the group of people clustered around Sung-Soo at the edge of the Dome. The music sounds muffled in the background, the LensCam software applying selective filters to the auditory data entering Mack's chip so Sung-Soo's voice can be heard more clearly.

"—if I thought I could do something but I can't. I've tried and she's just so . . . broken. And I've been standing here at this party and seeing how much you all care for one another here and I know how much you care for Ren and it feels wrong to stay quiet about it. I know you'd want to help her. But she keeps it all hidden from you, so how can you help if you don't know?"

I stumble, but I don't want to slow my pace.

"How bad is it?" Carmen asks.

"You can't walk in. You have to crawl through a tunnel made of garbage. She doesn't have a space to sleep. There's trash everywhere."

"I don't think this is something that should be discussed in a public place," Mack says.

"I didn't want to tell anyone—I don't want to break the trust she has in me—" Sung-Soo spreads his hands, the picture of the concerned friend, and I'm overwhelmed by a surge of hate-filled anger. "But I know I can't help her and it's going to kill her one day. It has to be public. Her problem is everyone's problem here."

"*Why?*" I mutter at the grass.

"It makes sense," Kay says in the footage and she swings into view as Mack looks at her instead. Kay's eyes are closed and her hands are pressed against her cheeks. When she opens her eyes again they are shining in a way that wrenches my heart. "She never let me into her house, even when we were so close."

"But if it's as bad as this, how could we not know about it?" Mack asks.

"She's very clever," Sung-Soo says. "And all of you are too polite to press her. You never even ask her anymore; you just leave her alone."

"We have to go there and help her," Carmen says.

"What about her privacy?" Mack asks.

"If it's as bad as Sung-Soo says, she's ill," Kay says. "We may have to force an intervention. It sounds like it's part of the OCD spectrum. Dr. Lincoln knows much more about this than I do. I'll contact him and I'll check on Ren. Make sure she's okay."

I close the recording as I reach the southern gate and veer toward my home. I open Mack's second message, now several minutes old. This time it's just one line.

I'm trying to stop them getting into your house.

The low dome of the house that is my sanctuary, my haven, comes into view and I can hear shouting. It's Mack.

"She has the right to her own space and what she does in there—"

There's the sound of scuffling and then grunts of effort as I round it to reach the front door, panting and sweating. I arrive as Sung-Soo and Nick are wrenching the door open between them, the sensor pad at the side of the door smashed.

Kay is there with Dr. Lincoln, having an intense discussion that pauses as the door opens. Pasha is there, Carmen, Mack and half a dozen other faces I can't bring myself to look at.

They are all staring into my house. Hands cover mouths and

noses, and tiny moans of disgust and distress slip through them. Carmen's eyes are wide with horror and blatant excitement.

I look at Kay, dreading what I'll see, but she's not looking at the house. She's looking at me. She stretches her hands toward me. I can't see any disgust, only . . . What is that? I don't—

"Ren . . . Ren, it's all going to be okay," she says and I can't face her a moment longer.

I look away and stumble a few steps closer to my house, feeling as naked as if they'd torn the clothes off my body. Their words and sounds and movements fade into an awful backdrop as I stare at the sensor pad. They didn't have to do that. They could have just bypassed the lock through the network. Why be so violent?

"Ren—" Sung-Soo steps toward me and I twist away to keep air between us. I reach the edge of the doorway, aware of pairs of eyes flitting between the contents within and me. The contents within me. Me.

"I had to tell them," Sung-Soo says and comes toward me again.

"Don't fucking touch me!" I scream at him and everyone draws in a breath sharply enough to be heard.

"You need help," Sung-Soo says. "I can't help you. I tried but—" He waves a hand toward the stuff. "I couldn't get through to you."

"Just don't—" I can't finish the sentence. There are too many words that need to fit into that space.

Dr. Lincoln takes a step forward. "Renata, you're suffering from a mental illness. I—we—can help you, but the first step is going to be the hardest for you. I understand that."

"You don't understand anything! You bastards! You can't . . . You don't have the right to break my door and—"

"That's my picture frame!" Nick's voice is like a sword

through me. He stomps over from the gathering crowd and pulls it from the top of the tunnel. "I put this in my chute. It's cracked. What is it doing here?"

I reach for it but he steps back, holding it close to his chest as if reclaiming ownership. But it's mine now. "I was going to fix it."

"It isn't yours to fix."

"You didn't want it anymore!"

Another movement in the crowd. "That's my comb!"

"That's the cup I threw out a couple of months ago!"

"Shit—that's the folder I used to keep my notes in!"

A surge of people rush forward, jostling to reclaim discarded things, made valuable once more by the fact that I own them now. I try to push Nick away as he starts to poke about looking for more of his ex-belongings, and he shoves me aside.

"This all needs to be cleared out," he says. "We need to just pull it all out and get this place sorted!" He looks at Sung-Soo, ignoring my distress. "Is it like this farther in?"

Sung-Soo nods. "Every room. It's been going on for years. You can hardly move in there."

There are five of them now, three pulling things from the pile to pass back to the others, who stack them outside. The tunnel collapses and I cry out, now trapped outside my home. I make another attempt to pull Nick away from my stuff but hands grab my shoulders and pull me back.

I'm spun around and now I'm facing Mack, who has been silent up until now. He's terribly pale beneath the black of his beard and I can feel his hands shaking as they hold me in front of him. "Why didn't you tell me?"

There's no answer to that. I try to twist free, knowing they're going to break my things and take those objects back even though it's wrong. But Mack holds me tight and pulls me farther away. "Why didn't you tell me!" It's almost a shout. There are tears in his eyes.

Why? I'm the one this is happening to!

"This isn't the way to handle this!" Dr. Lincoln's reedy voice calls out above the rabble, but nobody stops. I can hear comments filled with horror and loathing, the sounds of things falling and crunching underfoot, the din of my life being ripped open. "Renata needs to be a part of this process if we're going to help her!"

"We are helping her." That was Carmen. "How can she get better with a house full of trash?"

"No, you don't understand."

The argument fades into the background when I see a tear roll down Mack's cheek. I have never seen him cry. Not even after Planetfall. But there it is, sinking into the hair of his beard, another following it.

"I had no idea," he says, his voice strained. "I thought you just liked your privacy. I had no idea."

I look down at the buttons of his shirt, studying the pale plastic rather than his eyes. They're easier to stare at; they have nothing to say.

And then I'm outside of myself, detached from the storm of emotional shit raging through my body. There is an unspeakable calm. It's done now. They know. Sung-Soo no longer has any power over me. I don't have to be afraid of how bad the revelation of this secret life will be because it's happening now. I know that beast. I don't feel anything at all.

"Oh God, what's this?"

Nick's question pulls me back into my body like it's at the other end of a taut elastic band. I manage to turn to see him holding a cloth with blood on it, so old and dried out it's nothing more than a brown stain.

"I cut my hand. A while ago."

"But why did you keep it?"

"I must insist!" Now Dr. Lincoln is putting himself between them and my house, even taking a shoe from Carmen's hands and putting it back over the threshold. "Please stop and listen to me. This is already getting out of hand. This is deeply traumatic for Renata and I know you want to help, but the most important person in this process is her, not all of you."

I can't believe he's standing up for me. I can't believe I need him—or anyone else—to stand up for me. Who are these people tearing out my belongings, violating me and judging me? Have I really lived alongside them all these years? Did I really travel millions of miles with them, build their houses and construct the foundations of their colony?

"There's no 'process' here," I say. "I don't want your help. It's none of your business."

"But the Pathfinder said there was still work to be done!" Carmen is flushed too, like she's excited. Like she's enjoying this. "She spoke through Marco and this is what she meant! Who found out? Sung-Soo! He came here and found this . . . this . . . canker and exposed it and we have to act now! She meant this is the work—not the experiments, not the other distractions—it's this! That's what Marco meant!"

"Bullshit!" I shout back. "That was nothing but—"

Mack pulls me back around and starts manhandling me away from them. "You need a time-out," he says, loud enough for everyone else to hear. "Think about what you're saying," he hisses into my ear.

"I'm not going to let that stupid, crazy woman convince everyone that doing this to me is God's work! She's just bored and if they knew—"

"Ren!" He's steered me over the colony boundary and into

the grasses, at a direction that rapidly puts the entrance to my house out of sight. "Think about what you're saying!"

"So it's better for that stupid woman to feel entitled to do this than me tell the truth?"

"Just . . . just please don't . . . I know this is hard but please don't say anything."

The breath from his whisper is hot against my forehead. He's looking over the top of my head to my house, fearful someone will follow us and hear what he's saying.

"You don't give a fuck about anything but yourself, do you?"

"That's not true." Now he's looking at me properly. "Whatever help you need, I'll give it, but please don't do anything that could break this colony. I promise, we'll work out the best way to sort all that stuff out, but now isn't the time."

"I need you to get those people away from my house."

He nods and we go back. This time his arm is around my shoulders and feels like a tree branch that I don't want to carry. Piles of my things are accumulating outside, as is a crowd at the edges. I can see little mountains of clothing, trinkets and unloved things I adopted, all divided up without any thought or care about what I want. Carmen, Nick and Sung-Soo have formed a human chain, taking things passed from someone inside who I can't see as everyone else watches. I can hear Dr. Lincoln's voice coming from inside, but from the tone it sounds like he's trying—and failing—to stop whoever it is in there from passing more stuff out.

"But it doesn't make any sense," Pasha is saying. "How could so much be in there and not have an impact on the communal levels?"

"She changes the numbers," Sung-Soo says and then notices I'm there.

Pasha looks horrified. "But . . . none of us are supposed to take more than we need. There must have been points when supplies were far too low. If we'd had an emergency . . ."

"It's theft," someone shouts from the crowd.

"How can it be theft when no one wanted it anymore?" I shout back in that direction.

"Stopping it from being recycled deprives the community," Pasha says. I've never seen him look so stern. "The metals need to go to the Masher now."

I realize they have been giving some thought to what goes into each pile; they've been dividing them up by base material. They've looked at my belongings with the eyes of recyclers without a second thought about what might have been thrown in there, nor its value to me.

I lurch forward as Pasha scoops up an armful of things from one of the piles, clanking and knocking against one another as they settle in his thieving embrace. I feel the scrape of Mack's hand down my back as he tries to grab me, but I'm too fast. As soon as Pasha is close enough, I reach for whatever I can grab in the hope of saving it or at least seeing what it is before he takes it from me. I catch his arm and pull it enough to open the cradle he's formed beneath my belongings, sending them crashing to the ground.

"Ren!" His voice booms down at me as I drop to my knees and frantically look through the objects. I can see models, cutlery, an old-fashioned stylus to use with some of the early interfaces we had here. When his hands reach down I slap them away.

"This is mine!" I yell at him.

He picks up a tangled mess of cutlery, his fingers like the claws of some gigantic eagle from a children's story come to carry off poor adventurers. I grab his wrist but he shrugs me off and then I'm on my feet, my hand is a fist, and then there's pain in my knuckles and a clattering of stainless steel. Pasha is staggering backward, reaching for his cheek, and I know then that I hit him.

The background din of the crowd disappears and an awful silence descends. I don't care if they're staring or what they think. I scrape the fallen items closer together, so no one can grab anything from the edges of the collection. When I hear footsteps behind me, I pick up one of the knives, a bent and blunt thing but the first to come to hand, and round on the one behind me.

"Put it down," Mack says.

"I just want to be left alone," I say. It's a perfectly reasonable request. I didn't ask any of them to come here. I didn't want any of them to go in my house and I don't want any of them to come near me.

"She's gone mad." The wind carries the whisper from the crowd. It ignites a new fire of speculation and judgment.

Others close in and I throw the knife down. What am I doing?

"I'm sorry, Pasha," I say, but he just stares at me. "I just . . . I just want to . . ." I look around me. All of them want to take my things and I can see there's nothing I can do to stop them. I have to find a way to do it on my terms. "Just let me look through the stuff so I know what's going to the Masher."

With the scrutiny of the crowd pressing in on me, I try to sort through the cutlery, but I can't tell which is still good and which can be thrown away. It's all good. It's all mine and I can't look at it properly with them all staring at me.

"Just go home, for fuck's sake!" I scream at them. "I'm not your fucking entertainment! Leave me alone! Go on! Fuck off!"

None of them are paying attention, so I shout louder. I get on my feet and lean forward and my hands are fists again and my throat is getting raw but they still just stand there, watching. A dialog box flashes up from MyPhys, with some sort of warning in it, but I don't pay attention. I have to make them go away. I pick up the nearest thing to me, something hard that fits in my fist and is light enough to throw, just as the dialog box turns red and starts to flash. "Emergency intervention," the software says and then my vision tunnels as the chip in my brain is used to shut me down.

33

I WAKE ON Mack's bed. I've often wondered what it would be like, not because I envied those he took to his bed, but rather out of a morbid curiosity. I'm fully clothed and lying on top of the sheets with a blanket draped over me, the same one that covered Sung-Soo when Mack drugged him.

I sweep it off me as I remember what happened before I lost consciousness. As soon as I move, MyPhys gives me a verbal report, reassuring me that I am physically unharmed and there is no cause for alarm. Straight afterward, a compulsory notice opens in a text box, detailing how Dr. Kay Reed deemed it necessary to stage a full intervention due to violent behavior and obtained the necessary second electronic signature from Dr. Lincoln to force a neural shutdown against my will. I scan the rest of the notice, absorbing its true message: my violence contravened colony rules and I gave the colony physicians the right to direct chip access when I signed up for the trip, so there is no right to complain either. When that box closes, another appears, containing a notice of potential criminal prosecution for assault, theft and contravention of domestic environmental policy. The assault charge has been automatically logged by Pasha's chip; the rest has been reported by Nick, Carmen and at least twenty others.

I close the box and cover my face with my hands, pressing my head into the pillow beneath it. Everything is falling apart.

There's a single knock on the door and Mack comes in. I drag my hands down my face, pulling at my skin, and look at him in silence. He looks haggard and hesitant, pausing in the doorway as if checking whether I'm going to leap up and attack him too. When he sees that I'm keeping still he closes the door behind him and comes to sit next to me on the bed.

"How are you feeling?" His voice is low.

I look at the closed door. "Who else is here?"

"Kay. She had to—"

"I know. I got the message. Is Pasha all right?"

He nods. "He's fine, and he's not going to press charges. He wanted you to know that."

"It's still in the colony record." I feel sick at the thought of it. On Earth, that would follow me around forever, altering my chances of getting a job, seriously curtailing opportunities to work for any gov-corps or subsidiary organization, and all but ending any chance of romantic liaisons with any employees with high enough clearance to access my files. Not that I'd want to shag any of them anyway, but still, I'm tainted now. Seventy years of working hard to keep my file clean and now it's stained forever.

"It's automated."

"Not the other charges."

His lips press tight together, making the hairs growing beneath them shift orientation. They remind me of the cilia outside that room, but right now I don't care about any of that.

"Carmen shouldn't have done that," Mack says.

"It wasn't just her."

"The rest followed her suggestion. Interfering bitch." He sounds genuinely angry. "I doubt the council will take it any further. Dr. Lincoln will explain it's . . ." He trails off, uncertain of what to say. It's so unlike him. He always has an answer, a way to twist any conversation into whatever he wants. But he's just looking at me and no words are being spun into their usual silver strands. He sucks in a breath. "Don't worry. I'll handle all of it."

"And my house? My stuff? Did you stop them?" He shakes his head and I sit up. He puts a hand on my shoulder as I start to swing my legs off the bed. "They're not going to recycle anything yet; they're just emptying the house."

"So everyone can have a good look?"

He doesn't answer. I can't stand these little silences from him. They're too loud.

"It wasn't a problem until Sung-Soo decided it was. I have a right to privacy and to live the way I want and—"

"No, Ren, not like that. I've talked to Kay and Lincoln and I've read up on it. You're ill. And the illness won't let you realize that and it won't want us to help you."

He's one of them. There's no one here who will help me. I realize that now. I look to his throat, expecting to see a thong of leather there, but no pendant hangs from his neck. Perhaps Sung-Soo is still carving his.

All this stems from him. I should have been stronger. I should have been more careful, but I let him in and everything I feared the most is happening. Because I know what they're like. They don't understand.

There's always been a distance between Mack and me, a chasm filled with wreckage and memories and bizarre trees of loyalty and mutual dependency that have grown out of the stinking filth at the bottom. But that distance has widened and now he's on another emotional continent, not even a tiny speck on the horizon, even though he is sitting there, trying so hard to be present and probably silently congratulating himself for being such a good friend in these difficult circumstances.

He probably thinks he's always been a good friend and can't understand why this is happening.

I can't bear the sight of his face anymore. I'm torn between two impulses impossible to fight: to hide here or to go back to my house and . . . and what? I can't stop them. Not even Lincoln could do that. I can't stand the thought of them all looking at me again. I can't just let them take everything out of there and . . .

Muscles contract in my stomach and there's a cold ball of fear in my chest. I look at the window and see the darkness on the other side of the aquarium. A flush rises up my throat and I can feel sweat beading on my forehead.

"How long was I out?"

"A few hours."

I stand and wobble briefly. "I have to go home."

"I don't think that's a good idea," Mack says but I'm through the door before he can stop me, driven forward by the terror blooming through my body. I can't let them pull *everything* out.

Then Kay is between me and the outer door. Her face is puffy and her eyes are reddened, but I don't want to think about that, so I look at the pendant hanging at her throat. I have to remember to keep my guard up with her because she is one of his now. Carmen and Nick too. Sung-Soo has spent time with all the ones who are now against me.

"Dr. Lincoln is there, making sure nothing is disposed of." She thinks that fear is the only one motivating my flight from the house. "It might be best to—"

I step to one side, aiming to go around her, and she matches my movement. I can hear Mack following me out of the bedroom, so I turn to face him. "Am I under house arrest?"

"No," he says with the voice of an exhausted old man.

I move to go around Kay again and this time she doesn't try to get in my way. Instead she falls into step alongside me saying something about wanting to help and the usual bullshit they've all been trotting out since Sung-Soo betrayed me. I slap my hand against the sensor and the valve opens. Kay follows me out of the house but hangs back to conspire with Mack. I don't care what they're saying. All that matters is putting a stop to it all.

The paths are empty as I march across the colony and the Dome is dark. Perhaps the party has moved to my house now, one that has spectacle and schadenfreude instead of drink and drugs. I try to think of ways to halt the excavation as I half walk and half jog. I can't raise my voice or they'll think I'm being violent again and shut me down. Dr. Lincoln doesn't have the presence to stop them, but if I could get Mack to snap out of being so bloody flaccid, then he could stop them. I have to pretend to want to be part of the process Lincoln spoke about. I have to convince them that I've come around to seeing it their way and that I want to work with them instead of being obstructive. If I can convince them of that, they may force everyone else to work to my pace and I'll get them out of the house before they find the door down to the—

The crowd is huge. I reach the back of it several houses away from my own and have no desire to push my way through people desperate to see something to gossip about. I cut across the back edge of the human mass until I reach the colony boundary. I strike out into the grasses to go around them all and get to my house from the opposite direction.

"Ren," Mack calls from behind me. I don't reply. There isn't time to get sucked into his crap now.

There are so many people that their collective chatter sounds like the hum of machinery and air-conditioning at the old lab in Paris. I'd do anything to go back there now and find that younger self and tell her to split off from Suh and leave the city before it was too late. But then I hear my name bobbing up to the surface of the noise and the spell is broken.

"They've found another door!" someone calls back to the people behind them and the news ripples through the crowd in the opposite direction from the one I'm hurrying in, much faster than I can move.

"In the floor?" someone asks.

"No, at the end of the steps down from that one," the answer flies back and I sprint, ignoring the pain from my shoulder.

The crowd is thinner on the boundary side, unable to see into the drama from this side of the house. I shove my way through them and the crowd starts to open ahead of me as people hear that it's me. They're all too happy to make way for the crazy woman who's bound to do something more thrilling than anything they've experienced in the last ten years.

A cordon has been set up to keep the crowd back and I dive under the barrier closest to me. It was last used to keep people away from the foundation work we did on the Dome. Floodlights, used for that same activity, are now illuminating the small mountains of belongings taken from my house. I see my knitted doll on top of the one nearest to me and grab her, stuffing her into my sling to rest protected in the crook of my elbow.

There's no one outside the door, so I step inside. The sight of the empty hallway with its dead floor and grimy walls makes me hesitate, as if I've dashed into the wrong house. What used to be moss is now just a brown powder with footprints tracked through it. The lower parts of the walls I haven't seen for years are cracked and bruised with mold. Have I been breathing in its spores all this time? Is it native or something we brought with us? Is that possible considering all the—

I can hear voices up ahead. They must be in the room on the other side of the kitchen. As I pass that room I can't help but peer inside. I haven't used it for over ten years, thanks to the portable food printer in the bedroom. There's a sink, dark green with filth and a stench that makes me cover my face like so many people I've seen today.

This isn't my house. I drift through the hallway, leaving the ex-kitchen behind, feeling unanchored here. It's almost as if I can't feel the edges of myself with nothing to squeeze through or push past. I fancy that I'm turning into mist as I walk, just a cloud of diffuse misery haunting this broken place.

"We just focus on clearing the tunnel right now. We'll shift it all outside later. We need to know the scale of this." That's Pasha. He's in the room ahead of me.

"Is it safe down there?" Carmen asks.

"Ren's an engineer," Pasha replies. "She wouldn't create something structurally unsound underneath her own house."

"A sane engineer wouldn't," Carmen replies as I reach the door.

They're both wearing coveralls and masks to keep the dust and spores out of their lungs. It makes me feel like one of the contaminants.

Carmen's cheeks blush over the top edge of hers. "Ren. We've almost done it. Once this is all cleared out, we can clean and repair the—"

I ignore her and walk past her and Pasha as calmly as I can, aware, so painfully, of having to keep up the act. I wait for one of them to comment on how the underground excavation is illegal as it's not registered on the colony records, but neither of them say anything. It's beyond that now.

Crates of my belongings have been carried up to this room. I see the book my father wrote for me and brush the edge of the pages. I don't trust them to not throw it out, so I take it and tuck it in my sling with the doll. I would sit and leaf through it if there wasn't something more pressing to deal with. I promise myself that I'll look at it later, once I've stopped them going into the last room.

The door in the floor is smaller than I remember. It was white when I fitted it; now it is various shades of brown and black with occasional streaks of green. It looks like it's been camouflaged for a woodland environment. It's propped open and as I get to the edge with the steps leading down I can see the other side of the door is now gray.

They've taken portable lights down there that cast shadows across the steps. I carved them from the dirt with tools my great-grandfather would have recognized. I have to go down there, and fast, but the thought of it roots my feet to the top step. I'm trapped between the fear of going down there and the fear of them opening the door I made over twenty years ago.

"I can nearly reach the handle!" Sung-Soo's voice is like a cattle prod in my back. I'm down the steps in seconds and can see him at the far end of the corridor. It's less than five meters long and standing close behind him are Dr. Lincoln and Nabiha. There is a crate at Sung-Soo's feet. I can't see what's in it from here. As I watch he scoops up more of the things between him and the door to dump them in the crate with no care at all. He shifts the crate a couple of centimeters closer and dumps another armful into it.

I almost scream, "Get away from that door!" but I check

myself. It's as if someone had dropped me in a room full of snakes; I want to run and shout and be violent, but all that will achieve is them attacking me. I force a breath down my throat, breathing in the scent of their sweat. "I . . . I'm here to work with you," I say to Dr. Lincoln.

"Good." He smiles. "That's good."

"I can see you all want to help me." I wonder if that is too much but he just smiles again. "And I'm sorry about what happened before."

"We understand how hard this is for you." The patronizing tone makes me want to knee him in the balls. "It's taken a lot of bravery to come back here so soon, and I commend you for that."

"I want to . . . to get well again." Mack and Kay have come down the steps behind me. I'm trapped halfway down the corridor now. "But it has to be at my pace."

"Yes. I'm sorry it's happened this way. I understand."

"And I want to just slow it down a bit. Get my head around it."

Sung-Soo kicks the crate. "You're just trying to stop us," he says.

"It's not unreasonable," Dr. Lincoln says to him.

"But isn't this what the illness does?" Neela asks. "I'm sorry, Ren, but how do we know you're not just going to derail this?"

"Derail what?" I stop myself, realizing my voice is rising.

Sung-Soo exploits the pause. "What's behind this door, Ren?"

"None of your business."

"Is it the last room?" Dr. Lincoln asks. I nod, not thinking. "Then I propose we stay here and open it together. This is the last part of the hoard. It's no surprise it's creating resistance within you."

"I don't want to open it."

"Why?" Dr. Lincoln asks the question as if it's something simple. As if I'd said I'd rather drink tea instead of coffee.

Sung-Soo starts putting more things in the crate, steadily clearing the last meter before the door, but I still can't think of anything to say.

Lincoln comes closer and Neela steps back, giving us a modicum of privacy. "It's likely that whatever is behind that door has a great deal to do with the onset of your illness," Lincoln whispers. "It's perfectly natural to be afraid."

But it isn't just that. I know something terrible is behind it, but when I start to try to remember, there's nothing but slippery darkness. It seems as impossible to remember as trying to look directly at a faint star. When I try to focus on it head-on, there's nothing more than an emotional residue and the lingering knowledge that no one must ever come down here.

I turn to look at Mack. He's only a meter or so away, standing on the bottom step looking ghoulish in the lantern light. His arms are wrapped tight around himself and he seems smaller. "Stop him," I say.

"I agree with Dr. Lincoln," he says. "I bet whatever's in there isn't as bad as you think it is, Ren. And best that it's all out in the open now. We've come too far to leave the last part unfinished."

I can't remember what's behind the door, but something else has remained: a certainty that it will break him. But there's nothing in his face or the way he is standing to suggest he's going to do anything. I look at Lincoln and he meets my stare. He's probably trying to appear open and "there for me." He is anything but.

Sung-Soo has his back to me; his long hair is tied back and lies down his spine like a black snake. Why does he feel such a compulsion to press this? I want to think it's because he lost his friend, but something deep in my gut tells me there's another agenda here. Perhaps he's always had one. Perhaps he was always looking for something to get stuck into, a way to truly embed himself in colony life.

Neela slips past me to go to Kay. I can't look at either of them. The way to the door will be cleared in a matter of minutes and I'm just standing here, like someone waiting patiently next to the scaffold where they'll be beheaded. I know this is inevitable. If I try to stop them, they'll stop me. I lost control hours ago.

Sung-Soo grunts as he pulls the crate, now full, away from the door. It's made of a tough composite material, able to withstand all sorts of conditions. It hasn't warped or degraded over the years; it's just acquired a film of dirt. He reaches for the handle and I watch, numbed, as if it's a cut scene in a game I'm bored of. I have to see what happens even though there's no emotional investment here anymore. The flood has seeped away. There's nothing left of my tsunami panic save some mud gunging up my chest, making each breath harder to draw in.

The door isn't locked. There was no need. My entire house was the lock that prevented its opening. Now it opens on squeaking hinges and reveals not a room, rather a rough cube-shaped cubbyhole. It's two meters high, wide and deep. I remember that.

The long black box that lies within is familiar. It is 1.8 meters long, 80 centimeters deep and 1.5 meters high. The numbers are there, crystalline, in my mind. My brain, sculpted by engineering over all these years, is creating a wire frame of it from memory and spinning it around as if I'm working in my visengineering software. But I still can't recall what's inside, and when I try to think about that, the mud in my lungs spreads its cold through my chest, seeping into my throat and clogging that too. I can remember making it. I can remember sobbing over it and the tears running off its near frictionless surface to make dark splashes in the dirt left by my excavation. I know the top lid is made of plasglass so that I could see into the box, but when I try to do that in my memory, the darkness just folds in on itself.

Sung-Soo can't make out what's inside even though he's standing over it. He picks the lantern up from the floor and raises it. As the light hits the top of the box I know it's a sarcophagus and that Suh's body is inside.

34

IT WAS THE only thing Mack couldn't cope with in the days that followed Planetfall: recovering Suh's body from the place we left it in the city. His skin would turn pale and his lips a horrible gray at the mere thought of going back to that place and seeing her again. So I said I would handle it.

That we left her there had tormented me from the moment we returned to Atlas. I hadn't slept properly since; I knew the preservative we'd injected into her—standard practice after a death that would require autopsy—would fail eventually and the protection from her suit and helmet wouldn't last forever. Mack had bought a month at the most before her body would decompose in the normal fashion. The thought of her rotting in that place made me shiver in bed at night, even though I was beyond exhausted.

We left her in the tunnel near the valve hidden by the tendrils. That was how I found it; I was hunting for the corresponding spot on the outside to cut through and retrieve her body. In the small hours on day twenty planetside, I dragged her body from the city and took her to the newly printed dome of my house.

I decontaminated the suit exterior and her body using the same procedure I did with my own suit before entering my home's protective environment. We still needed those measures back then. I pulled the suit from her and felt how the preservative had made her skin clammy to the touch, as if she were recovering from an illness. I was almost sick and then that feeling passed faster than I expected. I washed her and it felt good. Respectful. I talked to her the whole time, telling her what I was about to do before I did so, as if she were able to hear, like in the coma. I asked her why she did it and of course there was no reply. I slept next to her that night.

When Mack asked, I told him it was all sorted and he didn't press for details. He was soothed and could carry on without it hanging over him anymore. But I couldn't burn her or bury her. I couldn't let her go. Making something to keep her safe was so easy. I had direct access to the biggest printer in the colony, linked by a short tunnel to my home to keep the air inside microbe free. I put a message on the network that something was malfunctioning but I had it under control and that the list of items required for the colony build would be printed as soon as possible. It was the first major lie I told: the first time I actively fabricated something instead of remaining silent. And it was so easy. Taking care of Suh was far more important than anything else.

I made the sarcophagus, placed her in it, disinfected everything and then poured in a resinlike compound, sealing her totally from the air and acting as a secondary preservative. She looked like Sleeping Beauty. I made a lid to protect the resin and make all of it airtight.

Then I slept.

When I woke I realized I couldn't keep the box in the center of my home indefinitely. I hadn't built the internal walls yet and dabbled with the idea of just hiding it in plain sight, boxed in next to a cupboard so no one would notice unless they studied the floor plan. But I'd never rest. I decided to put her underground, in a place of my making, where I knew she would be safe.

How could I have forgotten all that? Somehow I just stopped thinking about it. I stuffed things between her and myself until there wasn't even room for myself anymore.

Perhaps I am broken.

A guttural sound fills the tunnel and breaks the memory like a stone destroying a reflection on the surface of a pond. It sounds like an animal, but it's coming from Sung-Soo's throat as he looks down into the face of his dead grandmother. He drops the lantern and whirls around, his eyes huge and demonic in the shadows. He looks at me with an accusatory glare. Oh Lord. He thinks I killed her!

He launches himself down the tunnel toward me as Lincoln shouts, demanding to know what he saw, but there are no words penetrating the furious haze surrounding Sung-Soo.

"It wasn't me!" That's all I have time to yell before he reaches me. But he doesn't grab me or try to throttle me. He just knocks me aside. He does the same to the others behind me and I hear Mack hit the wall and swear. By the time I've turned around, all I see are Sung-Soo's heels as his feet leave the top step and he heads out of the house.

I lean against the wall, needing something solid to help keep me upright as my legs tremble. All of them—Lincoln first, then Mack, Neela and Kay—rush down the tunnel, ignoring me, desperate to see what would cause such a reaction. "It wasn't me," I whisper to Kay as she passes me, but she doesn't hear.

Soon after they reach the box, there are screams and cries of despair. Some of them are my own.

Carmen and Pasha race down the steps and Neela runs into his arms, distraught and snaring him in the expectation of comfort, when all he wants to do is find out what's going on. I glance down the tunnel to see Mack backing away from the sarcophagus, shaking his head, as Dr. Lincoln slides down the wall, the color of milk.

"I didn't kill her," I say, but none of them are listening. Carmen is well on her way to becoming hysterical and starts shouting that I've murdered the Pathfinder. When the notification envelope starts flashing, I realize she's broadcasting on the network, even propping herself up against the door into Suh's tomb to keep her LensCam footage as steady as possible.

"Now everyone knows how evil you are!" she screams at me once she's satisfied she's shown enough of the corpse.

"She killed herself!" I yell back. "I didn't kill her." My eyes meet Mack's. He looks terrified. "I can prove it."

This time Mack lunges for me. I don't know what he plans to do, but I doubt he's thinking of anyone but himself. I dart away from his grabbing hands and run up the stairs, my father's book jabbing into my ribs as I sprint. I know he's right behind me, but I don't look back, darting through the empty house to the front door, only to meet a surge of people pushing over the barriers to come in and see it all for themselves. I can't see Sung-Soo anywhere in the chaos up here.

"Stop!" I put all the power of my lungs behind the word and it actually works. People do stop, more easily than I thought they would, their shock working in my favor. "I didn't kill Suh," I say. "Just . . . just let me show you what happened."

"No, Ren!" Mack is in the doorway to my house behind

me. He's been hiding this so long he's incapable of seeing when he has to give it up.

"You can all see for yourselves," I say and call up the file I haven't been able to open since Planetfall. The footage of Suh's death.

I share the link on the network and almost a thousand people select it, an eerie silence descending over the crowd as their attention shifts inward. I start the playback about three hours in, the point when we're nearing the top of God's city on the outside. By then I'd stopped recording with full immersion, knowing that it would be too traumatic to be useful. But it still contains everything I could see and hear, and as the colonists around me begin to watch, they see and hear it all like I did then.

Hak-Kun and Mack are arguing as we climb, each of them with opposing opinions on how to progress. We were all exhausted by then, having been churned about inside the city for at least two hours by that point. All of us—except Suh—had vomited inside our own suits and felt every scrap of our feeble humanity. She was so distant by that point I wondered whether Suh had shut off the comms in her suit. She just kept her face focused on the topmost pod and pulled herself up, pausing only to fix more hexes for our climbing gear to register and follow.

We reached the second highest pod soon after; the only sound was all of us panting. I sprawled flat on top of it, letting the exhaustion take my body until Suh drove us on again. I was so drained I didn't care about the feeling of bile seeping down my neck as I shifted position. I could have slept there and then.

"We cut in here," Suh said. "Then we climb up the tunnel."

"But how do you even know it's where we need to go?"

Hak-Kun sounded like a whining child by then and Suh was losing her patience.

"I just do. You were happy to accept all the other things I've known. Why not this?"

It was enough to shut him up, but Winston wasn't satisfied. "It feels wrong to cut in like that."

"We can't go up the other way," Lois said. "Fuck knows we tried. And I'm not going through that again."

"It's like the city wanted to kill us," Mack said, sitting next to me.

"It's testing us," Suh said, pulling the cutting tool from her pack.

"So we're cheating," Winston said, but she just started to cut in.

She made a vertical slice into the base of the tendril reaching up toward the highest pod, about two meters long, and then put the tool away to reach in and part the fleshy wall.

When she opened it enough to force her way in, there was a puff of something like vapor from the space inside. It misted on the plasglass of her helmet, but it didn't faze her. She went in first and then we followed, like we had from Earth, full of doubts and terrible fears but compelled to see where she would lead us.

By then I was so mired in the physicality of exhaustion that I'd forgotten to be hopeful. We're such base creatures, so easily pulled from higher things by the needs of the body. I followed because everyone else did and as I squeezed into that last tunnel all I wanted was to not be sick again.

That last climb was easier; the tunnel was much narrower than the others, inclined steeply enough to walk up and thankfully not moving like so many of the others had. It almost felt too easy, after all we'd been through. I wondered if the city hadn't realized what we'd done yet.

There was another valve and Suh pressed her gloved hand against it. Everyone reached out and braced themselves against the walls of the tunnel, expecting it to pitch us into the air with a sudden change in orientation, but the only thing that happened was the opening of the door-like valve.

The room beyond was formed by half of the pod, reaching at least four meters into the air at the highest point and twice that across at its widest. It was unlike any other we'd seen so far; the walls were made of something that looked like stone and every spare centimeter of them was decorated elaborately.

"Is it bone?" Winston asked as he drifted to the nearest part of the wall, but no one answered him.

"What does it all mean, Hak-Kun?" Lois asked and I couldn't decide if it was a genuine question or some sort of dig at his self-assigned title.

"Give me a chance to look," he replied and then all of us went to different parts, marveling at the intricacy of the symbols.

Some looked familiar, undoubtedly because my human brain was desperately trying to form patterns and make me feel rooted in something that could make sense. Some parts seemed like art, perhaps abstract representations of the grasslands and the mountains we'd passed over. Others looked like hundreds of rows of neatly painted symbols that could be letters or numerical representations. Hak-Kun was already working with the Atlas AI, using his program to start digesting and interpreting the data. Mack and Lois were in discussion with Winston about some detail or other. Suh was silent. I turned away from the walls and watched her instead, standing in the center of the room, turning slowly, her eyes scanning the walls in a bizarre, almost mechanical movement. She seemed to see through the others, her eyes still tracking up and down, even when she was facing me.

I said her name, but she didn't acknowledge it. I said it again, louder, now frightened by her odd manner and fearful that something else had taken her over. Perhaps that had already happened, years before in that field in the Alps, but seeing her acting in such an . . . alien way was too much for me.

My concern attracted everyone else's attention and we all stared at her as she completed her sweep of the room. Then she smiled and looked at me and said, "I know what it means."

"Tell us!" Hak-Kun said but she turned her back and walked to the far side of the room, tracing her hand along a series of grooves incorporated so elegantly in a larger design that I hadn't even noticed them until that moment.

"God is waiting," she said and the wall she was standing in front of started to look fainter somehow, something more like a gauze with the designs painted on. Then she walked through it.

Hak-Kun shouted for his mother and ran to the place she had been just moments before, his desperate hands slapping stone. He fumbled for the grooves she'd touched, but nothing changed. When he rounded on it and looked at us, panicked, none of us had anything to say to reassure him. Or ourselves.

"Is this it?" Lois whispered eventually. "Is this what we're here for? For her to go and leave us here?"

"Perhaps she's speaking to God," Winston said. "Perhaps God is on the other side." He pointed at the wall that Hak-Kun still pawed at.

"Perhaps something else is," Mack said and looked at me. "What do you think, Ren?"

"I think we have to wait," I replied. It was the only sensible thing to say.

We drifted around the room like people in an art gallery after closing, waiting for another function to start, our minds too focused on that to really process anything on the walls. Hak-Kun revisited the footage I'd captured of his mother's behavior and then tried to replicate her movements exactly, over and over again. Winston and Mack both tried to calm him down as each replication became more frantic, but after five attempts he stopped himself and withdrew to a corner as far from everyone else as he could get. I couldn't bring myself to tell him that I believed she was the only person who could go through. She wasn't sick in the city like all of us and she knew exactly where she was heading. She wasn't like us anymore. It seemed absurd, to me at least, to even attempt to follow her. She'd said the city was testing us, but I think she believed she was the only one really being tested and that was why she was happy to cut in. She'd already proven she could cope and the rest of us were just keeping her back. That last bit of the real Suh didn't have the heart to just abandon us outside as she came up here, so she brought us as far as she could.

We all knew that we'd have to leave eventually, forced to do so by our finite air supply, but no one mentioned it out loud. Then only nine minutes and forty five seconds after she'd gone through the wall, it phased into its faint state again and Suh staggered through.

She was already lifting her helmet off as the wall became solid behind her again. She was distraught, wild-eyed with grief, almost howling with each tear-filled breath. "I took too long!" she said, sinking to her knees and lifting the helmet off before any of us could get to her.

"No! No, Suh!" Winston's pleas went unheeded and she let her helmet drop to the floor in front of her.

As he scrambled to open his medkit, her skin blotched with lurid red rosettes and her sobs became more labored. All the microbial life in the air was invading her body, so finely tuned to another planet's microbiology. "Nothing matters," she said to Winston as he fussed around her. "We're nothing. All this is nothing. God is already dead."

The poisonous air stole her words then and Hak-Kun cradled her as she collapsed in his arms. She had no tears for him, no parting smile or any attempt to make a final connection to her only son. All she could do was stare at the wall she had passed through until she died. We all watched as Winston frantically tried to bring her back, but I knew there was nothing that could be done. Her breath had been bubbling in her lungs; she'd coughed blood over Hak-Kun's and Mack's visors. She wasn't coming back from that.

I didn't cry then. I don't think I quite believed it. After decades of being with her, talking to her in the middle of the night when she couldn't sleep, watching her struggle with the ever widening gap between her and everyone else, I couldn't believe it was over so quickly. And so needlessly. The only thing I felt was anger. How could she do that to us! To her son! I couldn't begin to process what she'd said.

The playback stops and it feels like I'm dropped into my body again, outside my house, where I've been all along. Everywhere I look there are people crying or staring at the city, dumb with shock. Some are clinging to one another. Others have their arms wrapped around themselves as they all process what they saw.

I didn't choose to end the playback there though and when I check the network I'm unsurprised to see that Mack shut my link down. He's standing behind me, still close to the entrance to my house, staring at the crowd.

"Why didn't you tell us?" Pasha says to him, to both of us, as he comes outside too.

Mack looks at me and shakes his head, but I'll be damned if I'm going to hide what's left now. "We argued about it," I say. "The others wanted to take her back to Atlas and tell everyone what happened but he—"

"I did what I needed to," he cuts in. "I had to keep the colony together."

"The people who died," Pasha says, "the ones whose pods didn't make it here . . . You were covering it up, weren't you?"

"That was just a terrible accident," Mack says.

"That's a lie." This time I cut across him. "I should have spoken up about it and I'm sorry but—" I look at Mack. Do I reveal his crime? Is it my right to condemn him? But he killed those people. He is responsible for their deaths. And the reason I've kept quiet about this is no longer valid. "We argued after she died and it got violent; then Mack got Lois's gun and shut everyone up. He persuaded us all to keep quiet about Suh's death until the colony was established. We agreed that telling everyone when we went back with the air and soil samples would just destroy everyone and we needed to make sure everyone was focused on second Planetfall. We couldn't stay on Atlas. We had to make it work." I pause under the power of Mack's eyes, silently pleading me to protect him. But he could have killed me. He would have killed me, if he'd needed to. "When we got back to Atlas and were waiting for the first round of vaccinations to be produced, Hak-Kun came to see me. He said he didn't trust Mack to tell the truth once we landed and he tried to persuade me to make a new pact with him, Winston and Lois, to tell everyone the moment we made Planetfall, so Mack wouldn't have a chance to cover it all up. He didn't know—none of us did—that Mack was spying on us. I said we had to trust Mack. That's why I'm here, now, alive. Mack bided his time, monitored them closely and then sabotaged their pods. He cut them off from the network so that when they realized what was happening they couldn't tell the truth. Or ask for help. Not until it was too late. The other pod that went off course was to stop people thinking it was something to do with the original team."

When I stop speaking, there is silence. I've done it. I've broken the spell Mack cast and I've broken the colony with it. Pasha moves away from Mack as if being near him is unbearable now. I wait for someone to say something or do something, but no one knows how to handle this. It's all too big, too sudden, to lose so much in quick succession. Kay looks at me with a brief, cold glance. I know there will never be anything between us again now. Not after this.

Nick is the first to come to his senses. "We need time to come to terms with this," he says, stepping forward. "And there needs to be a trial. I think Ren and Mack should be held beneath the Dome until we're ready to deal with that. Does anyone have any objections?"

No one voices any, and Pasha, Nick and a couple of others surround me and Mack. He looks resigned and avoids eye contact with me. I look back at my house as we walk away, wondering if I'll ever be allowed back into it again.

35

WE END UP being escorted by a small entourage. At first I'm fearful that people are drawing closer to try to hurt us, but then I realize that's their fear too and they are actually protecting us. There are angry shouts thrown from the crowd, but most people are too caught up in their own shock and grief to be violent. Mack made sure he screened out those tendencies in the early stages of the selection process. In fact, aside from a few incidents of flared tempers, he is the only one who has ever committed a serious violent act since we left Earth. I suppose he didn't apply his entry criteria to himself.

As I walk I wonder where Sung-Soo has gone. There's no mention of him on the network. I want to explain to him what happened. He's the only one here who doesn't know the truth. It isn't so much the worry that he thinks I killed Suh; it's more the fact that if there's anyone here who deserves to know what happened, it's him. Will he come back? Or has he gone to fend for himself in the wilderness again?

Every now and then I look at Mack. He's fixated on the ground ahead of him, probably trying to work out how to handle this. He won't be able to talk his way out of this though. I want to say something to him but I can't settle on anything that doesn't seem ridiculous. Occasionally I want to apologize, but then another part of my mosaic feels that he should apologize to me, for putting me through this over the years. But I can't blame him for my actions. I could have told everyone a long time ago. And that's why Kay looked at me that way. I'll never be anything but a liar to her now. And out of all of this, that's what makes me start to weep.

Only meters away from the Dome, the darkness is rent apart by an explosion on the other side of the colony. Instinctively we all scream and hunker down as flaming scraps of debris rain down upon us. My ears are ringing and I don't realize one of the burning scraps has landed on my shoulder until I feel the heat. I brush it off and frantically sweep my hand over my head and back.

"Did you do that?" I yell at Mack, thinking he's lost all perspective and somehow set something off to cause a distraction. But he looks just as shocked and confused as everyone else. People are now running toward and then past us from that direction as another explosion tears through the colony not far from the first. There's a high-pitched note soon afterward, like a whistle that's at the topmost edge of my hearing range. I have no idea what makes it and no time to worry about it either.

Our entourage scatters and I'm knocked over, unable to steady myself well enough with a slinged arm. I bang my head and lose a couple of seconds to the pain, expecting MyPhys to make an instant report, but no dialog box pops up. I wonder if Kay has somehow disabled it, then check my stream to see if anyone knows what's going on. There's no new data coming into my feed. The network is down.

I struggle onto my knees wondering why people are still screaming when a movement next to me makes me twist toward Mack. He's on his knees too, presumably knocked over by the stampede as I was. But there's someone standing behind him, holding his hair in a fist, drawing a blade across Mack's throat. Sung-Soo.

The blood falling from the wound in a torrent paralyzes me. Sung-Soo is looking at me as he cuts, ending the act with a wide arc that flicks the blood away from his blade. He releases Mack's hair and he collapses in front of me. The smile that spreads across Sung-Soo's face as Mack drops speaks of relief and satisfaction.

He must have been in the crowd when I told them what Mack did.

Sung-Soo holds the knife to one side as Mack's blood drips from it. He's dead. His blood is soaking into the knees of my trousers. I'm going to be sick.

"I waited so long to do that."

Sung-Soo's comment not only chills me, but confuses me too. He sees that in my face and nods.

"Yes, I knew what he did. My father told me everything."

"You knew Suh was dead all the time you were here?"

"Yes. You started lying to me the first day I met you. Does a true word ever come out of that mouth?"

I say nothing, swallowing down waves of bile, keeping an eye on the knife I'm sure he's going to plunge into me.

"But I needed to work out what you knew. I needed proof. Your pod wasn't sabotaged, so Dad always wondered if you were in on it. He hoped you weren't." He kicks Mack's slack body in the back. "But he knew that bastard sent them off to die."

"Are you going to kill me now?"

"You're sick in the head, but you know so much."

Another statement that confuses me. What difference would either make to his revenge?

"You didn't kill anyone," he continues. "You're just a coward. You should have told everyone what he did. Then maybe they would have found Dad and the others. But you're too useful to die."

I struggle to my feet. Behind him I see someone running. It's hard to see who in the darkness, but I know it's a man. He drops suddenly, but I can't see why. What the fuck is going on?

"Sung-Soo!" It's a man's voice and it's unfamiliar. "We've got five. Are there many more?"

"Ten in total," Sung-Soo calls back over his shoulder and I bolt, using his momentary distraction to make my escape.

He's fitter than I am and uninjured and I know this is an act of futility above good sense, but I still obey my basic survival instinct and plunge myself into the nearest stream of running people. I need to get away from him as priority and I need to know if Kay is all right. I can't see her anywhere, and between the smoke from the fires and the soft glow of the path, it's practically impossible to make one person out from another.

I collide with a woman cutting across the direction I'm sprinting and as we bump off each other I realize I don't know her. There's something about her eyes that's familiar though, and the set of her nose that reminds me of Winston. Her clothes are a patchwork of old coveralls patched many times with strips of rough, untanned leather and she's holding a huge bowie knife that makes my stomach flip over. Its blade's silver has been dulled by blood.

She looks at me for a moment, then at my chest, then does the same with someone behind me and throws herself toward them. I have to dodge to one side to avoid being clipped by her knife. I see Christophe, a quiet man with a specialty in microbiology, is the target of her attack. There's something glowing on his upper chest, as if someone had fired a pellet of luminescent paint at him, splattered outward from a point just below his neck.

The woman doesn't stab him; instead she strikes him in the solar plexus with the flat of her free hand, and as the poor man staggers back, winded, she hits him on the top of his head with the butt of the knife handle. It knocks him out, and without looking at me or caring about anything else around her, the woman starts to tie Christophe's hands together.

I can hear Sung-Soo laughing. Abandoning Christophe, like the coward I am, I turn and run again. I can't fight that woman. I'd just get myself killed. I don't feel any better about my actions though.

I make it to the edge of the colony and get my bearings. I'm not very far from my house, not that there's anything there that could help me. I can't print a weapon with the network down and Mack owns the only gun I know of. I have no idea where he kept it and I'm not willing to go to his house to search for it and risk running into Sung-Soo or another knife-wielding stranger.

I run out into the grasses, hoping that the farther away I get from the colony, the harder I'll be to spot. I get as far as I can before I have to stop and drop down to my knees, gasping for breath.

"Where are you going, Ren?" Sung-Soo shouts. He sounds amused. "You think I won't find you out there? That's my world. I'll find you no matter where you go."

I know he's right, but I don't move. There's the faintest gray appearing on the horizon. The dawn is an hour away at most.

I'll be too easy to track in the grasses; anyone could follow the trampled path I made during my flight.

"I'm not going to kill you," he says. He doesn't sound any closer. "And you're going to come with us. Kay's coming too. This colony won't last a month. You'll be better off with us."

I twist the corner of my sling, biting into the fabric to try to let some of the tension out. Is he lying about Kay to draw me out?

Us. He said "us"—he wasn't the only one left from his group. It was all a lie; he just pretended to be alone so we'd lower our guard. Those strangers are his people—that woman with the knife is probably Winston's daughter. They're not just seeking revenge against Mack, but against all of us. They want to destroy what we have for depriving them.

"Carmen isn't coming, if that's what you're worried about. She's useless."

But how could they get so close without setting off the sensors? I shake my head. I'm forgetting that Lois knew how to get around that sort of thing effortlessly. She would have passed on her knowledge. Hell, she might be out there now—Sung-Soo lied about so much that the others may have survived. But if that were the case, why wait so long? And why not just come and join the colony? No. These are the actions of their children who heard stories about us that twisted them and set them against us. Ones that grew up in hardship and danger while we lived soft, cocooned lives of luxury.

I can't stay here. I can't go back. If I try to strike out on my own with no supplies, I'll be dead in a week. I don't know how to survive out there, but Sung-Soo does. He'll find me.

There's only one place I can go where he might not follow.

36

HE'LL SEE MY route through the grasses to the edge of God's city, but then my trail will end if I move fast enough. As I run, I use my chip to manually scan for the climbing hexes. They should still be broadcasting a low-level local signal so that the network would be able to find them, should a user be in the vicinity. Mack set them so that only I could connect and that works in my favor as now my chip will be able to handle the handshake in lieu of the network.

By the time I reach the secret place beneath the twisted tendrils, I've worked myself up into a terrible state of anxiety about whether the climbing gear will still be there. When I find that it is, except for the coverall and respirator I took home the night I dislocated my shoulder, I weep with relief and the memory of Mack training me to climb the outside of the city. He wasn't all bad. And I'm hardly blameless in all this mess.

The tears for him soon spill for Kay. I have no idea where

she is or what Sung-Soo really meant. But I wipe my face and pull out the harness and u-velcro crampons. I have to move now.

There's no way I can make this climb with only one arm in use, so I take off the sling. The woolen doll spills out and I realize then that my father's book must have fallen out when I was knocked over by the blast. I feel the wrench of loss like a physical blow to the stomach, doubling over slightly at the thought of it being trampled and potentially lost to me forever. But I force myself to focus on the practical matters of prepping for the climb and soon enough moving my shoulder is a painful distraction. It's much better than it was, but I resign myself to the fact that this will hurt and there's nothing to be done about it. I tuck the doll into the waistband of my trousers and hope she'll stay put.

I listen for Sung-Soo as I re-coil the tangled ropes, but there's no sign of him. Perhaps he's waiting for dawn before setting out. I can still hear all sorts of yelling and chaos coming from the colony. I know a couple of the colonists had swords and knives displayed in their homes, but I doubt anyone has the skills to use them effectively. We've evolved our way of life as top predators, thinking technology would be there to defend against any threat. But we assumed we'd have a network to deliver weapon patterns to printers and notice given by the far-range sensors. We didn't prepare for human cunning and our species' capacity to plan and execute a surprise attack against us.

Once the coiled ropes are slung into place and I've steeled myself against the inevitable pain, I move farther around to the back of the city, accept the climbing software's offer of help and begin the ascent. The adrenaline helps and I use the breathing techniques I was taught at prenatal class to manage the complaints from my shoulder. I've forgotten the pain of childbirth, but not the techniques to cope with it.

For the first twenty meters or so I'm only focused on the climb and making sure the rope is pulled up after me by using the remote opening command to release the grip from the hexes. I allow myself only the briefest pause to catch my breath, no more, as the sky is brightening in the north and I've got to get higher before the dawn breaks. The higher I go, the more tendrils and pods there are to hide behind. At least they can't use the network to find me now.

I reach the peak point of the climb as the sun comes up and I'm sweating and shaking as it breaks the horizon. The last time I was up here I was on my way to plant the fake seed and keep those lies alive for another year. All for nothing.

I hunker down on top of a pod that's partially covered by another tendril stretching upward to a larger pod above me. From here I can see down into the colony. The fires are still burning but haven't spread, sending thick plumes of black smoke into the air. There are four in total: one where the main colony server is housed, one where the backup system is kept, one pouring from the main vent out of the Masher, and the building containing the big communal printers. I don't recall four explosions, so they must have set fire to some with other means. They clearly knew what to target.

They. I can see them now in the gray light. Seven of them are clustered around the range vehicle used for expeditions and to mine the minerals we needed in the first phase of the colony. The soft roof cover has been rolled back to make room for a huge pile of supplies and what look like a few portable printers, tied down for travel. Seated on the rear benches that run the length of the rear compartment are nine colonists, hands tied to the loops that the roof is normally strapped to. All of them have the luminescent splashes on their chests. One of them is Kay. She looks barely conscious.

The pendants. Sung-Soo's gifts were markers and that material he carved them from had been somehow rigged to turn to a dye. Perhaps that whistling sound I heard at the start of the chaos had something to do with it. All this time he's been identifying people to steal, people with skills. He gave Kay her pendant only after he heard about her healing skills. I told him that. She's there because I made him realize she was useful.

No. I'm not going to feel guilty. She's there because they've caught her, because they are committing a crime in which I am not complicit.

I can't see anyone else from the colony moving around. There are dozens of bodies. I can't tell if they're dead or just unconscious. Everyone else must be hiding, terrified. It doesn't look like there's been any serious resistance; none of Sung-Soo's people are injured. I spot another one of them heading to the vehicle from the direction of my house, shaking her head at Sung-Soo, who comes out from the other side of the truck and walks over to meet her. There's a discussion and five of them split off from guard duty to go with Sung-Soo in the direction he last saw me leave the colony. The proper hunt is beginning.

I look back at the truck, at my colleagues and my former lover held prisoner, and I know I'm not going to save them. If this were a game, like the countless stupid things I've played over the years, I'd be heading down there to pick off the guards one by one and free them. Then we'd take back the colony and put an end to this terror. But I don't have the skills or the weapons that my character would have. There aren't handy weapon caches stored in secret places that I can raid to arm myself and my fellows. None of the games I've ever played have built in total failure from the start. I wouldn't have the first idea of how to tackle one of the guards and take their weapon. There's no engine to interpret my clumsy actions and translate them into flawless silent assassinations. There is no heroism in me without the supporting game narrative.

I shuffle back until the sight of the truck disappears below the lip of the pod and I weep for Kay and the others, hating my incompetence. My skin is clammy and I can't stop shivering.

They're coming for me now. What to do? Without the network, I can't connect to Atlas to find some sort of tracking software to keep one step ahead of my hunters. There's no way I can go off into the grasslands yet. From the look of the others in the truck, I've been picked to run their stolen printers and build things for them. They're not going to give up their search easily.

I could hide up here for a couple of days, three at a push, but then my need for water would drive me down there. Even though they look like they want to leave, I'm not sure if they will without me. They might leave the colony, fearful that someone will get themselves together enough to organize a retaliation, but Sung-Soo could easily wait in the grasslands and come back.

And what would I find down in the colony? I can't see how we'll survive in the meantime. There are limited water supplies in the houses, raw materials we could extract from the kitchen printers to make food. We could cobble something together perhaps. But the damage he's done to this place is so deep that I'm not sure we'll ever recover the easy life we had. Perhaps that's the point. Sung-Soo wanted to snatch that luxury away and force us to struggle like they have all their lives.

The thought of scrabbling to survive among the same people who watched my home being ripped open makes me feel nauseous. I can't trust any of them. Some of them will think it's my fault. Mack and I are—were—associated with bringing Sung-Soo into the colony. They'll think Sung-Soo's attack was retaliation for what he found beneath my house. I'll be the scapegoat.

The alternative is to give myself up. Perhaps we could find a way to escape. Perhaps, seeing as we have skills they need, we'd be treated well. It seems, for a moment at least, to be the easiest option. The fear of the chase would be over. But I still don't move. Even when I decide that's the path of least resistance, I don't stand up and call down to the captors. There's too much of a gap between the reality and my scared little fantasy. Some part of me refuses to give myself up to any sort of slavery. If only that part of my mosaic was louder when I meekly obeyed Mack's orders. Fuck. I hate myself.

I lie flat on top of the pod, stuck. I can't go down there, I can't climb any higher and there's nowhere else to go. Then I feel the pod shift its position by just a fraction, but enough to make me wonder what triggered it.

There is another place to go.

I'm moving before I've even had a chance to think how terrible an idea it is. There are no other options I'm willing to take and no other places I'm willing to go. I don't want to hand my survival chances over to Sung-Soo and his people. But I am willing to give myself up to another judge. I'm ready to be tested. I'm going into God's city and I'm not going to leave until I understand it or until it kills me.

37

THE COURTYARD IS empty and for the first time in over twenty years there are no greeters outside the entrance. Even if the colony hadn't been attacked, there would be no one there. Now they all know that Suh isn't coming back.

I slide off the top of the tendril I cut through before and land on the old platform that Pasha stood on just a couple of days ago. I detach the rope, coil it and sling it over my shoulder. I'll need it in there. After clambering over the rail, I step across the gap between the waiting platform and the top of the slope leading up to the entrance to the city. Less than twenty-six hours ago Marco stood here with the whole colony watching. Sung-Soo was just meters away, knowing it was all false and keeping his silence.

I'm putting this off. I press my hand against the join like Marco did and the valve opens. I see the plant inside near the entrance, now just stalk and leaves, and the tunnel stretching ahead of me.

This will be the death of me, surely? I'll survive in the tunnel, but once I'm past the valve at the far end leading deeper into the city, I'll be poisoned. A flash of Suh's last moments and the blotches spreading across her skin returns along with the sound of her wheezing as her airway closed. The bubbling in her lungs . . . all of it plays out without any need of my chip to enhance the memory.

But that was before we adapted to this planet. Her body was geared up for a sanitized memory of Earth's environment. No new viruses or diseases introduced for all that time during the journey on Atlas. My body has been altered to thrive in this environment since then. I'm more likely to survive.

It doesn't take away the fear though. As a scientist, I know this is madness. But I also know this is an act of faith. I step inside and wait until the doors close behind me.

I have no headlamp. No respirator, not even a pair of gloves. I pull my sleeve down until I can wrap it over my fist and reach out to the side until my knuckles brush the wall. With something to guide me now I take a few tentative steps forward in the darkness, doing everything I can to try to keep my breathing steady as my heart's percussion threatens to overwhelm me.

All I can think about is Suh's death. After all these years of doing everything I could to avoid even a reminder of what happened, I find myself walking toward it. Is this actually a desire for suicide disguised as a desire to understand this place?

"Oh, shut up!" I jump at the sound of my own voice and then laugh, the terror tipping over into mild hysteria.

My hand is wet and the laughter chokes off. The skin on the back of my hand is tingling. I try to work out if that's because of what's soaked through my sleeve or if it's the cold or just plain panic. In the darkness I can't check for any discoloration and the sensation is spreading.

I turn around to go back but misjudge it and walk into the opposite side of the tunnel. My forehead slaps against the wet slime coating the inside of the wall and I yelp at the direct contact. In moments my whole face is tingling, like I've been outside in snow and then plunged my face in a bowl of hot water. Stupidly I turn, looking for some crack of light to guide me out, but there's nothing except darkness. I blink frantically, trying to work out if I really do have my eyes open as the tingling spreads up my arm and down my neck. It's then that I know I don't want to die. There is no romantic notion of following Suh on that last journey. There's just fear and waiting for my windpipe to close and my lungs to fill with liquid.

But neither of those things happens. Instead, a pale blue light fills the tunnel, seeming to glow from the walls rather than from a single source. I can see the tunnel stretching away from me to the valve that I entered and another valve much farther away. I can even see my footprints as darker depressions in the slick floor.

I look at my wet hand and my stomach drops when I can't see it. I can feel myself waving it about in front of me, I touch my face with it to reassure myself it's still there, and I can feel it against my cheek. But all I can see is the tunnel, as if my body is still in darkness.

"There has to be an explanation," I whisper to myself. A hypothesis emerges from the roiling mess of my panic. Perhaps it's still dark in here, but somehow I can now see the tunnel via a different spectrum. I rub my wet fingers together, thinking of the sensation contact first created that is subsiding now. Perhaps something in this substance has altered me, enabling me to see the interior of the tunnel.

Cut off from the environment in our suits and helmets, we had no contact with this part of the city when we first stepped in. I've never allowed any of the gunk to come into contact with me after my illegal visits. But perhaps that was our first mistake. Perhaps, just like the pheromones released by that plant, the city releases something here in the entrance tunnel to prepare us for its depths. We kept ourselves blind.

I feel normal now, my skin no longer tingles, and I can cope with not being able to see myself now that I can see where I'm going. I look at my footprints to get my bearings and walk away from the doors, deeper into God's city.

38

THE TUNNEL IS longer than I appreciated and every step is filled with thoughts of Suh's death. They're no longer laced with the fear that I'll die the same way. I'm finding that I can think about it calmly now, without the threat of being overwhelmed by pure emotion. Perhaps I'm still keeping it at bay. No, I don't really think that. There's a relief I've never felt before, now that the secret is out. I worry briefly about what will happen to her body now but only in the most abstract way. In here, it seems that all those things are much further away than they've ever been before.

I want to find a way to that topmost room, the one in which Suh said God was already dead. I didn't believe her then and I don't now. I was willing to follow her so far, but not to that place without hope. She saw something on the other side of that veil that made her lose belief in everything. I want to face whatever she did and see what is left behind. I've lost so much in the last few hours I need to see what is left.

I reach the valve and press my hand against it, trusting that whatever I'll come into contact with won't kill me. The valve opens and another stretch of tunnel lies beyond, this time curving upward. There's a pungent scent that reminds me of burned toast mixed with the taste of aniseed and I realize I'm breathing in a different kind of chemical mix. I pause, waiting to see if there are any side effects, but all I feel is light-headed. That could be from the exertion and lack of food and water for a few hours. I step over the threshold and wait for the valve to close behind me.

When it shuts, the color of the tunnel shifts to a deeper blue. A variation in the shading slowly becomes apparent, revealing what seems to be a pathway up the right-hand side of the tunnel. Is that the right way to interpret it? I move over to the right with a couple of steps until I'm aligned with it and tentatively put a foot at the start of the darker color.

Nothing happens. I breathe out and take another step, then another. My feet sink into the surface as if there are steps below it, hidden beneath a spongy slime-covered material. I pause and prod the area to the left of the path. There are no depressions there and the incline is getting steep enough to make it impossible to climb without these hidden steps. I climb a little higher before I realize I didn't see any difference when I was prodding the floor, as if my foot was invisible.

I stop, jarred out of the excitement of finding a path by the thought that my understanding of what happened to me in the previous tunnel was wrong. I hold up my hand and press it against the wall next to me, feeling the slight sticky depression form in its surface. I can see the dent but not my hand. It's like I'm not there.

It makes me shudder. I'm certain I would have noticed that before. Has another chemical entered my brain and altered my perception further?

I slip and fall to the bottom of the tunnel, my back hitting the valve door.

"Focus," I say out loud, half to chastise myself and half to see if I can still perceive my own voice. It's a welcome sound.

I stand up, my clothes now damp and clinging to my skin, clogged with the mucus. I try not to think about that and instead concentrate on the way ahead. The darker line I saw before has gone, and when I try to step where I did before there's no depression to a step beneath.

Doubting my memory, I stare at the tunnel until the darker line coalesces again. This time it's stretching up the middle with a slight curve to the left. I don't question it. I walk and feel the steps there as before.

This is the beginning of being tested. I start to remember early immersion games from my childhood but pull myself back into focusing on the path. I mustn't overthink it. I look. I follow. I climb.

Toward the end of the tunnel I have to use my hands, still repulsed by the way my fingers sink into the stickiness, but it's getting so steep I need to use the hidden steps like a ladder. A new valve comes into view above me and I go through. There is a tangle of possible ways onward, instead of the interior of another pod, as if several tendrils have partially merged with one another and formed an internal junction.

I don't remember climbing down the outside of any such tangle and feel horribly disoriented as I try to match what I have found with what I remember of the outside; then I remind myself that it's not important now. I breathe in and out, studying the different tunnels, hoping that there will be some sort of shift to indicate the route on.

Just as I'm starting to doubt my idea, a flash of light ripples along the interior of a tunnel stretching off to the left. Instinctively I go to activate the goggles I'm not wearing and swear. Another tunnel starts to flicker with a different rhythm and any moment now I expect the migraine and vomiting to begin.

I lean back against the door, taking care not to touch its center and accidentally open it. There are six possible ways to go and now all of them are pulsating with different-colored lights. Thinking that these lights are the ones picked up by my goggles on previous occasions, I raise my hands hopefully, thinking I might be able to see them now. I don't see anything and feel that lurch in my stomach again at my own invisibility. An awful sound like a screeching animal breaks me out of that worry and I press myself against the door harder as all the lights stop.

Did I do something wrong?

I take a moment to steady myself, letting the memory of the sound fade. I try not to think about where it came from and the possibility of some alien creature bounding down the tunnel to eat me. Instead, I try to remember what I was doing before. Yes. That was it. I was looking for the way on.

The lights begin again. Different colors in different tunnels, pulsing at different rates. Which one do I choose?

I pick a tunnel and try to study the light to see if there is a pattern, but it keeps shifting and seems random. I try with two more and suspect I'm taking the wrong approach. I try to think of a way to interpret the different colors, but there's no reason to suggest that the meanings my European upbringing have associated with each one have any validity here.

At least the migraine hasn't started yet. I focus on my breath, trying to relax and step back from the puzzle, like I do with any engineering problem that foxes me for more than a few minutes.

My gaze settles on one of the tunnels without my realizing it. Something about the pulsing light seems familiar. As the thought occurs to me, a sound gets louder, a steady, rapid beat. It's my heart, sounding as loud as if it were being amplified down the tunnel. The pulsing light has fallen into phase with it. I confirm my theory with a minute of my hand on my chest, feeling the beat through my palm. That's the way on.

As soon as I step into that tunnel, the other lights stop. The light in this one fades to a pleasant, soft red, moving in the direction I'm walking now as if to confirm I've made the right choice. Soon enough it starts to curve upward and I'm filled with same elation as defeating a gaming puzzle.

39

I CLIMB. I listen to the sound of my heartbeat. I follow the direction of the pulsing light. I haven't been so absolutely present in such a long time. When I reach the next valve, I have no idea how long I've been walking or how high I've climbed relative to the place I entered.

I've reached my first pod. When I did that with the first team, we'd all been sick—apart from Suh—and were feeling pretty wretched. I feel fine. Even my shoulder has stopped hurting. As I step through the opening, I remember Sung-Soo, but it's a fleeting fear, part of *out there* and feeling so distant now as to seem like a memory of a bad dream.

I'm not afraid of him now.

I've been here before. Or, at least, a room very similar, filled with the roughly hewn pots and tools. I can't see any spaces that my thieving would have left, so I decide it's a different room. It feels more like a museum display, something to be looked at passively on the way to somewhere else. As soon as

I think that, a path appears through the center of the room, this time a bold neon purple. I follow it.

It leads me through a succession of rooms and the museum feel of it all intensifies. The pots and tools get more sophisticated with each collection, leaving me with the idea of technological development. Some of the items aren't familiar to me in the later rooms, but there are universals throughout relating to basic survival needs and then higher needs such as art and written language. If I had access to my files, I'd match some of the latter to the things I saw in the top room. Instead I'm left in ignorance.

Each room is higher, housed in individual pods reached by a short climb up steps revealed by the guide path. No wonder we couldn't progress before.

By the time I reach the eighth pod I'm feeling relaxed and gently inquisitive. There's a pleasant scent that reminds me of vanilla. I'm even looking forward to the next rooms, hoping they'll join up the simple things I understand from the early displays and the massively advanced synthetic biotech I'm walking through and interacting with. But when the valve opens, I step into a room that breaks the pattern.

There are many pedestals, but only a handful are topped by objects. Each one is so very different from the next that there's no sense of a collection, not like the previous rooms. All the items are small. None of them are familiar in design or function. There's no path to guide me through the room and I can't see a way out.

I start to walk around the boundary, but that screeching sound begins again and I stop, returning to the entrance quickly.

I move from one pedestal to the next, trying to fathom a connection between the objects displayed upon them. As I walk the screeching stops, and even though I feel I'm moving toward the right action, I have no idea what to do next.

The only thing each one has in common is being well used. A piece of metal that could be a bracelet has chips in its decoration. A rounded piece of stone on the next pedestal is smooth with a groove in it, perhaps made by frequent use. I get to the end of the filled pedestals and stand in front of the next empty one.

I have a thought that I immediately discard. It returns, like a dog that's been kicked but still loves its owner.

Perhaps I need to leave something here too.

A soft blue glow spreads up the pedestal and I know it's what I need to do. But I have nothing that seems right. The rope is hardly worthy of such a place and my clothes are damp and covered with drying mucus.

Then I remember the doll tucked into my waistband. I pull her free. Even though I can't see my hand, somehow I can see her in the glow from the pedestal. It looks like she's floating there, buoyed up by some celestial force. The urge to keep hold of her fills every part of me. I look at her little stitched eyes and the arm I knitted for her. I feel my own warmth held in the wool. I know that I have to give her up.

But she's the last thing I have. All my treasures are gone now. All those beloved pieces of my life are now dumped outside my house and left to the mercy of the elements. I can feel tears running down my cheeks. I know I have to let it all go. I can't go back there. I have to let her go too. I put her on the pedestal and think of my child in the box at the end of the Parisian church, of my father's words trampled beneath the feet of our attackers, of my mother's painting buried under a pile of things I spent years collecting. I release the doll from my fingers, see her rest on the stone and take a step back.

The purple color deepens on the floor until it coalesces into a path again. I see a way out now.

THERE ARE A few more rooms. There is more art, and more artifacts that look like they could have many functions, none of which are fathomable from looking at them. But the message is clear enough. This is human development. I see more stylized representations of human forms. This place is showing me our tendency to evolve and discover and create.

I don't know if these have been collected from different planets or if they're just theoretical or just a story being told in a universal language. But I'm left with the feeling that whoever put them here expected people to come from places other than Earth. I think of the seed again, the real one, and how the thought of it being one of many sent to bring the right person here seems more likely.

It makes me pause. Suh was the one it called here. Not me. Should I progress even though I'm not much more than a stowaway in this scheme?

The light and the path fade. My concentration has drifted and the doubts are creeping in.

"It's not for me to decide," I say. "If I'm able to progress, I will."

The path is restored with my resolve. I have faith, not in God but in this city and the fail-safes put into place here. Suh hacked this system even though she was the one called here. She said she understood when we were in that topmost room, but I'm not sure she could have. This city is changing me, preparing me in ways I don't understand. I can't see how she could have changed enough without contact.

I'm climbing all the time now and feeling lighter than I have in so long. I think back to my house, to the things I stuffed between its walls and how much energy I wasted keeping it all hidden. It seems so strange to me now, so long ago. I was a different person then. Who I am now . . . I can't tell.

Through another valve and I'm in a narrow tunnel. Is this the last one? The one we all squeezed through exhausted and despairing?

The room is unchanged. I look at the place Suh died and can almost see her there in front of me. Mack and Winston, Lois and Hak-Kun, all dead now. Only I remain, the one least likely to survive.

There is no path marked on the floor to guide me. It's of no concern to me as I want to pause here and see if the markings mean anything to me now.

I walk along the walls, not caring if they are lit or if I can see myself anymore. I let myself trace the shapes and the colors, sometimes trying to find meaning, sometimes stepping back and waiting. Neither yields results.

Thinking of Suh before she went through the wall, I stand

in the same place and try to read the symbols the way she did, moving from the bottom to the top at speed.

They are still unfathomable.

She said that she knew what it all means. Was she even telling the truth? Or is my poor, normal brain simply incapable of interpreting all of this without the seed's influence?

But I got here. I passed the city's tests. I turn and look at the central wall. There is a sense of someone waiting. Is it me or someone else?

"If you think I'm ready, I'm here," I say to it. Then I shake my head. "I know I'm ready."

The wall fades and I walk through.

I have no expectations. I feel empty but not hollow. As I cross through the translucent wall I become aware of my body again. I feel blisters on my feet and tongue, the pain in my shoulder and a gnawing hunger. My head is aching, and my clothes are uncomfortably damp and have chafed my skin in places.

It's the most human I've felt since I left the first tunnel.

At first I think the room is open to the sky, but then I see a slight distortion in the air suggesting a barrier of some kind. It's a full circle, rather than the other half of the pod, and even though I don't understand it, I don't try to work it out. It's not important.

There is nothing else in the room except a slab of stone and on it lies a body. Not obviously male or female but most definitely human. The limbs are long and delicate, the hair gray and hanging down to the floor in soft curls, the jawline square but not heavy. The skin is painted with symbols and artwork I recognize from the rooms below and the one on the other side of the wall that's now solid behind me. Blues and greens and golds and black.

The chest isn't moving.

"Are you the one who made all this?" I ask but there's no response.

Did Suh think this was God?

The floor is pale gray and bright in the morning sunshine. Through the haze of the barrier I see Diamond Peak and the clouds scudding across the flawless sky. I look down at my hands and see liver spots and wrinkles and strength and potential.

That person isn't God.

This isn't the last room.

I don't know why I think that—no—why I know that.

I go to the slab and kneel beside it. There's a decorative edge carved into the stone so delicate that it's easy to miss. In the center of the length I'm looking at there's a tiny spike of stone. I press my forefinger against it without thinking and watch as a bead of blood rolls down it to collect at a groove around its base. I suck at the little wound as the blood thins and begins to run along the carved grooves as if the slab were on a slope.

Soon it's as thin as cotton threads and they reveal something I can understand. First an image of Diamond Peak. Then something that looks like lots of people. Then only one figure, alone, throwing something depicted as tiny dots upward.

I crawl around the edge, following the pictures as they're revealed, interpreting a story that is so simple anyone could understand it. After the others left, the lone figure sent the seeds out into the stars and then a long time passed. The sender created the city and then people came from lots of different places to enter it, all much smaller than the sender. A segment shows the tiny people inside stylized tunnels and pods, each one showing the person getting bigger until there's one of the topmost pod with a symbol that has to be the sun above it. The sender is above the city now and the little people who have grown during their passage through the city are reaching up. The next shows this room, seen from above, the visitor lying on it and then—

The body on the slab begins to crumble as if it has been formed from powder all along. The dust left behind is repelled by the material the slab is made from and slips off to plume in the air briefly, leaving it pristine.

I haven't decorated my body. My clothes are filthy. It doesn't matter. I lie down on the slab.

It feels soft beneath me, like I'm lying on a cushion of air. I feel all the tightness in my muscles flow out of me. I look up at the sky and I know that I'm ready and that it's time to go. I've worn this body long enough.

And as I lie there I think of those I've loved and those I've hurt. Sometimes they were one and the same. I think of the ones who have hurt me and see them as I see myself. We were all just little broken things, trying so hard to protect ourselves when all we were doing was keeping ourselves blind and alone.

There is something beautiful happening above and below me. My body is between and will be left behind when I go on. I know that soon I'll be with the one who built the city to prepare those who make it this far, so they too can reach that higher place.

And in time another will come and will trust the city and will find my body. And if they are ready, they'll know what to do.

Return to the universe of *Planetfall* . . .

After Atlas

Turn the page for an extract

1

IT'S TIMES LIKE these, when I'm hunkered in a doorway, waiting for a food market of dubious legality to be set up, that I find myself wishing I could eat like everyone else. I watch them scurry past, hurrying back to their warm little boxes with their bright lights and distractions, a hot meal just the press of a button away. They'll stand there in front of their printers, watching that artificial shit being spurted out of dozens of tiny nozzles with clinical precision to form lasagna or something, and their stomachs will rumble and their mouths will water and, oh God, just the thought of it is making me nauseous. As much as it disgusts me, I envy them.

It's cold and damp, the November sun is setting in the middle of the afternoon and I am beyond tired. The satisfaction of finishing my latest case didn't last long in the face of my hunger, and I just want the truck to arrive, to buy what I need, to get home and to shut the door on it all. I'll make a casserole, I promise myself, like a parent promising a grumbling toddler he'll get a toy if he behaves. There's some beef left in the freezer. And if there's flour (I try not to get my hopes up), I'll make dumplings, stodgy and crisped on the top like the Brits make them. I haven't eaten since an early and inadequate breakfast, and just imagining what that casserole could smell like makes me close my eyes and smile to myself, just for a moment. I turn my collar up and tuck my hands back into my pockets. I'm hoping that here in this little nook no one will see me and feel they're entitled to come and talk to me just because they've seen me on the news and docu-feeds.

A woman walks in front of the doorway and looks straight at me, pausing midstride as if she's listening for something I'm about to say. I pull back into the shadows when she laughs, worried that she's recognized me, before realizing she's talking to an avatar projected by her chip. She's experiencing walking with a friend, chatting and laughing away. When I shift to the other side of the doorway she blinks with a yelp, seeing me for the first time, and mutters an apology in Norwegian.

I rest my head against the door behind me, waiting for my pulse to settle again.

"Would you like to play a game while you're waiting?" Tia asks.

"No." Now I'm the one looking like I'm talking to myself. Not that it matters. Most of the people I can see in this dingy London backstreet are talking to either projected avatars or, like me, just the voices of their Artificial Personal Assistants, delivered directly into their brains via neural implant.

"We're next to a node for a new urban-enhancement game with a free trial to—"

"No."

"Would you like me to stop making urban-environment interactivity suggestions when you are off duty?"

"Yes. Why are you making them, anyway?"

"A recent change in the licensing agreement between—"

"Save it, Tia. I don't need to know." It's the first rule of any change to a licensing agreement: it's not for the benefit of the end user, no matter what they say.

Where the fuck is the van?

I check the time and it's only five p.m. It feels like two in the morning. There's a steady pounding throb at the back of my head, and my hunger has moved from gnawing, through occasional bouts of light-headedness, to making me want to kill someone. Then I hear the low whine of the van's engine and step out as it parks, pulling my small wheeled case behind me, ready to muscle my way to the front when it opens its back doors.

Everyone in the loitering crowd has their public profile set to private, as do I. I recognize some of them from other markets. There's the man with the tiny dog that bites anyone who goes near, the little shit. There's the woman with the umbrella that's almost taken my eye out several times, and she knows she's doing it but has no fucks to give for a rival consumer. There's the old dear who looks like she could be the sweetest grandma straight out of a department store Christmas mersive advert, but I know she's just as willing to grind her bootheels into someone else's toes if they push too much from the back.

The driver gets out, moves to the side of the van and slides the side door across just enough to pull out the folding table, while his passenger jumps out and scans the street. They've just made a delivery to a supermarket down the road, one that's—like all of them—too expensive for most people to shop in. It has aisles filled with perfect vegetables and a counter with the freshest meat—actual real meat cut from real animals—all sparkling and brightly lit. I only know about it because of the mersive adverts that weasel their way in every few months or so before Tia closes the loophole they've exploited to get to me. Cooking with real, fresh food is the province of the rich. Rich enough to buy it, or rich enough to have the space for dirt to grow it, or rich enough to hire space and equipment to have other people grow it just for them.

This impromptu market is a testament to mankind's ability to exploit every possible consumer niche. The driver has come from a wholesaler who has realized that there are people willing to pay good money for the stock that the supermarkets won't take. So all the rejects get put into boxes and loaded onto the last delivery of the day, to be sold in a backstreet that smells of piss and misery. Now it's filled with people who are doing well enough to spend money on food items considered luxuries, but not quite well enough to afford to do it in a nice building with beautiful staff and real champagne given at the door.

I'm not doing well enough to have the money to do this. I've made greater sacrifices to get this food. I doubt any of the others have given up years of freedom to be able to buy a few misshapen vegetables every week. I frown to myself, trying to stop thinking that way. I try to reframe it, the way Dee would. "It was a shitty choice," she'd say. "But at least it was one you got to make for yourself."

It doesn't have the same effect when she's not here with me. No matter how much I try to spin it into something else, it doesn't alter the sheer injustice of it all. But as much as I want it to, my sacrifice doesn't give me a place at the front of the jostling throng that is slowly, reluctantly morphing into a queue. In moments I find myself behind the old woman and take care where I'm putting my feet. The man with the dog is farther back, his irritation expressed perfectly by the tiny, vicious snarling of the overgrown rat in his arms. There's a sharp, painful tap on the top of my head and I twist to see the woman with the umbrella.

"So sorry," she says with a fake smile.

"It's not raining," I say through gritted teeth.

"Oh, has it stopped?" She pretends not to have noticed and still doesn't fold the damn thing away. There's a slight narrowing of her eyes as she stares at me and I face front again, worrying that she's thinking she's seen me somewhere before.

I turn my collar up as if against the wind, but it's more to cover as much of my face as possible. Crates of produce have been hauled out of the van and the driver has cranked one open already. He scoops out a few carrots, all huge, malformed things, looking like fetishes from some ancient magical ritual. He holds one up for the crowd, who laugh when they see how much it looks like a man running, with its split root and arm-like offshoots. Turnips are dumped next to them, then onions. It's as if the universe knew I wanted to cook a casserole.

"No need to push," the driver calls. "Plenty for sale tonight. Cooking apples too, when this doughnut"—he jerks a thumb at his assistant—"digs 'em out for ya."

Tia informs me that the seller's APA has made contact and the handshake has been successful. All I need to do is pick what I want and our APAs will handle the rest. I swipe away a notification warning me that the ingredients I plan to buy will amount to an extra three hours on my contract to pay off the credit required.

The queue shuffles forward as the first purchases are swiftly made. Only four people away from the table, I'm already earmarking the ones I hope will still be there when it's my turn. The seller glances down the line, sees me and winks. A recorded audio message comes in from him moments later and I give Tia permission to play it to me.

"I got some flour in the van for you and some sugar. You need to sieve 'em 'cos they was spillages, but it's all good 'cos it's a clean processing plant. No charge. My boy'll give 'em to ya round the front of the van after you got your veggies."

Has it been sent to me in error? The message continues.

"I know you was the copper who got that bloke who was killin' the babies up north. Saw it on the feed. I know 'im, I thought, he's the one who buys me veggies. So there's extra for you whenever you come. Just don't tell no one. Next time I'll bring some beef if I can sneak it out. I got a baby grandson, see? Same age as that young lad, the last one that bastard got."

The message ends, and for the first time in years I choose to seek out eye contact with another real human being because I genuinely want to. He meets my gaze and nods and I smile. I actually smile at someone I don't know. He looks away to serve the next customer and I'm left reeling from the body blow of the first act of kindness I can remember in years.

The queue moves forward again, and even though the umbrella hits my head once more I don't have any anger left in me now. I ignore it and wait with newfound patience. There will be something left for me by the time I get there; I know it now.

Minutes pass and then the hairs on the back of my neck prickle. I have the distinct impression someone is watching me. It's not the woman behind me—I can hear her arguing with the man behind her, who's also been hit by the umbrella. It's someone else. I tuck my chin into my coat and whisper to Tia.

"Who's in this crowd?"

"Everyone within a ten-meter radius, with the exception of

the driver and sales assistant, have their public profiles set to private."

"Read them anyway."

"You are not currently assigned to a case. Please state your justification."

I can't give the real reason, so I need to lie. If I push it too far, my breach of their personal privacy will be flagged in the system. "Possible criminal activity in progress." I pause, hoping that's enough.

The gamble pays off; I'm in good standing at the Ministry of Justice and there's nothing in the system to suggest I ever abuse my privileges, so it gives me the benefit of the doubt. Tia pulls in the information that all the people around me would display about themselves if they had their profiles set to public, overlaying it across my vision as if the text is floating above the tarmac next to me. Before I even have the chance to scan the list, Tia highlights one and pulls it to the front, in line with a command I programmed years ago. That profile is now larger than the rest with a single keyword flashing.

Journalist.

Oh JeeMuh. Oh fuck, no. Not now.

The omnipresent paranoia ratchets up a gear and my palms start to sweat. He must have followed me from the train station, old-school style. I read his profile and select the link to his portfolio. He's written several pieces about the Pathfinder. Of course he has; half of the journalists alive now have written some bullshit about that crazy woman who built a spaceship called Atlas and took the faithful off into space to find God. His most recent piece is an article on the capsule they left behind to be opened forty years later that will soon be opened, the one I've instructed Tia to remove all mentions of from my feeds. The grand opening is less than two weeks away and the speculation about its contents has gone from occasional and irritating to constant and unbearable.

I force myself to appear calm, telling myself that I overreact to these people, and if I don't get a lid on this soon, it could be reported to my psych supervisor.

"Show him in the crowd, Tia."

A small blue arrow appears at the right-hand edge of my vision and I twist until the arrow disappears and a bald black man in a heavy gray overcoat is outlined in blue. He's staring right at me and just a second of eye contact is sufficient to send my heart rate high enough to flash a notification from MyPhys. I look away as fast as I can, silently hoping he'll stay where he is.

It's a ridiculous hope.

There's only one person in front of me now, and the vegetables I've got my eye on are still there. I want to run but I need the food. I add a "Do not disturb" to my personal profile but I know it won't make any difference to that parasite. If anything, it'll probably make him even more keen to bother me. Journos are twisted sods.

He's walking over and I ball my fists in my pockets. I fix my attention on the table ahead, tucking my nose beneath the top rim of the turned-up collar, even though it won't do a thing. I have to satisfy this primal urge to duck and hide somehow.

"Mr. Moreno," he says, even though his APA will be reminding him of the DND notice on my profile.

"I don't have anything to say."

"I don't want to talk to you about the case."

I channel my contempt into a long sideways glance. "I know."

"It's just a—"

"Leave me alone," I say as the person in front of me finishes her transaction.

"That's not very polite."

"Neither is harassment," I reply, and point out the vegetables I want, furious at this asshole ruining my chance to give the vendor a personal thank-you for his kindness. I pass over the small canvas bag I've brought with me and watch the carrots, onions and turnip being put inside. Even though it's gone out of fashion, I extend my hand to the seller and he shakes it firmly. "Thank you," I say to him as our APAs handle the transaction.

He winks at me again. "You need to queue properly if you want to buy," he says to the journo. "These good people have been waitin' awhile."

"You pushed in right in front of me!" umbrella lady says, sparking protests from the others behind her. As the journo extricates himself, I nip round the side of the van and collect two small sacks that I put straight into my case with more thanks to the seller's son.

I manage to get a few meters away before the journo catches up. "Mr. Moreno, I'm not like the others. I want to work with you. Surely you want some control over what people say about you? About your mother?"

"I deny permission to use any footage of this interaction or any recording of this conversation. If it's published online I'll use every fucking contact I have in the Ministry of Justice to—"

He smiles, holds up his hands as he puts himself in my way, forcing me to stop. "There's no need to threaten me. I'm not stupid. I'm not going to fuck with an SDCI, am I?"

"You already are." I move to go around him, mindful of the fact he's taller than me.

"I just want to explore the impact of—"

"Piss off." I push past him, but he follows. "I'm recording this," I say, even though he knows I will be. I still have to cover my ass.

"There are a lot of people who want to know who you are, Mr. Moreno. They want to know how you're doing. The network had more than three million messages after that first documentary was shown about you and your father. Three million people who cared so much they got in touch. Thousands sent cards and gifts. Did you know that? Just because of that documentary. Imagine what a second one could do."

That documentary. I stop, struggling to control the rage as a string of warnings from MyPhys scroll down the left-hand side of my vision. It details elevated blood pressure, increased cortisol and high adrenaline levels, forming a cold report of my need to punch this fuck into next week.

"Those people want to love you, Carlos. They want—"

I round on him, the bag slipping from my fingers, the case handle dropping into a puddle. "They want whatever the fuck you tell them to want," I spit through my teeth. "Let's tell the fucking truth for once. You want me to make you money. You're not interested in me or my story."

"On the contrary," he says, teeth bright white against his dark brown skin, "I'm very interested in why you spent all that money on a few shitty vegetables. On your pay grade? Bit indulgent, isn't it?"

I can hear Dee telling me to back off, just like she did on the first day I met her, when I almost hit the hot-houser who'd tried to make out that kidnapping us was an act of mercy. Even when Dee's hundreds of miles away, I carry her with me. I push down the rage, telling myself over and over again that he's not worth it. This journo isn't the first to harass me and he won't be the last. I can't risk a black mark on my file. "I'm going to walk away now, and if you follow me, I'll call in a team that'll make the counterterrorism forces look like the Boy Scouts."

I pick up the bag and the handle of my case and I force myself to walk away from him. I listen for his footsteps and breathe again when I realize my bluff has worked and he is walking in the opposite direction.

"MyPhys is reporting elevated stress levels," Tia says as I start to shake. "Would you like to play a game to calm you down while we walk to the station?"

"No, Tia. Call Dee for me. I . . . I need to talk to Dee."

ABOUT GOLLANCZ

Gollancz is the oldest SF publishing imprint in the world. Since being founded in 1927 Gollancz has continued to publish a focused selection of bestselling and award-winning authors. The front-list includes **Ben Aaronovitch**, **Joe Abercrombie**, **Charlaine Harris**, **Joanne Harris**, **Joe Hill**, **Alastair Reynolds**, **Patrick Rothfuss**, **Nalini Singh** and **Brandon Sanderson**.

As one of the largest Science Fiction and Fantasy imprints in the UK it is no surprise we have one of the most extensive backlists in the world. Find high-quality SF on Gateway written by such authors as **Philip K. Dick**, **Ursula Le Guin**, **Connie Willis**, **Sir Arthur C. Clarke**, **Pat Cadigan**, **Michael Moorcock** and **George R.R. Martin**.

We also have a strand of publishing in translation, which includes French, Polish and Russian authors. Gollancz is home to more award-winning authors than any other imprint, with names including **Aliette de Bodard**, **M. John Harrison**, **Paul McAuley**, **Sarah Pinborough**, **Pierre Pevel**, **Justina Robson** and many more.

The SF Gateway
More than 3,000 classic, rare and previously out-of-print SF novels at your fingertips.
www.sfgateway.com

The Gollancz Blog
Bringing you news from our worlds to yours. Stories, interviews, articles and exclusive extracts just for you!
www.gollancz.co.uk

GOLLANCZ
LONDON